S0-BRX-167

THE CAVALIER

01659

BY

GEORGE W. CABLE

WITH ILLUSTRATIONS BY

HOWARD CHANDLER CHRISTY

CHARLES SCRIBNER'S SONS
NEW YORK ::::::::::::::::: 1901

TROW DIRECTORY
PRINTING AND BOOKBINDING COMPANY
NEW YORK

CONTENTS

Contents

Contents

Illustrations

The Cavalier

I

SHE WANTED TO LAUGH

OUR camp was in the heart of Copiah County, Mississippi, a mile or so west of Gallatin and about six miles east of that once robber-haunted road, the Natchez Trace. Austin's brigade, we were, a detached body of mixed Louisiana and Mississippi cavalry, getting our breath again after two weeks' hard fighting of Grant. Grierson's raid had lately gone the entire length of the State, and we had had a hard, vain chase after him, also.

Joe Johnston's shattered army was at Jackson, about forty-five miles to northward; beleaguered Vicksburg was in the Northwest, a trifle farther away; Natchez lay southwest, still more distant; and nearly twice as far in the south was our heartbroken New Orleans. We had paused to recuperate our animals, and there was a rumor that we were to get new clothing. Anyhow we had rags with honor, and a right to make as much noise as we chose.

It was being made. The air was in anguish with the din of tree-felling and log-chopping, of stamping, neighing, braying. whooping, guffawing, and singing—all the daybreak charivari beloved of a camp of Confederate " critter companies." In the midst of it a chum and I sat close together on a log near the mess fire, and as the other boys of the mess lifted their heads from their saddle-tree pillows, from two of them at once came a slow, disdainful acceptance of the final lot of the wicked, made unsolicited on discovering that this chum and I had sat there talking together all night. I had the day before been wheedled into letting myself be detailed to be a quartermaster's clerk, and this comrade and I were never to snuggle under the one blanket again. The thought forbade slumber.

" If I go to sleep," I said,—" you know how I dream. I shall have one of those dreams of mine to carry around in my memory for a year, like a bullet in my back." So there the dear fellow had sat all night to give me my hourly powders of reassurance that I could be a quartermaster's clerk without shame.

" Certainly you can afford to fill a position which the leader of Ferry's scouts has filled just before you."

But my unsoldierly motive for going to headquarters kept my misgivings alive. I was hungry for the gentilities of camp; to be where Shakespeare was part of the baggage, where Pope was quoted, where Coleridge and Byron and Poe were recited, Macaulay criticized, and " Les Misérables "—Madame Le Vert's Mobile translation—lent round ; and where men, when they did steal, stole portable volumes, not currycombs. Ned Ferry had been Major Harper's clerk, but had managed in several instances to display such fitness to lead that General Austin had lately named him for promotion,

She Wanted to Laugh

and the quartermaster's clerk was now Lieutenant Ferry, raised from the ranks for gallantry, and followed ubiquitously by a chosen sixty or so drawn from the whole brigade. Could the like occur again? And could it occur to a chap who could not comprehend how it had ever occurred at all?

By and by we breakfasted. After which, my precious horse not having finished his corn, I spread my blanket and let myself doze, but was soon awakened by the shouts of my companions laughing at me for laughing so piteously in my sleep.

"Would I not tell my dream, as nice young men in the Bible always did?"

"No, I would not!" But I had to yield. My dream was that our General had told me a fable. It was of a young rat, which seeing a cockerel, whose tail was scarcely longer than his own, leap down into a barrel, gather some stray grains of corn and fly out again, was tempted to follow his example, but having got in, could only stay there. The boys furnished the moral; it was not complimentary.

"Well, good-bye, fellows."

"Good-bye, Smith." I have never liked my last name, but at that moment the boys contrived to put a kindness of tone into it which made it almost pleasing. "Good-bye, Smith, remember your failings."

Remember! I had yet to make their discovery. But I was on the eve of making it.

As I passed up the road through the midst of our nearly tentless camp I met a leather-curtained spring-wagon to which were attached a pair of little striped-legged mules driven by an old negro. Behind him, among the curtains, sat a lady and her black maid. The mistress was of strikingly graceful figure, in a most tasteful gown and broad Leghorn hat. Her small hands were daintily gloved. The mules stopped, and through her light veil I saw that she was handsome. Her eyes, full of thought, were blue, and yet were so spirited they might as well have been black, as her hair was. She, or fate for her, had crowded thirty years of life into twenty-five of time.

For many a day I had not seen such charms of feminine attire, and yet I was not charmed. Every item of her fragrant drapery was from the world's open market, hence flagrantly un-Confederate, unpatriotic, reprehensible. Otherwise it might not have seemed to me that her thin nostrils had got their passionateness lately.

" Are you not a New Orleans boy? " she asked as I lifted my képi and drew rein.

Boy! humph! I frowned, made myself long, and confessed I had the honor to be from that city. Whereupon she let her long-lashed eyes take on as ravishing a covetousness as though I had been a pretty baby.

" I knew it! " she said delightedly. " But tell me, honor bright," — she sparkled with amusement— " you're not regularly enlisted, are you? "

I clenched my teeth. " I am nineteen, madam."

Her eyes danced, her brows arched. " Haven't you got "—she hid her smile with an embroidered handkerchief—" haven't you got your second figure upside down? "

She Wanted to Laugh

I glared, but with one look of hurt sisterliness she melted me. Then, pensive just long enough to say, " I was nineteen once," she shot me a sidelong glance so roguish that I was dumb with indignation and tried to find my mustache, forgetting I had shaved it off to stimulate it. She smiled in sweet propitiation and then came gravely to business. " Have you come from beyond the pickets? "

" No, madam."

" Have you met any officer riding toward them? "

I had not. Her driver gathered the reins and I drew back.

" Good-bye, New Orleans soldier-*boy*," she said, gaily, and as I raised my cap she gave herself a fetching air and added, " I'll wager I know your name."

" Madam,"—my cap went higher, my head lower— " I never bet."

I could not divine what there was ridiculous about me, except a certain damage to my dress, of which she could not possibly be aware as long as I remained in the saddle. Yet plainly she wanted to laugh. I made it as plain that I did not.

" Good-day, sir," she said, with forced severity, but as I smiled apologetically and moved my rein, she broke down under new temptation and, as the wagon moved away, twittered after me unseen,—" Good-bye, Mr. Smith."

The Cavalier

II

LIEUTENANT FERRY

I PASSED on, flattered but scandalized, wasting no guesses on how she knew me—if she really knew me at all—but taking my revenge by moralizing on her, to myself, as a sign of the times, until brigade headquarters were in full view, a few rods off the road; four or five good, white wall-tents in a green bit of old field backed by a thicket of young pines.

Midway of this space I met Scott Gholson, clerk to the Adjutant-general. It was Gholson who had first spoken of me for this detail. He was an East Louisianian, of Tangipahoa; aged maybe twenty-six, but in effect older, having from birth eaten only ill-cooked food, and looking it; profoundly unconscious of any shortcoming in his education, which he had got from a small church-pecked college of the pelican sort that feed it raw from their own bosoms. One of his smallest deficiencies was that he had never seen as much art as there is in one handsome dinner-plate. Now, here he was, riding forth to learn for himself, privately, he said, why I did not appear. Yet he halted without turning, and seemed to wish he had not found me.

" Did you "—he began, and stopped; " did you notice a "—he stopped again.

" What, a leather-curtained spring-wagon? "

" No-o! " he said, as if nobody but a gaping idiot would expect anybody not a gaping idiot to notice a leather-curtained spring-wagon. " No-o! did you

6

notice the brown horse that man was riding who just now passed you as you turned off the road?"

No, I barely remembered the rider had generously moved aside to let me go by. In pure sourness at the poverty of my dress and the perfection of his, I had avoided looking at him higher than his hundred-dollar boots. My feet were in uncolored cowhide, except the toes.

"He noticed you," said Gholson; "he looked back at you and your bay. Wouldn't you like to turn back and see his horse?"

"Why, hardly, if I'm behindhand now. Is it so fine as that?"

"Well, no. It's the horse he captured the time he got the Yankee who had him prisoner."

"Who?" I cried. "What! You don't mean to say—was that Lieutenant Ferry?"

"Yes, so called. He wa'n't a lieutenant then, he was a clerk, like you or me."

"Oh, I wish I had noticed him!"

"We can see him yet if you——"

"Do you want to see him?" I gathered my horse.

"Me!—No, sir. But you spoke as if——"

I shook my head and we moved toward the tents. This was worse than the dream; the rat had not seen the cockerel, but the cockerel had observed the rat—dropping into the barrel: the cockerel, yes, and not the cockerel alone, for I saw that Gholson was associating him with her of the curtained wagon. By now they were side and side. I asked if Ferry came often to headquarters.

The Cavalier

" Yes, quite as often as he's any business to."

" Ah, ha! " thought I, and presently said I had heard
he was a great favorite.

" Well,—yes,—he—he is,—with some."

" Don't you like him? "

" Who, me? Oh!—I—I admire Ned Ferry—for a
number of things. He's more foolhardy than brave;
he's confessed as much to me. Women call him handsome. He sings; beautifully, I suppose; I can't sing a
note; and wouldn't if I could. Still, if he only wouldn't
sing drinking-songs—but, Smith, I think that to sing
drinking-songs—and all the more to sing them as well
as some folks think he does—is to advocate drinking,
and to advocate drinking is next door to excusing
drunkenness! "

" Then Ned Ferry doesn't drink? "

" Indeed he does! I don't like to say it, and I don't
say he drinks ' too much ', as they call it; but, Smith, he
drinks with men who do! Oh, I admire him; only I do
wish——"

" Wish what? "

" Oh, I—I wish he wouldn't play cards. Smith, I've
seen him play cards with the shells bursting over us! "

For my part I privately wished this saint wouldn't
rub my uninteresting surname into me every time he
spoke. As we dismounted near the tents I leaned
against my saddle and asked further concerning the
object of his loving anxiety. Was Ned Ferry generous, pleasant, frank?

" Why, in outward manner, yes; but, Smith, he was
raised to be a Catholic priest. I could a heap-sight

easier trust him if he'd sometimes show distrust, himself. If he ever does I've never seen it. And yet—Oh, we're the best of friends, and I'm speaking now only as a friend and *toe* a friend. Oh, if it wa'n't for just one thing, I could admit what Major Harper said of him not ten minutes ago to me; that you never finish talking to Ned Ferry without feeling a little brighter, happier and cleaner than when you began; whereas talking with some men it's just the reverse."

I looked carefully at my companion and asked him if the Major had said *all* of that. He had, and Gholson's hide had turned it without taking a scratch. "That's fine!—as to Ferry," I said.

"Oh, yes,—it would be—if it was only *so*. Trouble is, you keep remembering he's such a stumbling-block to any real spiritual inquirer. Yes, and to himself; for, you know, spiritually there's so much less hope for the moralist than what there is for the up-and-down reprobate! You know that,—*Smith.*"

My silence implied that I knew it, though I did not feel any brighter, happier or cleaner.

"Smith, Ned Ferry is not only a Romanist, he's a romanticist. We—you and me—are religionists. *Our* brightness and happiness air the brightness and happiness of faith; our cleanness is the cleanness of religious scruples. Worst of it with Ned is he's satisfied with the difference, I'm afraid! That's what makes him so pleasant to fellows who don't care a sou marquee about religion."

I said one might respect religion even if he did not—

"Oh, he's always *polite* to it; but he's—he's read

Voltaire! Oh, yes, Voltaire, George Sand, all those men. He questions the Bible, Smith. Not to me, though; hah, he knows better! Smith, I can discuss religion and not get mad, with any one who don't question the Bible; but if he does that, I just tell you, I wouldn't risk my soul in such a discussion! Would you?"

I could hardly say, and we moved pensively toward Major Harper's tent. Evidently the main poison was still in Gholson's stomach, and when I glanced at him he asked, "What d'you reckon brought Ned Ferry here just at this time?"

I made no reply. He looked momentous, leaned to me sidewise with a hand horizontally across his mouth, and whispered a name. It was new to me. "Charlie Toliver?" I murmured, for we were at the tent door.

"The war-correspondent," whispered Gholson; "don't you know?" But the flap of the tent lifted and I could not reply.

III

SHE

MAJOR HARPER was the most capable officer on the brigade staff. I had never met a man of such force and dignity who was so modestly affable. His new clerk dined with him that first day, at noon in his tent, alone. Hot biscuits! with butter! and rock salt. Fried bacon also—somewhat vivacious, but still bacon. When the tent began to fill with the smoke of his meerschaum pipe, and while his black boy cleared the table for us

to resume writing, we talked of books. Here was joy!
I vaunted my love for history, biography, the poets, but
spoke lightly of fiction.

The smoker twinkled. " You're different from Ned
Ferry," he said.

" Has he a taste for fiction?" I asked, with a de-
preciative smirk.

" Yes, a beautiful story is a thing Ned Ferry loves
with a positive passion."

" I suppose we might call him a romanticist," said I,
" might we not?"

The patient gentleman smiled again as he said, " Oh
—Gholson can attend to that."

I took up my pen, and until twilight we spoke there-
after only of abstracts and requisitions. But then he
led me on to tell him all about myself. I explained
why my first name was Richard and my second name
Thorndyke, and dwelt especially on the enormous dif-
ferences between the Smiths from whom we were and
those from whom we were not descended.

And then he told me about himself. He was a grad-
uate of West Point, the only one on the brigade staff;
was a widower, with a widowed brother, a maiden sister,
two daughters, and a niece, all of one New Orleans
household. The brothers and sister were Charleston-
ians, but the two men had married in New Orleans,
twin sisters in a noted Creole family. The brother's
daughter, I was told, spoke French better than English; the Major's elder daughter spoke English as perfectly as her father; and the younger, left in her aunt's
care from infancy, knew no French at all. I wondered

if they were as handsome as their white-haired father, and when I asked their names I learned that the niece, Cécile, was a year the junior of Estelle and as much the senior of Camille; but of the days of the years of the pilgrimage of any of the three " children " he gave me no slightest hint; they might be seven years older, or seven years younger, than his new clerk.

To show him how little I cared for any girl's age whose father preferred not to mention it, I reverted to his sister and brother. She was in New Orleans, he said, with her nieces, but might at any moment be sent into the Confederacy, being one of General Butler's " registered enemies." The brother was—

" Out here somewhere. No, not in the army exactly; no, nor in the navy, but—I expect him in camp to-night. If he comes you'll have to work when you ought to be asleep. No, he is not in the secret service, only in *a* secret service; running hospital supplies through the enemy's lines into ours."

I was thrilled. *I* was taken into the staff's confidence! Me, *Smith!* That *Major Harper* would tell me part of a matter to conceal the rest of it did not enter my dreams, good as I was at dreaming. The flattery went to my brain, and presently, without the faintest preamble, I asked if there was any war-correspondent at headquarters just now. There came a hostile flash in his eyes, but instantly it passed, and with all his happy mildness he replied, " No, nor any room for one."

Just then entered an ordnance-sergeant, so smart in his rags that the Major's affability seemed hardly a

She

condescension. He asked me to supper with his mess —"of staff *attatchays*," he said, winking one eye and hitching his mouth; at which the Major laughed with kind disapprobation, and the jocose sergeant explained as we went that that was only one of Scott Gholson's mispronunciations the boys were trying to tease him out of.

I found the clerks' mess a bunch of bright good fellows. After supper, stretched on the harsh turf under the June stars, with everyone's head (save mine) in some one's lap, we smoked, talked and sang. Only Gholson was called away, by duty, and so failed to hear the laborious jests got off at his expense. To me the wits were disastrously kind. Never had I been made a tenth so much of; I was even urged to sing " All quiet along the Potomac to-night," and was courteously praised when I had done so. But there is where affliction overtook me; they debated its authorship. One said a certain newspaper correspondent, naming him, had proved it to be the work—I forget of whom. But I shall never forget what followed. Two or three challenged the literary preëminence of that correspondent, and from as many directions I was asked for my opinion. Ah me! Lying back against a pile of saddles with my head in my hands, sodden with self-assurance, I replied, magnanimously, " Oh, I don't set up for a critic, but—well—would you call him a better man than Charlie Toliver? "

" Who—o? " It was not one who asked; the whos came like shrapnel; and when, not knowing what else to do, I smiled as one dying, there went up a wail of mirth that froze my blood and then heated it to a fever. The company howled. They rolled over one another, crying, "Charlie Toliver!—Charlie Toliver!—Oh, Lord, where's Scott Gholson!—Charlie Toliver!"— and leaped up and huddled down and moaned and rolled and rose and looked for me.

But, after all, fortune was merciful, and I was gone; the Major had summoned me—his brother had come. I went circuitously and alone. As I started, some fellow writhing on the grass cried, "Charlie Tol—oh, this is better than a tcharade!" and a flash of divination enlightened me. While I went I burned with shame, rage and nervous exhaustion; the name Scott Gholson had gasped in my ear was the name of her in the curtained wagon, and I cursed the day in which I had heard of Charlotte Oliver.

IV

THREE DAYS' RATIONS

In the vocabulary of a prig, but in the wrath of a fishwoman, I execrated Scott Gholson; his jealousies, his disclosures, his religion, his mispronunciations; and Ned Ferry—that cockerel! Here was I in the barrel, and able only to squeal in irate terror at whoever looked down upon me. I could have crawled under a log and died. At the door of the Major's tent I paused to learn why there was laughter in there also, and in the bewilderment and joy of one to whom comes reprieve when the rope is on his neck, I overheard Harry Helm,

Three Days' Rations

the General's nephew and aide-de-camp, who had been with us, telling what a howling good joke Smith had just got off on Gholson!

"We shall have to get Ned Ferry back here," the Major was saying as I entered, "to make you boys let Scott Gholson alone."

The young man laughed and turned to go. "Why doesn't Ned Ferry make *her* let Gholson alone? He can do it; he's got her round his finger as tight as she's got Gholson round hers."

"Harry," replied the Major, from his table full of documents, "don't you know that any man who's got a woman wrapped round his finger has also got her wrapped round his throat?"

The aide-de-camp laughed like a rustic and vanished. "Smith," said the Major, "your eyes are—"

"I've been awake for forty-eight hours, Major. But —oh, I'm not sleepy."

"Well, go get some sleep.—No, go at once; you'll be called when needed."

But I was not needed; while I slept, who should come back and do my work in my stead but Ned Ferry. When I awoke it was with a bound of alarm to see clear day. The command was breaking camp. I rushed out of the tent with canteen, soap and comb, and ran into the arms of the mess-cook. We were alone. "Oh, yass, seh," he laughed as he poured the water into my hands, "th'ee days' rairtion. Seh? Lawd! dey done drawed and cook' befo' de fus' streak o' light. But you all right; here yo' habbersack, full up. Oh, I done fed yo' hoss. Here yo' jacket an' cap; and here yo'

15

saddle an' bridle—Oh, you welcome; I dess tryin' to git shet of 'em so's I kin strak de tent."

As I mounted, our wagonmaster rode by me, busy as a skipper in a storm. "Oh, here!" he cried, wheeled, and reaching something to me added, "that's your pass. Major Harper wants you as quick as you can show up. He says never mind the column, ride straight after him. Keep this road to Hazlehurst and then go down the main Brookhaven road till you overtake him. He's by himself—nearly."

As the rider wheeled away I blurted out with anxious loudness in the general hubbub, "Isn't his brother with him?"

He flashed back a glare of rebuke and then bellowed to heaven and earth, "Oh, the devil and Tom Walker! I don't keep run of sutlers and citizens!" He took a circuit, standing in his stirrups and calling orders to his teamsters, and as he neared me again he said very gently, "Good Lord! my boy, don't you know better than to shoot your mouth off like that? You'll find nobody with the Major but Ned Ferry, and I don't say you'll find him."

I galloped to the road. Away down through the woods it was full of horsemen falling into line. With the nearest colonel was Lieutenant Helm, the aide-de-camp. I turned away from them toward Hazlehurst, but looked back distrustfully. Yes, sure enough, the whole command was facing into column the other way! My horse and I whirled and stood staring and swelling with indignation—we ordered south, and the brigade heading westward! He fretted, tramped, neighed, and began hurriedly to paw through the globe to head them off on the other side. He even threatened to rear; but when I showed him I was ashamed of that, he bore me proudly, and I sat him as proudly as he bore me, for he made me more than half my friends. And now as the aide-de-camp wheeled about from the receding column and came our way saluting cordially, we turned and trotted beside him jauntily. Our first talk was of saddles, but very soon I asked where the General was.

"Out on the Natchez Trace waiting for the command. I'm carrying orders to Fisher's battery, down here by the cross-roads. Haven't you seen the General this morning? What! haven't seen him in his new uniform? Whoop! he's a blaze of glory! Look here, Smith, I believe you know who brought it to him!"

"How on earth should I know?"

"Oh, how innocent you always are! Look here! just tell me this; was it the Major's brother brought it, or was it Ned Ferry?"

"Suppose it wasn't either."

"I knew it! I knew it was her! Ah, you rogue, you know it was her!"

"Well, that *might* depend on who 'her' is." We had reached the cross-roads and he was turning south.

"Look!" he said, and gave the glance and smile of the lady in the curtained wagon so perfectly that I cackled like a small boy. "Oh, you know that, do you? I dare you to say she didn't bring it!"

"I give you my word I don't know!" called I as the distance grew between us.

The Cavalier

" And I give you my word I don't care!" he crowed back as we galloped apart. His speech was two or three words longer, but they are inappropriate at the end of a chapter, and I expurgate.

V.

EIGHTEEN, NINETEEN, TWENTY

On entering Hazlehurst I observed all about the railway-station a surprising amount of quartermaster's stores. A large part were cases of boots and shoes. Laden with such goods, a train of shabby box-cars stood facing south, its beggarly wood-burner engine sniffing and weeping, while the cork-legged conductor helped all hands wood up. Though homely, the picture was a stirring one. Up through the blue summer morning came the sun, bringing to mind the words of the dying Mirabeau, " If that is not God, at least it's his first cousin."

Even in the character of the goods there was eloquence, and not a drollery in the scene, not even an ugliness, but was touched, was rife, with the woe of a war whose burning walls were falling in on us. And outward, too, upon others; a few up-ended cotton-bales leaned against each other ragged and idle, while women and babes starved for want of them in far-away Lancaster.

One of the cars furthest from the engine had no freight proper, only a number of trunks; and these were nearly hidden by the widely crinolined flounces of an elegant elderly lady who sat on the middle one. And now she, too, was hidden, and the wide doorway in the side of the car more than filled, by the fashionable gowns of three girls. On the ground below there stood a lieutenant in a homemade gray uniform, and at his back half a dozen big, slouching, barefoot boys squirted tobacco juice and gazed at the ladies. The officer scanned me, spoke to the ladies, scanned me again, and threw up an arm. "Ho—o! Come here! Hullo! Come here—if you please."

If he had not said please he should have ho'd and hullo'd in vain, but at that word I turned. Before I had covered half the distance I read New Orleans! my dear, dear old New Orleans! in every line of those ladies' draperies, and at twenty-five yards I saw one noble family likeness in all four of their sweet faces. Oh, but those three maidens were fair! and I could name each by her name at a glance: Camille, Cécile, Estelle; eighteen, nineteen, twenty!

There was a hush of attention among them as the lieutenant and I saluted. His left hand was gone at the wrist and the sleeve pinned back on itself. He asked my name; I told him. In the car there was a stir of deepening interest. I inquired if he was the post-quartermaster here. He was.

"Ain't you Major Harper's quartermaster-sergeant?" he asked.

"I am his clerk." In the car a flash of joy and then great decorum.

As he handed me a writing he glowed kindly. It proved to be from Major Harper; a requisition upon this officer for shoes and clothing; not for a brigade, regiment or company, but for me alone, from hat to shoes. I tendered it back silently, and saw that he knew its purport already from the Major, and that the ladies knew it from him. The good fellow looked quite happy a moment, but then reddened as they joyfully crowded the car's doorway to see me fitted!

"We can select out sev'l pair—" he began, but heard a puerile titter and lost his nerve. "Now, you boys that ain't got any business here, jest clair out!—Go! I tell you, aw I'll—" The boys loitered off toward the engine. "We can select out sev'l si-izes," he drawled, uncovering a box, "and fit you ove' in my office. You ain't so pow'ful long nor so pow'ful slim, but these-yeh gov'ment contrac's they seldom ev' allow fo' anybody so slim in the waist bein' so long in the, eh,—so, eh,—so long f'om thah down. But yet still, if you'll jest light off yo' hoss and come and look into this-yeh box—"

Hmm! yes! I wouldn't have got off my horse and leaned over that box to save the Confederacy. "I thank you, Lieutenant, but I can't stop. If you'll hand me up a jacket and pair of shoes I'll sign for them and go. I don't want a hat, but I reckon I'd as well include shoes, although really,—" I glanced down brazenly at the stirrup-leathers that so snugly hid my naked toes.

As the quartermaster lifted out a pair of brogans as broad as they were long, there came a cry of protestation from the freight-car group, that brought the entire herd of rustics from the woodpile and the locomotive.

Eighteen, Nineteen, Twenty

Miss Harper rose behind her nieces, tall, slender, dark, with keen black eyes as kind as they were penetrating. "My boy!" she cried, "you cannot wear those things!"

Camille, the youngest, whispered to her, whereupon she beckoned. "Oh!—oh, do come here!—Mr. Smith, I am the sister of Major Harper. You're from New Orleans? Does your mother live in Apollo Street?"

"Yes, madam, between Melpomene and Terpsichore."

"Richard Thorndyke Smith! My dear boy," she cried, while the nieces gasped at each other with gestures and looks all the way between Terpsichore and Melpomene, and then the four cried in chorus, "We know your mother!"

"We've got a letter for you from her!" exclaimed Camille.

"And a suit of unie-*fawm!*" called Cécile, with her Creole accent.

"We smuggled it through!" chanted the trio, ready to weep for virtuous joy. And then they clasped arms like the graces, about their aunt, and let her speak.

"We all helped your mother make your uniform," she said. "In the short time we've known her we've learned to love her dearly." With military brevity she told how they had unexpectedly got a pass and were just out of New Orleans—"poor New Orleans!" put in Estelle, the eldest, the pensive one; that they had come up from Pontchatoula yesterday and last night, and had thrown themselves on beds in the "hotel" yonder without venturing to disrobe, and so had let her

21

The Cavalier

brother pass within a few steps of them while they slept!
"Telegraph? My dear boy, we came but ten miles an
hour, but we outran our despatch!" Now they had
telegraphed again, to Brookhaven, and thanks to the
post-quartermaster, were going down there at once on
this train. While this was being told something else
was going on. The youngest niece, Camille, had put
herself entirely out of sight. Now she reappeared with
very rosy cheeks, saying, "Here's the letter."

My thanks were few and awkward, for there still
hung to the missive a basting thread, and it was as
warm as a nestling bird. I bent low—everybody was
emotional in those days—kissed the fragrant thing,
thrust it into my bosom, and blushed worse than Camille.

"Poor boy!" said the aunt. "It's the first line
you've had for months. Your sweet mother wrote, but
her letters were all intercepted, and the last time she
was warned that next time she'd be dealt with according to military usage! I'm glad we could give you
this one at once. We can't give you the uniform, for
we—why, girls, what—why, what nonsense!"

Maybe I did not say vindictive things inside me just
then! The three nieces had turned open-mouthed upon
one another and sunk down upon their luggage with
averted faces.

"I say we can't give it to you now," Miss Harper
persisted, with a motherly smile; "we're wearing it
ourselves. We've had no time to take it off. I couldn't
get the boots off me last night. And even if you had
the boots, the other things—"

"Aunt Martha!" moaned some one—

A Handsome Stranger

"Well, in short," said the aunt, twinkling like her brother, "we can't deliver the goods, and—" She started as though some one had slapped her between the shoulder-blades. It was the engine caused it, whistling in the old, lawless way, putting a whoop, a howl, a scream and a wail into one. The young ladies quailed, the train jerked like several collisions, the bell began tardily to clang, and my steed whirled, cleared a packing case, whirled again, and stood facing the train, his eyes blazing, his nostrils flapping, not half so much frightened as insulted. The post-quarter-master waved to the ladies and they to us. For a last touch I lifted my cap high and backed my horse on drooping haunches—you've seen Buffalo Bill do it—and then, with a leap like a cricket's, and to a clapping of maidens' hands that made me whooping drunk, we stretched away, my horse and I, on a long smooth gallop, for Brookhaven.

VI

A HANDSOME STRANGER

CERTAINLY no cricket ever dropped blither music from his legs than did my beautiful horse that glorious morning as we clattered in perfect rhythm on the hard clean road of the wide pine forest. Ah! the forest is not there now; the lumbermen—

For an hour or so the world seemed to have taken me for its center as smoothly as a sleeping top. Only after a good seven miles did my meditations begin to reveal any bitter in the sweet; but it was in recalling

for the twentieth time the last sight of Camille, that
I heard myself say, I know not whether softly or
loudly,

"Oh, hang the uniform!"

The morning was almost sultry. As I halted in the
clear ripples of a gravelly "branch" to let my horse
drink, I heard no great way off the Harpers' train
shrieking at cattle on the track, and looking up I noticed just behind me an unfrequented by-road carefully
masked with brush, according to a new habit of the
"citizens". The next moment my horse threw up his
head to listen. Then I heard hoofs and voices, and
presently there came trotting through the oak bushes
and around the mask of brush two horsemen unusually
well mounted, clad and armed. Their very dark gray
uniforms were so trim and so nearly blue that my heart
came into my throat; but then I noticed they carried
neither carbines nor sabres, but repeaters only, a brace
to each. They splashed lightly to either side of me,
and the three horses drank together.

"Good-morning," we said. One of the men was a
sergeant. He scanned my animal, and then me, with a
dawning smile. "That's a fightin'-cock of a horse
you've got, sonny."

"Yes, bub," I replied. The two men laughed so ex-
plosively that my horse lifted his head austerely.

"Jim," said the younger, "I don't believe all the
conscripts we've caught these three days are worth the
powder they've cost!"

"No," replied Sergeant Jim, "I doubt if the most of
'em are."

A Handsome Stranger

I turned to him and drew down my under eyelid. " Will you kindly tell me, sir, if you see any unnatural discoloration in there? "

He smiled. " No, but I can put some there if you want it."

" Thank you, I couldn't let you take so much trouble —or risk."

The three of us pattered out of the stream abreast. " No trouble," replied the sergeant, " it wouldn't take half a minute."

" No," I rejoined, " the first step would be the last."

The men laughed again. " You must a-been born with all your teeth," said the private, as we quickened to a trot. " What makes you think we ain't after conscripts? "

" Oh, if you were you wouldn't say so. You'd let on to be looking for good crossings on Pearl River, so that if Johnston should get chewed up we needn't be caught here in a hole, Ferry's scouts and all."

The pair looked at each other behind my neck for full ten seconds. Then the younger man leaned to his horse's mane in a silent laugh while Sergeant Jim looked me over again and remarked that he would be horn-swoggled !

" I'm willing," I responded, and we all laughed. The younger horseman asked my name. " Smith," I said, with dignity, and they laughed again, their laugh growing louder when I would not smile.

" Well, say ; maybe you'll tell us who this is we're about to meet up with."

Through the shifting colonnades of pine, a hundred

yards in front of us, came two horsemen in the same
blue-gray of the pair beside me. "Whoever he is," I
said, "that gray he's riding is his second best, or it's
borrowed," for his mount, though good, was no match
for him.

"Borrowed!" echoed the sergeant. "If he doesn't
own that mare no man does."

"Nor no woman?" I asked, and again across the
back of my neck my two companions gazed at each
other.

"By ganny!" exclaimed one, and— "You're a
coon," murmured the other, as the new-comers drew
near. The younger of these also was a private. Behind his elbow was swung a Maynard rifle. Both carried revolvers. The elder wore a long straight sword
whose weather-dimmed orange sash showed at the front
of a loose cut-away jacket. Under this garment was
a shirt of strong black silk, made from some lady's
gown and daintily corded with yellow. On the jacket's
upturned collar were the two gilt bars of a first lieutenant, but the face above them shone with a combined
intelligence and purity that drew my whole attention.

A familiar friendship lighted every countenance but
mine as this second pair turned and rode with us, the
lieutenant in front on Sergeant Jim Longley's right, and
the two privates with me between them behind. For
some minutes the sergeant, in under-tone, made report
to his young superior. Then in a small clearing he
turned abruptly into a neighborhood road, and at his
word my two companions pricked after him westward.
I closed up beside the lieutenant; he praised the weath-

A Handsome Stranger

er, and soon our talk was fluent though broken, as we moved sometimes at a trot and often faster. In stolen moments I scanned him with the jealousy of my youth. Five feet, ten; humph! I was five, nine and a thirty-second. In weight he looked to be just what I always had in mind in those prayers without words with which I mounted every pair of commissary scales I came to. The play of his form as our smooth-gaited horses sped through the flecking shades was worth watching for its stanch and supple grace. Alike below the saddle and above it he was as light as a leaf and as firm as a lance. I had long yearned to own a pair of shoulders not too square for beauty nor too sloping for strength, and lo, here they were, not mine, but his. No matter; the slender mustache he sported he was welcome to, I had shaved off nearly as good a one; wished now I hadn't. As once or twice he lifted his képi to the warm breeze I took new despair from the soft locks of darkest chestnut that lay on his head in manly order, ready enough to curl but waiving the privilege.

" Cock-a-doodle-doo," thought I; " if those are not the same hundred-dollar boots I saw yesterday morning, at least they are their first cousins!"

The Cavalier

VII

ONCE more I measured my man. Celerity, valor, endurance, they were his iridescent neck and tail feathers. On a certain piece of road where we went more slowly I mentioned abruptly my clerkship under Major Harper and watched for the effect, but there was none. Did he know the Major? Oh, yes, and we fell to piling item upon item in praise of the quartermaster's virtues and good looks. Presently, with shrewdest intent, I said the Major was fine enough to be the hero of a novel! Did not my companion think so?

Yes, he thought so; but I believed the glow in his tone was for novels. I extolled the romance of actual life! I denounced that dullness which fails to see the poetry of daily experience, and goes wandering after the mirages of fiction! And I was ready to fight him if he liked. But he agreed with me most cordially.

"And yet," he began to add,—

"Yet what?" I snapped out, with horse eyes.

"Doesn't a good story revive the poetry of our actual lives?" He wiped the rim of his cap with a handkerchief of yellow silk enriched at one corner with needlework.

"Um-hm!" I thought; "Charlotte Oliver, eh?" I responded tartly that I had that very morning met four ladies the poetry of whose actual, visible loveliness had abundantly illustrated to me the needlessness and impertinence of fiction! By the way, did he not think

A Plague on Names!

feminine beauty was always in its ripest perfection at eighteen?

Well, he thought a girl might be prettiest at eighteen and handsomest much later. And again I said to myself, " Charlotte Oliver! " But when I looked searchingly into his eyes their manly sweetness so abashed me that I dropped my glance and felt him looking at me. I remembered my fable and flinched. " Isn't your name—" I cried, and choked, and when I would have said Ferry, another word slipped out instead. He did not hear it plainly:

" Cockerel, did you say? "

A sweet color was I. " Yes, that's what I said; Cockerel. Isn't your last name Cockerel? "

" No," he said, " my last name is Durand." He gave it the French pronunciation.

" Mine is Smith," I said, and we galloped.

A plague on names! But I was not done with them yet. We met other scouts coming out of the east, who also gave reports and went on westward, sometimes through the trackless woods. At a broad cross-road which spanned the whole State from the Alabama line to the Mississippi River stood another sergeant, with three men, waiting. They were the last.

Again we galloped alone; and as our horses' hoofs beat drummers' music out of the round earth our dialogue drifted into confessions of our own most private theories of conduct, character and creation. Now that this man's name was not—Cockerel, my heart opened to him and we began to admit to each other the perplexities of this great, strange thing called Life. Espe-

cially we confessed how every waking hour found us
jostled and torn between two opposite, unappeasable
tendencies of soul; one an upward yearning after
everything high and pure, the other a down-dragging
hunger for every base indulgence. I was warmed and
fed. Yet I was pained to find him so steeped in pre-
sumptuous error, so wayward of belief and unbelief.
The sweet ease with which he overturned and emptied
out some of my arguments gave me worse failure of the
diaphragm than a high swing ever did. Nevertheless
I responded; and he rejoined; and I rejoined again,
and presently he gave me the notion that he was suffering some cruel moral strain.

VIII

ANOTHER CURTAINED WAGON

Upon whatever fundamental scheme we persever-
ingly concentrate our powers, upon whatever main road
of occupation we take life's journey,—art, politics, com-
merce, science,—if only we will take its upper fork as
often as the road divides, then will that road itself,
and not necessarily any cross-road, lead us to the noblest, truest plane of convictions, affections, aspirations.
Such a frame of mind may be quite without religiosity,
as unconscious as health; but the proof of its religious
reality will be that, as if it were a lighthouse light and
we its keeper, everybody else, or at any rate everybody
out on the deep, will see it plainer than we. Such is the
gist of what this young man was saying to me, when

Another Curtained Wagon

our speculations were brought to an end by our over-taking a man well mounted, and a woman whose rough-gaited mare was followed by a colt.

The pair took our pace, the man plying me with questions, and his wife, in front, telling Lieutenant Durand all the rumors of the day. Her scant hair was of a scorched red tone, she was freckled down into her collar, her elbows waggled to the mare's jog, and her voice was as flat as a duck's. Her nag had trouble to keep up, and her tiny faded bonnet had even more to keep on. Yet the day was near when the touch of those freckled hands was to seem to me kinder than the breath of flowers, as they bathed my foul-smelling wounds, and she would say, in the words of the old song, " Let me kiss him for his mother," and I should be helpless to prevent her. By and by the man raised his voice:—

" Why, yo' name *is* Smith, to be sho'! I thought you was jest a-tryin' to chaw me. Why, Major Harper al-ludened to you not mo'n a half-ow ago. Why, Miz Wall! oh, Miz Wall!"

But the wife was absorbed. " Yayse, seh," she was saying to the lieutenant, " and he told us about they comin' in on the freight-kyahs f'om Hazlehurst black with dust and sut and a-smuttyin' him all oveh with they kisses and goin's-on. He tol' me he ain't neveh so enjoyed havin' his face dirty sence he was a boy. He would a-been plumb happy, ef on'y he could a-got his haynds on that clerk o' his'n. And when he tol' us what a gay two-hoss turn-out he'd sekyo'ed for the ladies to travel in, s' I, Majo', that's all ri-ght! You

The Cavalier

jest go on whicheveh way you got to go! Husband and me, we'll ride into Brookhaven and bring 'em out to ow place and jest take ca'e of 'em untel yo' clerk is *found*."

" Miz Wall! " cried the husband—" She's busy talkin'.—Miz Wall!—she don't hyuh me. I hate to interrupt heh.—Oh, Miz Wall! hyuh's Majo' Harper's clerk, right now! "

" Law, you hain't! " cried Mrs. Wall, smiling back as she jounced. " If you air, the Majo's sisteh's got written awdehs fo' you."

I shot forward, but had hardly more than sent back my good-bye when around a bend of the road, in a wagon larger than Charlotte Oliver's, with the curtains rolled up, came the four Miss Harpers, unsooted and radiant. The aunt drove. We turned, all four, and rode with them, and while the seven chatted gaily I read to myself the Major's note. It bade me take these four ladies into my most jealous care and conduct them to a point about thirty miles west of where we then were. A dandy's task in a soldier's hour! I ground my teeth, but as I lifted my glance I found Camille's eyes resting on me and read anxiety in them before she could put on a smile of unemotional friendliness that faded rapidly into abstraction. She was as pretty as the bough of wild azaleas in her hand, yet moving forward I told her aunt the order's purport and that it implied the greatest despatch compatible with mortal endurance. The whole four seemed only delighted.

But Mrs. Wall protested. No, no, her hospitality first, and a basket of refreshments to be stowed in the

Another Curtained Wagon

vehicle, besides. "Why, that'll *sa-ave* ti-ime. You-all goin' to be supprised to find how hungry y'all ah, befo' you come to yo' journey's en', to-night, and them col' victuals goin' taste pow'ful fi-ine!"

Our acceptance was unanimous. I even decided not to inform Lieutenant Durand until after the repast, that ladies under my escort did not pick acquaintanceship with soldiers on the public highway. But before the brief meal was over I was wishing him hanged. Hang the heaven-high theories that had so lately put me in love with him! Hang his melodious voice, his modest composure, his gold-barred collar, his easy command of topics! Hang the women! they feasted on his every word and look! Ah, ladies! if I were mean enough to tell it—that man doesn't believe in hell! He has a down-dragging hunger for every base indulgence; he has told me so!

How fast acquaintance grew! When he addressed himself to Cécile, the cousin of the other two, her black eyes leapt with delight; for as calmly as if that were the only way, he spoke to her in French—asked her a question. She gave answer in happiest affirmation, and explained to her aunt that her Durand schoolmates of a year or two back were cousins to the Lieutenant. When the throng came out to the carry-all I was there and mounted. Squire Wall took me a few rods to point out where a fork of his private road led into the highway. Then the carry-all came merrily after, and with a regret that surprised me I answered our Lieutenant's farewell wave, forgave him all his charms, and saw him face westward and disappear by a bridle-path.

The Cavalier

IX

THE DANDY'S TASK

WESTWARD likewise we soon were bickering. The morning sun shone high; the thin, hot dust blew out over the blackened ground of some forest "burn" or through the worm fence of some field where a gang of slave men and women might be ploughing or hoeing between the green rows of young cotton or corn. The level stretches were many, the slopes gradual, and to those sweet city-bred ladies everything was new and delightful; a log cabin!—with clay chimney on the outside!—a well and its well-sweep!—another cabin with its gourd-vines! They knew that blessed alchemy which turns all things into the poetry of the moment. Sweet they would have been anywhere to any eye or mind; but I was a homeless trooper lad, and sweeter to the soldier boy than water on the battlefield are short hours with ladies who love him for his banner and his rags.

These four were charmed with an old field given up to sedge, its deep rain-gullies as red as gaping wounds, its dead trees in tatters of long gray moss. Estelle became a student of flowers, Cécile of birds, Camille of trees. All my explanations were alike enchantingly strange. To their minds it had never occurred that the land sloped the same way the water ran! When told that these woods abounded in deer and wild turkey they began to look out for them at every new turn of the road.

The Dandy's Task

And the turns came fast. Happy miles, happy leagues; each hour was of a mellower sweetness than the last; they seemed to ripen in the sun. The only drawback was my shame of a sentimental situation, but once or twice I longed to turn the whole equipage into the woods—or the ditch. As, for instance, when three pine-woods cavalrymen had no sooner got by us than they set up that ribald old camp-song,

> " We're going to get married, mamma, mamma ;
> We're going to get married, but don't tell pa——"

" Deserters, I don't doubt! " was my comment to the ladies. Tongue revenge is poor, but it is something.

Except in such moments, however, the war seemed farther away than it had for months and months. But about eleven o'clock we began to find the way scored by the fresh ruts of heavy wheels and the dust deepened by hundred of hoofs. The tops and faces of the road-side banks were newly trampled and torn by clambering human feet. Here was a canteen, smashed in a wheel-track; yonder a fragment of harness; here lay a broken hame, there was the half of a russet brogan and yonder a ragged sock stained and bloody.

" Why, what does all this mean? " asked Miss Harper amid her nieces' cries.

I said it meant Fisher's battery hurrying to the front. Twenty miles since five that morning was a marvel, horse artillery though they were, for, as I pointed out by many signs, their animals were in ill condition. " We shall have to go round them by neighborhood

35

roads," I said, and presently we were deeper than ever in woodland shades and sources of girlish wonderment. The humid depths showed every sort of green and gray, their trunks, bushes and boughs, bearded with hanging moss, robed with tangled vines and chapleted with mistletoe. We seemed to have got this earth quite to ourselves and very much to our liking.

One o'clock. Miss Harper suggested a halt to feed the horses. I, knowing what it would cost me to dismount and go walking about, said no, thrice no; let us first get back upon the main road in front of that battery. On, therefore, we hurried, and soon the reality of the war was vivid to us again. In a stretch of wet road where the team had mutely begged leave to walk and the ladies had urged me to sing we had at length paused in a pebbly rivulet to allow the weary animals to drink, and the girls and the aunt and the greenwood and I were all in chorus bidding somebody

" Unloose the west port and let us go free,"

when, just as our last note died among the trees one of us cried, " Listen! " and through the stillness there came from far away on our right the last three measures of a bugle sounding The March.

My eyes rested in Camille's and hers in mine. A musical license gave us the courage. At the last note our gaze did not sink but took on more glow, while out of the forest behind us a distant echo answered the last measure of the strain.

The Dandy's Task

Then our eyes slowly fell; and however it may have seemed to her, to me it was as if the vanished strains were not only or chiefly of bugle and echo, but as though our two hearts had called and answered in that melodious unison.

All that warm afternoon we paid the tiresome penalty of having pushed our animals too smartly at the outset. We grew sedate; sedate were the brows of the few strangers we met. We talked in pairs. When I spoke with Miss Harper the four listened. She asked about the evils of camp life; for she was one of that fine sort to whom righteousness seems every man's and woman's daily business, one of the most practical items in the world's affairs. And I said camp life was fearfully corrupting; that the merest boys cursed and swore and stole, or else were scorned as weaklings. Then I grew meekly silent and we talked in pairs again, and because I yearned to talk most with Camille I talked most with Estelle. Three times when I turned abruptly from her to Camille and called, " Hark!" the fagged-out horses halted, and as we struck our listening pose the bugle's faint sigh ever farther in our rear was but feebly proportioned to the amount of our gazing into each other's eyes.

Once, when we were not halted or harkening, we heard overmuch; heard that which brought us to an instant stand and caused even Miss Harper to gaze on me with dismayed eyes and parted lips, and the blood to go thumping through my veins. From a few hundred yards off in the northwest, beyond the far corner of an old field and the woods at its back, two gunshots together, then a third, with sharp, hot cries of alarum and command, and then another and another shot, rang out and spread wanderingly across the tender landscape.

X

THE SOLDIER'S HOUR

To regain the highroad we had turned into a northerly fork, and were in as lovely a spot as we had seen all day. Before us and close on our right were the dense woods of magnolia, water-oak, tupelo and a hundred other affluent things that towered and spread or clambered and hung. On the left lay the old field, tawny with bending sedge and teeming with the yellow rays of the sun's last hour. This field we overlooked through a fence-row of persimmon and wild plum. Among these bushes, half fallen into a rain-gully, a catalpa, of belated bloom, was loaded with blossoms and bees, and I was directing Camille's glance to it when the shots came. Another outcry or two followed, and then a weird silence.

"Some of our boys attacked by a rabbit," I suggested, but still hearkened.

"That was not play, Mr. Smith," Miss Harper had begun to respond, when a voice across the sedge-field called with startling clearness,

"Hi! there goes one of them!—Halt!—Halt, you blue—" pop!—pop!—pop!

"Prisoners making a break!" I forgot all my tatters and stood on tiptoe in the stirrups to overpeer the

The Soldier's Hour

fence-row. The next instant—"Sh—sh!" said I and slid to the ground. "Hold this bridle!" I gave it to Camille. "Don't one of you make a sound or a motion; there's a Yankee coming across this field in the little gully just behind us."

I bent low, ran a few steps, cocking my revolver as I went. Then I rose, peeped, bent again, ran, rose, peeped, waited a few seconds behind the catalpa, and without rising peeped once more. Here he came! He was an officer. His uniform was torn and one whole side of him showed he had at some earlier hour ridden through a hedge and fallen from his horse. On he came! nearer—nearer—oh, what a giant! Quickly, warily, he crouched under the fence where it hung low across the gully, and half through it in that huddled posture he found my revolver between his astonished eyes. I did not yell at him, for I did not want the men he had escaped from to come and take him from me; yet when I said, "Halt, or you die!" the four ladies heard me much too plainly. For, frankly, I said more and worse. I felt my slenderness, my beardless youth, my rags, and his daring, and to offset them all in a bunch, I—I cursed him. I let go only one big damn and I've never spoken one since, though I've done many a worse thing, of course. I protest it was my modesty prompted it then.

"I surrender," he said, with amiable ease. I stepped back a pace and he drew out and straightened up—the tallest man I had ever seen. I laughed, he smiled, laughed; my eyes filled with tears, I blazed with rage, and in plain sight and hearing of those ladies he said,

The Cavalier

"That's all right, my son, get as scared as you like; only, you don't need to cry about it."

"Hold your tongue!" I barked my wrath like a frightened puppy, drawing back a stride and laying my eye closer along the pistol. "If you call me your son again I'll send you to your fathers."

His smile darkened. "I am your prisoner," he said, with a sudden splendid stateliness, and right then I guessed who he was.

"Yess, ssir, you are!" I retorted. "Move to that wagon! And if you take one step out of common time you'll never take another."

The aunt and her nieces were standing in the carryall, she majestic, they laughing and weeping in the one act. I waved them into their seats.

"Halt!" We halted. "About face!" As the prisoner eyed me both of us listened. His equanimity was almost winsome, and I saw that friendliness was going to be his tactics.

"Guess I'm the first Yankee y' ever caught, ain't I?" His smile was superior, but congratulatory.

"You'll be the first prisoner I ever shot if you get any funnier!"

We listened again. "They've gone the wrong way," I said, still savage.

"No," he replied, "I came the wrong way."

The ladies smiled; I glowered. "Take those horses by their heads and turn them to me!"

An instant his superb eye resented, but then he pleasantly did my bidding. "Suits me well; rather chance it with you than with those I've just left."

"I surrender," he said, with amiable ease.

Captain Jewett

"Easier to get away, you think?" I asked, with a worse frown than ever, as he stepped into the carry-all and took the lines.

"No, not so easy; but those fellows are Arkansans, and they're in a bad humor with me."

I took the hint and grew less ferocious. "While you," I said, "are Captain Jewett."

"I am," was his reply, and my heart leaped for joy. We hurried away. My captive was the most daring Union scout between Vicksburg and New Orleans; these very Harpers knew that. The thing unknown to us was that already his fate was entangled with Ned Ferry's and Charlotte Oliver's, as yet more it would be, with theirs and ours, in days close at hand.

XI

CAPTAIN JEWETT

ONCE more we were in the by-road which had brought us westward parallel with the highway. The prisoner drove. Aunt Martha sat beside him, slim, dark, black-eyed, stately, her silver-gray hair rolled high à la Pompadour. With a magnanimity rare in those bitter days she incited him to talk, first of New Orleans, where he had spent a month in camp on one of the public squares, and then of his far northern home, and of loved ones there, mother, wife and child. The nieces, too, gave a generous attention. Only I, riding beside the hind wheels, held solemnly aloof.

"Front!" I once snapped out with a ring that made

the trees reply and the ladies catch their breath. "If you steal one more look back here I'll put a ball into your leg."

He smiled, chirped the horses up and resumed his chat. I heard him praise my horse and compare him not unfavorably with his own which he had lost that morning. He and a few picked men had been surprised in a farmhouse at breakfast. They had made a leap and a dash, he said, but one horse and rider falling dead, his horse, unhurt, had tumbled over them, and here was his rider.

I prompted Camille to ask if he had ever encountered Ned Ferry, and he laughed.

"No," he said, but Ned Ferry had lately restored to him, by proxy, some lost letters, with an invitation to *come and see him.*

I laughed insolently. The young ladies sparkled, and so did Miss Harper, as she asked him who had been the proxy.

He said the proxy was a young woman who had a knack of getting passes through the lines, and the three girls exchanged looks as knowing as they were delighted.

"I tell her as a friend," he said, "she'll get one into Fortress Monroe yet!"

Miss Harper's keen eyes glittered. "You northerners hardly realize our feelings concerning the imprisonment of women, I think."

"My dear madam, you don't realize ours. We don't want to imprison women."

So there came a silence, and then a gay laugh as

Captain Jewett

three of us at once asked if he had ever heard of Lieutenant Durand. "Durand!" he cried, and looked
squarely around at me. I lifted the cocked revolver,
but he kept his fine eyes on mine and I rubbed my
ear with my wrist. "What?" he said, "an elegant,
Creole-seeming young fellow, very handsome? Why,
that fellow saved my life this very afternoon."

The young ladies were in rapture. Miss Harper
asked how he had done it.

"If I tell you that," said the Captain, "you won't
like me the least bit."

Whereat Cécile replied, "Ah—well! we cou'n' like
you the leaz bit any-'*ow*."

"I suppose that's so," laughed the officer. "I'll
tell you how it was. My guard were just about to
hang me for saying I thought we had a right to
make soldiers of the darkies, when your friend came
galloping along, saw the thing, and rushed in and cut
the halter with his sword. And when they demanded
to know who and what he was, he told them Durand,
and that they'd hear it again, for he should report
them."

"Oh, sir," cried Estelle, whose eyes, brows, lashes
and hair were all of the same luminous red-brown,
and in whose cheeks the rose seemed always to burn
through the olive, "how can you and your people seek
to kill such men as that?"

"Such as which?" asked the Yankee, with a twinkle. "There were two kinds."

"But, o-oh! sir!" exclaimed the trio, when Miss
Harper waved them to forbear.

The Cavalier

There was yet some daylight left as we trundled into a broad highroad and turned northward. We passed a picket guard and then a whole regiment of cavalry going into camp. They scrambled to the sides of the road and stormed us with questions, chaffing us cruelly when I remained silent. " Lawd! look a' this-yeh Yank a-bringin' in ow desertehs! " " Hey, you big Yank, you jest let that po' little conscrip' go! "

Headquarters, we heard from a courier who said he was the third sent out to find us, were at the " Sessions house " two miles further on. We sent him galloping back there, and after a while here came Major Harper and three or four others of the staff, including Harry Helm. What a flood of mirthful compliment there was at sight of us and our captive; Harry was positively silly. In the series of introductions that followed he was left paired with Camille, and I said things to myself. Major Harper rode by the prisoner. " Well, Captain," he said, " you've had some experiences since you left me this morning. Don't you want to give us your parole this time, temporarily, for an hour or so, and be more comfortable? "

" Thank you, Major," the Federal affably replied, " that would be a great relief to this most extraordinary youngster that I've brought with me." He gave it and we turned into a lofty grove whitened with our headquarters tents.

" Smith," said the Major, " your part is done, and well done. You needn't report to me again to-night; the General wishes to see you a moment. Captain, will you go with this young man to General Austin's tent? "

In the General's Tent

XII

IN THE GENERAL'S TENT

I WENT to Gholson. He told me I was relieved of my captive and bade me go care for my horse and return in half an hour. In going I passed close by the Sessions plantation house. Every door and window was thrown wide to the night air, and preparations were in progress for a dance; and as I returned, a slave boy ran across my path, toward the house, bearing a flaming pine torch and followed by two ambulances filled with daughters of the neighborhood in clouds of white gauze. I found the General in fatigue dress. His new finery hung on the tent-pole at his back. Old Dismukes, the bull-necked colonel of the Arkansans, lounged on a camp-cot. Both smoked cigars.

The General asked me a number of idle questions and then said my prisoner had called me a good soldier. Old Dismukes smiled so broadly that I grew hot, believing the Yankee had told them of my tears.

"Smith," said the Colonel, and then smoked and smiled again till my brow beaded,—"tired?"

"No, sir."

"That's a lie," he pleasantly remarked, and lay back, enjoying my silent wrath. "Send him, General," he added, "he's your man."

The General looked at me between puffs of his cigar. "I hear you've ridden over fifty miles to-day."

"Yes, General."

The Cavalier

"If I give you a good fresh horse can you go twenty-three miles more by midnight?"

"Yes, General, if I don't have to save the horse."

"The horse may have to save you," drawled the Arkansan.

"I think you know Lieutenant Durand?" asked the General, with a quizzical eye.

"Slightly."

"Well, Smith, on his suggestion approved by Major Harper, I have detailed another clerk to the Major."

Rills of perspiration tickled my back like flies. "Can't one man do the work?"

"Yes, the new man is detailed in your place."

I almost leaped from the ground in consternation. My whole frame throbbed, my mouth fell open, my tongue was tied.

The man who had got me into this thing—this barrel—lifted the tent-flap. "Mr. Gholson," said the General, "write an order assigning Smith to Ferry's scouts."

The flap fell again and my panic was turned into a joy qualified only by a reduced esteem for my general as a judge of character.

Old Dismukes rose. "Good-night. Shall I send this boy that Yankee's horse?"

"Oh I was forgetting that; yes, do!"

At the door the Colonel gave me a last look. "Good-night, Legs."

I dared not retort, but I looked so hard at his paunch that the General smiled. Then he asked me if I knew where we were then camped, and I said we were on

In the General's Tent

the Meadville and Fayette road, near Franklin, twenty miles southeast of Fayette and—

"That will do. Now, beyond Fayette, about seven miles north, there's a place—"

"Clifton?"

"Don't interrupt me, Smith. Yes, Clifton. You're not to reach there to-night—"

"I can do it, General."

"You can do as you're told; understand?" I understood.

"The enemy are in Fayette to-night," he continued. "So when you get half-way to Fayette, just across Morgan's Creek, you'll take a dim fork on the right running north along the creek. Ever travel by the stars?"

I began to tell how well I knew the stars, but he stopped me. "Yes; well, keep straight north till you strike the road running east and west between Fayette and Union Church. You'll find there a little polling-place called Wiggins. Turn west, toward Fayette, and on the north side of the main road, opposite the blacksmith's shop, you'll come to a small—"

"I see."

"What do you see?" His frown scared me to my finger-tips.

"Why, I suppose I'm to find there a road down Cole's Creek to Clifton."

"Smith, if you interrupt me again, sir, you'll find the road back to your regiment. Opposite that blacksmith's shop you'll see a white cottage. There's a young lady stopping there to-night, a stranger, a traveller. The old lady who lives there has taken her in at my request. See that the young lady gets this envelope. It's no great matter, merely a pass through our lines; but it's your ostensible business till you get there; understand?"

I thought I did until I glanced at the superscription: Miss Coralie Rothvelt.

" Now, here is another matter of much more importance." He showed, but retained, another envelope. " Behind the house where you're to find Miss Rothvelt there's a road into Cole's Creek bottom. The house you're to stop at to-night, say from twelve o'clock till three or half-past, is on that road, about five miles from Wiggins, from Clifton and from Fayette. I'm sending you there expecting the people in that house will rob you if you give them half a chance."

" I understand, General; they'll not get it."

" Smith, I want them to get it. I want them to rob you of this." He waggled the envelope. " I want this to fall into the hands of the enemy; as it will if those people rob you of it."

I snapped my eyes. He smiled and then frowned. " I don't want a clumsy job, now, mind! I don't want you to get captured if you can possibly avoid it; but all the same they mustn't get this so easily as to suspect it's a bait. So I want you to give those villains that half-chance to rob you, but not the other half, or they may—oh, it's no play! You must manage to have this despatch taken from you totally against your will! Then you must reach Clifton shortly after daylight. Ferry's scouts are there, and you'll say to

In the General's Tent

Lieutenant Ferry the single word, Rodney. Understand?" He pretended to be reconsidering. "I—don't know but—after all—I'd better send one of my staff instead of you."

"Oh, General, if you send an officer they'll see the ruse! I can do it! I'll do it all right!"

"I'm most afraid," he said, abstractedly, as he read my detail, which Gholson brought in. "Here,"—he handed it to me — "and here, here's the despatch too."

"What's the name, General, of the man whose house I'm to go to?"

"You'd best not know; I want you to seem to have stumbled upon the place. You can't miss it; there's no other house within two miles of it. Good-bye, my lad;"—he gave me his hand;—" good luck to you."

Gholson, in the Adjutant-general's tent, told me Ned Ferry had named me to the General as a first-class horseman and the most insignificant-looking person he knew of who was fit for this venture.

"Ned Ferry! What does Ned Ferry know about my fitness?"

"Read the address on your despatch," said Gholson, resuming his pen.

I snatched the document from my bosom, into which I had thrust it to seize the General's hand "Oh, Gholson!" I said, in deep-toned grief, as I looked up from the superscription, "is that honest!"

He admitted that by the true religionist's standard it was not honest, but reminded me that Ned Ferry —in his blindness—was only a poor romanticist. The despatch was addressed to Lieutenant Edgard Ferry-Durand.

Major Harper's black boy brought me the Yankee's horse with my bridle and saddle on him; an elegant animal as fresh as a dawn breeze. Also he produced a parcel, my new uniform, and a wee note whose breath smelt of lavender as it said,—

"Papa tells us you are being sent off on courier duty to-night. What a heart-breaking thing is war! How full of cruel sepa'—"

That piece of a word was scored out and "dangers" written in its place. The missive ended all too soon, with the statement that I was requested to call, on my way out of camp, at the side gallery of the house—Sessions's—and let the writer and her sister and her cousin and her father and her aunt see me in my new uniform and bid me good-bye.

XIII

GOOD-BYE, DICK

I FOUND but one white figure under the dim veranda eaves. " Miss Camille? "

"Wh'—who is that?" responded a musical voice. "Why, is that Mr. Smith?" as if I were the last person in the world one should have expected to see there. The like of those moments I had never known. I saw her eyes note the perfect fit of my uniform, though neither of us mentioned it. I tried to tell her that Lieutenant Durand was Ned Ferry and that I was now

Good-Bye, Dick

one of his scouts, but she had already heard both facts, and would not tell me what her father had said about me, it was so good. Standing at the veranda's edge a trifle above me, with her cheek against one of the posts and her gaze on her slipper, she asked if I was glad I was going with Ned Ferry, and I had no more sense than to say I was; but she would neither say she was glad nor tell why she was not.

Through the open windows we could see the dancers. Now and then a pair of fanning promenaders came down the veranda, but on descrying us turned back. I said I was keeping her from the dance. To which she replied, drooping her head again, that she shouldn't dance that night.

" Too tired? "

" No."

" Too warm? "

" Oh, no, not too warm."

" Why, then? "

" Oh—I—just don't feel as if I could, that's all."

My heart beat wildly and I wanted to ask if it was on my account; but I was too pusillanimous a coward, and when I feebly tried to look into her eyes she would not let me, which convinced me that she lacked candor. A dance ended. Gold-laced fellows came and sat on the veranda rail wiping wrists and brows with overtasked handkerchiefs, and explaining the small mishaps of the floor. Two promenaders mentioned the hour. I gasped my amazement and extended my hand. " Good-bye."

" Wait a moment," she murmured, and watched the

The Cavalier

promenading pair turn back. Then she asked if I had read my mother's letter. I said I had. And then, very pensively, with head bent and eyes once more down, she inquired if I liked to get letters. Which led, quite accidentally, to my asking leave to write to her.

She replied that she did not mean that. Nevertheless, I insisted, would she? She only bent lower still. I asked the third time; and with nothing but the parting of her hair for me to look at, she nodded, and one of her braids fell over in front, and I took the pink-ribboned live end of it timorously between thumb and finger and felt as if I had hold of an electric battery.

She backed half a step, and quite needlessly I let it go. Then she bade me not forget I had promised her the words of a certain song. "Want them? Indeed, yes! Did you not say it was an unpublished song written by a messmate of yours?—oh, Mr. Smith! I see why you stammer! You said 'a member of your mess'! oh!—oh!—oh!—you wrote it, yourself! And you wrote it to-day! That explains—" She drew an awesome breath, rose to her toes and knit her knuckles under her throat.

I was in the sweetest consternation. With the end of her braid once more in my fingers I made her promise to keep the dark secret, and so recited them.

" Maiden passing fair, turn away thine eyes!
    Turn away thine eyes ere my bosom burn,
  Lit with foolish hope to hear thy fondling sighs,
    Like yon twilight dove's, breathe, Return, return!
  Turn away thine eyes, maiden passing fair.
    O maiden passing fair, turn away thine eyes!

Good-Bye, Dick

"Maiden passing fair, turn again thine eyes!
   Turn again thine eyes, love's true mercy learn.
Breathe, O! breathe to me, as these love-languid skies
   To yon twilight star breathe, Return, return!
Turn again thine eyes, maiden passing fair.
   O maiden passing fair, turn again thine eyes!"

"Mis-ter Smith! you wrote that?—to-day! Wh'—who is she?"

"One too modest," I murmured, "to know her own portrait." I clutched the braid emotionally and let it go intending to retake it; but she dropped it behind her and said I was too imaginative to be safe.

I stiffened proudly, turned and mounted my steed, but her eyes drew mine. I pressed close, bent over the saddle-bow, and said, "Good-bye, Camille."

"Good-bye." I could barely hear it.

"Oh!— good-bye, just anybody?" I asked; and thereupon she gathered up all her misplaced trust in me, all her maiden ignorance of what is in man, and all her sweet daring, to murmur—

"Good-bye,—Dick."

I caught my breath in rapture and rode away. She was there yet when I looked back—once—and again—and again. And when I looked a last time still she had not moved. Oh, Camille, Camille! to this day I see you standing there in pink-edged white, pure, silent, motionless, a summer-evening cloud; while I, my body clad in its unstained—only because unused—new uniform, and my soul tricked out in the foolhardiness and vanity of a boy's innocence, rode forth into the night and into the talons of overmastering temptation.

53

The Cavalier

XIV

CORALIE ROTHVELT

THE night was still and sultry. At one of the many camp-fires on the edge of the road I saw the Arkansas colonel sitting cross-legged on the ground, in trousers, socks and undershirt, playing poker.

Out in the open country how sweet was the silence. Not yet have I forgotten one bright star of that night's sky. My mother and I had studied the stars together. Lately Camille, her letter said, had learned them with her. Now the heavens dropped meanings that were for me and for this night alone. While the form of the maiden—passing fair—yet glimmered in the firmament of my own mind, behind me in the south soared the Virgin; but as some trees screened the low glare of our camp I saw, just rising into view out of the southeast, the unmistakable eyes of the Scorpion. But these fanciful oracles only flattered my moral self-assurance, and I trust that will be remembered which I forgot, that I had not yet known the damsel from one sun to the next.

I was moving briskly along, making my good steed acquainted with me, testing his education, how promptly, for instance, he would respond to rein-touch and to leg-pressure, when I saw, in front, coming toward me, three riders. Two of them were very genteel chaps, though a hand of each was on the lock of his carbine. The third was a woman, veiled, and clad in some dark stuff that in the starlight seemed quite black and contrasted strongly with the paleness of her horse. Her hat, in particular, fastened my attention; if that was not the same soft-brimmed Leghorn I had seen yesterday morning, at least it was its twin sister. I halted, revolver in hand, and said, as they drew rein,—" Good-evening."

" Good-evening," replied the nearer man. " How far is it to camp—Austin's? "

" A short three miles."

" To what command do you belong? " he asked.

" Ferry's scouts. What command is yours, gentlemen? "

" Ferry's scouts." He scrutinized me. " What command do you say you—"

" Ferry's scouts," I repeated. " F-e-r-r-y-apostrophe s, Ferry's—s-k-o-w-t-s—scouts."

The trio laughed, the young woman most musically. " How long have you belonged to Ferry's scouts? " sceptically demanded their spokesman.

" About an hour and a quarter."

" Oh! that-a-way."

" Yes," I replied, " in that direction."

The three laughed again and the men sank their carbines across their laps, while in a voice as refined as her figure their companion said, " Good-evening, Mr. Smith." She laid back her veil and even in the darkness I felt the witchery of her glance. " I was just coming to meet you," she continued, " to get the letter you're bringing me from General Austin. I feared you might try to come around by Fayette, not knowing the Yankees are there. These gentlemen didn't know it."

" She just did save us! " laughed the man hitherto silent.

" I'm Miss Coralie Rothvelt," she added, and then how she sparkled in the dark as she said, " I see you remember me."

" I am but human."

" And yet you never take a lady's name for granted? "

" I am to know Miss Rothvelt by finding her in a certain place." My honeyed bow implied that her being just now very much out of place was no fault of mine.

" Nonsense! " muttered both men, and I liked them the better.

" My dear Smith," said Miss Rothvelt, " keep your trust. But if I part here with these two kind gentlemen—"

" Who don't belong to Ferry's scouts at all," I still more sweetly added.

" No," she laughed, " and if I go back with you to Wiggins—to the little white cottage, you know, opposite the blacksmith's shop,—you'll give me what you've got for me, won't you? " She dropped her head to one side and a mocking-bird chuckle rippled in her throat.

" I shall count myself honored," said I, and we went, together and alone.

Venus and Mars

XV

VENUS AND MARS

SINCE those days men have made " fire-proof " buildings. You know them; let certain aggravations combine—they burn like straw. We had barely started when I began to be threatened with a conflagration against which I should have called it an insult to have been warned. The adroit beauty at my side set in to explain more fully her presence. From her window she had seen those two trim fellows hurrying along in a fair way to blunder into the Federal pickets within an hour, had cautioned them, and had finally asked leave to come with them, they under her guidance, she under their protection.

" You were so anxious to get the General's letter? " I asked.

" I was so anxious about you," she replied, with feeling, and then broke into a quizzical laugh.

I had not the faintest doubt she was lying. What was I to her? The times were fearfully out of joint; women as well as men were taking war's licenses, and with a boy's unmerciful directness I sprang to the conclusion that here was an adventuress. Yet I had some better thoughts too. While I felt a moral tipsiness going into all my veins, I asked myself if it was not mainly due to my own inability to rise in full manliness to a most exceptional situation. Her jaunty method of confronting it, was I not failing to regard *that* with due magnanimity? Was this the truth, or after all

ought I really to see that at every turn of her speech,
by coy bendings of the head, by the dark seductions of
dim half-captive locks about her oval temples, and by
many an indescribable swaying of the form and of the
voice, I was being—to speak it brutally—challenged?
Even in the poetic obscurity of the night I lost all
steadiness of eye as I pertly said—

" And so here you are in this awful fix."

" I'm enjoying one advantage," she replied, " which
you do not."

" What is that? "

" Why, I can read my safety in your face. You can't
read anything in mine; you're afraid to look."

All I got by looking then was a mellow laugh from
behind her relowered veil; but we were going at a
swift trot, nearing a roadside fire of fence-rails left by
some belated foraging team, and as she came into the
glare of it I turned my eyes a second time. She was
revealed in a garb of brown enriched by the red beams
of the fire, and was on the gray mare I had seen that
morning under Lieutenant Edgard Ferry-Durand.

" You recognize her? " the rider asked, delightedly.
" She's not stolen, she's only served her country a little
better than usual to-day; haven't you, Cousin Sallie? "
(Cousin Sallie was short for Confederate States.)

The note of patriotism righted me and I looked a
third time. The one art of dress worth knowing in
'63 was to slight its fashions without offending
them, and this pretty gift I had marked all day in
the Harpers. But never have I seen it half so successful as in the veiled horsewoman illumined by the

Venus and Mars

side-lights of those burning fence-rails. The white apparition at the veranda's edge gleamed in my mind, yet swiftly faded out, and a new fascination, more sudden than worthy heaved at my heart. Then the fire was behind us and we were in the deep night.

On the crest of a ridge we slackened speed and my fellow-traveller lifted her veil and asked exultantly what those two splendid stars were that overhung yonder fringe of woods so low and so close to each other. The less brilliant one, I said, the red one, was Mars.

"And the one following, almost at his side?"

"Don't you know?" I asked.

Her eyes flashed round upon me like stars themselves. "Not—Venus?" she whispered, snatched in her breath, bit her lip, and half averting her face, shot me through with both "twinklers" at once. Then she took a long look at the planets and suddenly exclaimed with a scandalized air—

"They're going down into the woods together!"

"Yes," I responded, "and without even waiting for Diana."

She dropped the rein and lifted both arms toward them. "Oh, blessings on your glorious old heathen hearts, what do you want of Diana, or of any one in heaven or earth except each other!"

Foolish, idle cry, and meant for no more, by a heart on fire with temptations of which I knew nothing. But then and there my poor adolescent soul found out that the preceptive stuff of which it had built its treasure-house and citadel was not fire-proof.

The Cavalier

XVI

AN ACHING CONSCIENCE

YET great is precept. Precept is a well. Up from its far depths by slow, humble, constant process you may draw, in a slender silver thread, and store for sudden use, the pure waters of character.

It has happened, however, that a man's own armor has been the death of him. So the moral isolation of a young prig of good red blood who is laudably trying to pump his conduct higher than his character—for that's the way he gets his character higher—has its own peculiar dangers. Take this example: that he does not dream any one will, or can, in mere frivolity, coquette, dally, play mud-pies, with a passion the sacredest in subjection, the shamefulest in mutiny, and the deepest and most perilous to tamper with, in our nature. As hotly alive in the nethermost cavern of his heart as in that of the vilest rogue there is a kennel of hounds to which one word of sophistry is as the call to the chase, and such a word I believed my companion had knowingly spoken. I was gone as wanton-tipsy as any low-flung fool, and actually fancied myself invited to be valiant by this transparent embodiment of passion whose outburst of amorous rebellion had been uttered not because I was there, but only in pure recklessness of my presence. Of course I ought to have seen that this was a soul only over-rich in woman's love; mettlesome, aspiring, but untrained to renunciation; consciously superior in mind and soul to the

An Aching Conscience

throng about her, and caught in some hideous gin of iron-bound—convention-bound—or even law-bound—foul play. But I was so besotted as to suggest a base analogy between us and those two sinking stars.

Unluckily she retorted with some playful parry that just lacked the saving quality of true resentment. How I rejoined would be small profit to tell. I had a fearful sense of falling; first like a wounded squirrel, dropping in fierce amazement, catching, holding on for a panting moment, then dropping, catching and dropping again, down from the top of the great tree where I had so lately sat scolding all the forest; and then, later, with an appalling passivity. And at every fresh exchange of words, while she laughed and fended, and fended and laughed, along with this passivity came a yet more appalling perversity; a passivity and perversity as of delirium, and as horrid to her as to me, though I little thought so then.

We came where a line of dense woods on our left marked the bottom-lands of Morgan's Creek. With her two earlier companions my fellow-traveller had crossed a ford here shortly after sunset, seeing no one; but a guard might easily have been put here since, by the Federals in Fayette. Pretty soon the road, bending toward it, led us down between two fenced fields and we stealthily walked our horses. Close to a wayside tree I murmured that if she would keep my horse I would steal nearer on foot and reconnoitre, and I had partly risen from the saddle, when I was thrilled by the pressure of her hand upon mine on the saddle-bow. " Don't commit the soldier's deadliest sin, my dear Mr.

Smith," she said under her breath, and smiled at my agitation; " I mean, don't lose time."

I was about to put a false meaning even on that, when she added " We don't need the ford this time of year; let us ride back as if we gave up the trip—for there may be a vidette looking at us now in the edge of those bushes—and as soon as we get where we can't be seen let us take a circuit. We can cross the creek somewhere above and strike the Wiggins road up in the woods. You can find your way by the blessed stars, can't you—being the angel you are? "

My whole nature was upheaved. You may smile, but my plight was awful. In the sultry night I grew cold. My bridle-hand, still lying under her palm, turned and folded its big stupid fingers over hers. Then our hands slid apart and we rode back. " I wish I were good enough to know the stars," she said, gazing up. " Tell me some of them."

I told them. Two or three times my voice stuck in my throat, I found the sky so filled, so possessed, by constellations of evil name. At our back the Dragon writhed between the two Bears; over us hung the Eagle, and in the south were the Wolf, the Crow, the Hydra, the Serpent—" Oh, don't tell any more," she exclaimed. " Or rather—what are those three bright stars yonder? Why do you skip them? "

" Those? That one is the Virgin's sheaf; and those two are the Balances."

I failed to catch her reply. She spoke in a tone of pain and sunk her face in her hand. " Head ache? " I asked.

An Aching Conscience

" No." She straightened, and from under her coquettish hat bent upon me such a look as I had never seen. In her eyes, in her tightened lips, and in the lift of her head, was a whole history of hope, pride, pain, resolve, strife, bafflement and defiance. She could not have chosen to betray so much; she must have counted too fully on the shade of her hat-brim. The beautiful frown relaxed into a smile. " No," she repeated, " only an aching conscience. Ever have one? "

I averted my face and answered with a nod.

" I don't believe you! I don't believe you ever had cause for one! " She laid a hand again upon mine.

I covered it fiercely and sunk my brow upon it. And thereupon the wave of folly drew back, and on the bared sands of recollection I saw, like drowned things, my mother's face, and Gholson's and the General's, and Major Harper's, and Ned Ferry's, and Camille's. Each in turn brought its separate and peculiar pang; and among those that came a second time and with a crueler pang than before was Camille's.

" You're tired! " murmured the voice beside me, and the wave rolled in again. I lifted my brow and moved one hand from hers to make room on it for my lips, but her fingers slipped away and alighted compassionately on my neck. " You must be one ache from head to foot! " she whispered.

I turned upon her choking with anger, but her melting beauty rendered me helpless. Black woods were on our left. " Shall we turn in here? " I asked.

" Yes." She stooped low under the interlacing boughs and plunged with me into the double darkness.

The Cavalier

XVII

TWO UNDER ONE HAT-BRIM

"Is this the conservatory?" playfully whispered Miss Rothvelt; and if a hot, damp air, motionless, and heavy with the sleeping breath of countless growths could make it so, a conservatory it was. Every slightest turn had to be alertly chosen, and the tangle of branches and vines made going by the stars nearly impossible. The undergrowth crowded us into single file. We scarcely exchanged another word until our horses came abreast in the creek and stopped to drink. Conditions beyond were much the same until near the end of our détour, when my horse swerved abruptly and the buzz of a rattlesnake sounded almost under foot. The mare swerved, too, and hurried forward to my horse's side.

"That was almost an adventure, itself," laughingly murmured my companion, as if adventures were what we were in search of. While she spoke we came out into a slender road and turned due north. "Did you," she went on, childishly, "ever take a snake up by the tail, in your thumb and finger, and watch him try to double on himself and bite you? I have, it's great fun; makes you feel so creepy, and yet you know you're safe!"

She laughed under her breath as if at hide-and-seek. Then we galloped, then trotted again, galloped, walked and trotted again. Two miles, three, four, we reckoned off, and slowed to a walk to come out cautiously upon the Union Church and Fayette road. A sound brought us to a halt. From the right, out on the main road, it came; it was made by the wheels of a loaded wagon. I leaned sidewise until her hat-brim was over me and whispered "Yankee foragers;" but as I drew my revolver we heard voices, I breathed a sigh of relief, and with her locks touching mine we chuckled to each other in the dark. The passers were slaves escaping to the Federal camp.

Now they came into view, on the broader road, two whole ragged families with a four-mule team. They passed on. And then all at once the whole situation was too much for me. In the joy of release I groped out caressingly and touched my companion's cheek. Whereat she took my fingers and drew them to her lips—twice. The next moment I found—we found— my lifted wrists in the slender grasp of her two hands and she was murmuring incoherent protests. Suddenly she grew eloquent. "Oh, think what you are and have always been! Do you think I don't know? Do you suppose I would have put myself into this situation, or taken the liberties I have taken with you, if I had not known you, and known you well, before ever I saw you? Ah! I have heard such good things of you! and the moment I saw you I saw they were true!—Yes,— yes, I tell you they were, they are! And I'm not going to take my trust away from you now! You shall keep my trust as you have kept all others. You shall be as miserly of it as of your general's. You will keep it!" Her whispers grew more and more gentle. "My dear friend, my dear friend! what is this trust compared to the trust I wish I might lay on you?"

The Cavalier

What did she mean by that! Had she some schemer's use for me? I could not ask, for her little hands had gradually slipped from my wrists to my fingers and were softly, torturingly fondling them. Suddenly she laughed and threw her hands behind her back. "I'm blundering! Oh, Richard Smith, be kind to a woman's poor wits, and let me say to-morrow that I know one man who can be trusted—who I *know* can be trusted— to make a woman's folly her protection. Do you know, dear, that any woman who can say that, is richer than any who cannot? And I am but a woman, sometimes a bit silly. Trouble is I'm a live one and a whole one! —or else I'm a live one and not quite a whole one— I wonder which it is!"

I mumbled something about never wishing to tempt any one.

"Oh, you haven't tempted me," she replied, with kind amusement. "You couldn't if you should try. You're a true soldier, with a true soldier's ideals; and I'm pledged to help you keep them."

"What do you mean?" I demanded. "To whom are you pledged for any such—"

"Oh!—don't you wish you knew! Why, to myself, for instance. Come! duty calls."

"Come!" I echoed. We swung into the broader road and followed the contrabands.

We came as close to them as was wise, and had to walk our horses. I could discern Miss Rothvelt's features once more, and felt a truer deference than I had yet given her. Near the blacksmith's shop, in the dusk of some shade-trees, she once more touched my

Two Under One Hat-Brim

shoulder. I turned resentfully to bid her not do it, but her shadowy gaze stopped me.

"Don't be moody," she said; "the whole mistake is four-fifths mine. And anyhow, repining is only a counterfeit repentance, you know. Come, I don't want to tease you. It's only myself I love to torment. I'm the snake I like to hold up by the tail. Did you never have some dull, incessant ache that seemed to pain less when you pressed hard on it?" She laughed, left me and rode into the cottage gate.

What do you say?—Yes, she might have spoken more wisely. Yet always there vibrated in her voice a wealth of thought, now bitter, now sweet, and often both at once, and a splendor of emotions, beyond the scope of all ordinary natures. How far beyond my own scope they were, even with my passions at flood-tide and turbid as a back-street overflow, I failed to ponder while I passed around the paling fence alone.

In the edge of the woods at the rear of this enclosure I found the road that led into Cole's Creek bottom, and there turned and waited. A corner of the cottage was still in view among its cedars and china-trees. In an intervening melon-patch blinked the yellow lamps of countless fireflies. And now there came the ghost of a sound from beyond the patch, then a glimpse of drapery, and I beheld again the subject of my thoughts. Such thoughts! Ah! why had I neither modesty, wit nor charity enough to see that yonder came a woman whose heart beat only more strongly than the hearts of all the common run of us, with impulses both kind and high, although society, by the pure defects of its awk-

The Cavalier

ward machinery, had incurably mutilated her fate; a woman wrestling with a deep-founded love that, held by her at arm's length, yielded only humiliations and by its torments kept her half ripe for any sudden treason even against that love itself.

She came without her horse, pointing eagerly at the brightness of the sky above the unrisen moon. " Diana! " she whispered, and tossed a kiss toward it. " You saw me put the mare into the stable and go into the house by the back door? "

" Yes," I said, and handed her, as I dismounted, the General's gift, the pass.

She snatched it gaily, loosed a fastening at her throat and dropped the missive into her bosom. Then with passionate gravity she asked, " Now, are you going straight on to Clifton to-night—without stopping? "

" I haven't been ordered to tell any one where I'm going."

" Neither was Lieutenant Ferry," she dryly responded, " yet I have it from him."

" He told you?—Ah! you're only guessing," I said, and saw that I was helping her to guess more correctly.

" Pooh! " she replied, ever so prettily, " do you suppose I don't know? Ferry's scouts are at Clifton, and you've got a despatch for Lieutenant—eh,—Durand—hem! " She posed playfully. " Now, tell me; you're not to report to him till daylight, are you? Then why need you hurry on now? This house where I am is the only safe place for you to sleep in between here and Clifton. I'll wake you, myself, in good time."

Two Under One Hat-Brim

My heart pounded and rose in my throat, yet I managed to say, "My orders are plain." I flinched visibly, for again I had told too much. I pretended to listen toward the depths of the wood.

She struck a mock-sentimental attitude and murmured musically—

> "'The beating of our own hearts
> Was all the sound we heard.'

Yes,"—she put away gaiety—"your orders are plain; and they're as cruel as they are plain!"

"Cruel to you?" I took her hand from my arm and held it.

"Oh! cruel to you, Richard, dear; to you! And—yes!—yes!—I'll confess. I'll confess—if only you'll do as I beg! Yes, ah yes, cruel to me! But don't ask how, and we'll see if you are man enough to keep a real woman's real secret! And first, promise me not to put up at that house which the General and Lieutenant Ferry—"

"Lieutenant Ferry is not sending me to any house."

"Pardon me, I know better. This is his scheme." She laid her free hand on our two. "Tell me you will not go to that house!"

I attempted an evasion. "Oh—a blanket on the ground—face covered up in it from the mosquitos—is really—"

"Right!" She laughed. "I wish a woman could choose that way. Oh! if you'll do that I'll go with you and stand guard over you!"

Dolt that I was, I would have drawn her close, but

69

she put me off with an outstretched arm and forbidden smile. " No!—No! this is a matter of life and death."

I stepped back, heaving. " Who and what are you? Who and what are you? "

" Why, who and what should I be? "

" Charlotte Oliver! "

" Hmm; Charlotte Oliver. Are you sure you have the name just right? "

" Why haven't I got it right? "

" Oh, I don't doubt you have; though I didn't know but it might be Charlie Toliver or something. "

I dilated. " Who told—did Ned Ferry tell you that story? "

" He did. Or, to be accurate, Lieutenant Ferry-Durand. My dear Richard, we cannot be witty and remain un-talked-about. "

" I—I believe it yet! You are Charlotte Oliver! "

She became frigid. " Do you know who and what Charlotte Oliver is?—No? Well, to begin with, she's a married woman—but pshaw! you believe nothing till it's proved. If I tell you who and what I am will you do what I've asked you; will you promise not to stop at Lucius Oliver's house? " She softly reached for my hand and pressed and stroked it. " Don't stop there, dear. Oh, say you will not! "

" Is it so dangerous? "

" General Austin believes it is. You're being used to bait a trap, Richard. "

I laughed a gay disdain. " Who is Lucius; is he Charlotte's husband? "

The reply came slowly. " No; her husband is quite

another man; this man's wife has been dead for years. No, Charlotte Oliver lives in—hark!"

The sound we had heard was only some stir of nature in her sleep. "I must go," I said.

"Oh, no, no! I cannot let you!" She clutched the hand she had been stroking.

"Coralie! Coralie Rothvelt!"—my cry was an honest one—"you tempt me beyond human endurance."

She threw my hand from her. "I know I do! I'm so unworthy to do it that I wouldn't have believed I could. You thought I was Charlotte Oliver—Heavens! boy, if you should breathe the atmosphere Charlotte Oliver has to live in! But understand again, for your soul's comfort, you haven't tempted me. Go, if you must; go, take your chances; and if you're spared ever to see your dear, dear little mother—"

"My mother! Do you know my mother?"

"Tell her I tried to keep my promise to her."

"You promised her—what did you promise her?"

"Only to take care of you whenever I had the chance. Go, now, you must!"

"And was care for me your only motive in—"

"No, no, Richard, I wanted, and I still want, you to take care of me! But go, now, go! at once or not at all! Good-bye!" She laughed and fluttered away. I sprang upon my horse and sped into the forest.

Another mile, another half; then my horror and dismay broke into gesture and speech, and over and over I reviled myself as a fool, a traitorous fool, to be fooled into confession of my errand! I moaned with physical pain; every fatigue of the long day now levied payment, and my back, knees, shoulders, ached cruelly. But my heart ached most, and I bowed in the saddle and cried—

"What have I done, oh, what have I done? My secret! my general's, my country's secret! That woman has got it—bought it with flatteries and lies! She has drawn it from my befouled soul like a charge from a gun!"

For a moment I quite forgot how evident it was that she had gathered earlier inklings of it from some one else. Suddenly my thought was of something far more startling. It stopped my breath; I halted; I held my temples; I stared. What would she do with a secret she had taken such hazards to extort? Ah! she'd carry it straight to market—why not? She would give it to the enemy! Before my closed eyes came a vision of the issue—disaster to our arms; bleeding, maiming, death, and widows' and orphans' tears.

"My God! she shall not!" I cried, and whirled about and galloped back.

At the edge of the wood, where we had parted, I tied my horse, and crept along the moonlight shadows of the melon-patch to the stable. The door was ajar. In the interior gloom I passed my hands over the necks and heads of what I recognized to be the pair of small mules I had seen at Gallatin. Near a third stall were pegs for saddle and bridle, but they were empty. So was the stall; the mare was gone.

"Gone to the Yankees at Fayette!" I moaned, and hurried back to my horse. To attempt to overtake one within those few miles would only make failure com-

plete, and I scurried once more into the north with
such a burden of alarm and anguish as I had never
before known.

XVIII

THE JAYHAWKERS

It was well that I was on the Federal captain's
horse. He knew this sort of work and could do it
quicker and more quietly than mine. Mine would have
whinnied for the camp and watched for short cuts to
it. Another advantage was the moon, and the hour
was hardly beyond midnight when I saw a light in
a window and heard the scraping of a fiddle. At the
edge of a clearing enclosed by a worm fence I came
to a row of slave-cabins. Mongrel dogs barked
through the fence, and in one angle of it a young white
man with long straight hair showed himself so abruptly as to startle my horse. Only the one cabin was
lighted, and thence came the rhythmic shuffle of bare-
footed dancers while the fiddle played " I lay ten dollars down." There were three couples on the floor,
and I saw—for the excited dogs had pushed the door
open—that two of the men were white, though but
one wore shoes. On him the light fell revealingly as
he and the yellow girl before him passed each other in
the dance and faced again. He was decidedly blond.
The other man, though silhouetted against the glare of
burning pine-knots, I knew to be white by the flapping
of his lank locks about his cheeks as he lent his eyes
to the improvisation of his steps. His partner was a

young black girl. I burned with scorn, and doubtless showed it, although I only asked whose plantation this was.

"This-yeh pla-ace?" The rustic dragged his words lazily, chewed tobacco with his whole face, and looked my uniform over from cap to spur. "They say this-yeh place belong to a man which his name Lu-ucius Ol-i-veh."

So! I honestly wished myself back in my old rags, until I reflected that my handsome mount was enough to get me all the damage these wretches could offer. Still I thought it safest to show an overbearing frown.

"To what command do you fellows belong?"

He spurted a pint to reply, "Fishe's batt'ry."

"Oh! And where is the battery?"

"You sa-ay 'Whah is it?' — ow batt'ry " — he champed noisily—"I dunno. Does you? Whah is it?"

"It's twenty miles off; why are you not with it? What are you doing here?"

"You sa-ay 'What we a-doin' hyuh?' Well, suh, I mought sa-ay we ain't a-doin' nuth'n'; but I "— he squirted again—"*will* sa-ay that so fah as you *see* what we a-doin', you *kin* see, an' welcome; an' so fah as you don't see, it ain't none o' yo' damn' busi-*ness*."

"Oh, that's all right, I was only asking a friendly question."

"Yaas; well, that's all right, too, suh; I uz on'y a-givin' you a frien'ly aynsweh. I hope you like it."

Our intercourse became more amiable and the fel-

The Jayhawkers

low dragged in his advice that I spend the rest of the night at the house of Mr. Oliver. His acquaintance with that gentleman seemed to grow while we talked, and broke into bloom like a magician's rosebush. He described him as a kind old bird who made hospitality to strangers his meat and drink. A conjecture darted into my mind. "Why, yes! that is his married son, is he not, yonder in the cabin; the one with the fair hair?"

"Who?—eh,—ole man Ol-i-veh? You sa—ay 'Is that his ma'-ied son, in yondeh; the one 'ith the fah hah?'—Eh,—no—o, suh,—eh,—yass, suh,—yass! Oh, yass, suh, thass his—tha'—thass his ma'ied son, in thah; yass, suh, the one 'ith the fah hah; yass, suh. I thought you meant the yetheh one."

"I don't believe," said I, "I'd better put myself on the old gentleman when the mistress of the house is away."

"*She* ain't awa-ay."

"Is she not! Isn't she the Mrs. Oliver—Charlotte Oliver—who is such friends—she and her husband, I mean, of course,—"

"*Uv* co'se!" The reptile giggled, squirted and nodded.

"—With General Austin," I continued, "—and with Lieutenant Ferry?"

"She air!" He was pleased. "Yass, we all good frien's togetheh."

"But if she—oh, yes!—Yes, to be sure; she could easily have got here yesterday afternoon."

"Thass thess when she arrove!" It was fascinating to watch the animal's cunning play across his face. The fiddle's tune changed and the dance quickened.

"I naturally thought," resumed I, with a smile meant to refer to the blond dancer, "that the madam *must* be away somewhere."

My hearer grinned. "Oh, that ain't no sign. Boys will be boys. You know that, yo'se'f. An' o' co'se she know it. Oh, yass, she at home."

"Well, I reckon I'll stop all night." I began to move on. His eyes followed greedily.

"Sa-ay! I'll wrastle you fo' them-ah clo'es."

I waved a pleasant refusal and rode toward the house.

XIX

ASLEEP IN THE DEATH-TRAP

THE dwelling was entirely dark. I came close in the bright moonlight and hallooed. At my second hail the door came a small way open, and after a brief parley a man's voice bade me put up my horse and come in. The stable was a few steps to the right and rear. Returning, I took care to notice the form of the house: a hall from front to rear; one front and one rear room on each side of it; above the whole a low attic, probably occupied by the slave housemaids.

I was met in the bare unpainted hall by a dropsical man of nearly sixty, holding a dim candle, a wax-myrtle dip wrapped on a corncob. He had a retreating chin, a throat-latch beard and a roving eye; stepped with one foot and slid with the other, spoke in a de-

Asleep in the Death-Trap

jected voice, and had very poor use of his right hand. I followed him to the rear corner chamber, the one nearest the stable, feeling that, poor as the choice was, I should rather have him for my robber and murderer than those villains down at the quarters. I detained him in conversation while I drew off my boots and threw my jacket upon the back of a chair in such a way as to let my despatch be seen. The toss was a lucky one; the document, sealed with red wax, stuck out arrogantly from an inside pocket. Then, asking lively questions the while as if to conceal a blunder and its correction, I moved quickly between him and it and slipped the missive under a pillow of the four-post bedstead.

He was not wordy, and he tarried but a moment, yet he explained his paralysis. In the dreary mono-tone of a chronic sour temper he related that some Confederates, about a year before, had come here im-pressing horses, and their officer, on being called by him "no gentleman," had struck him behind the ear with the butt of a carbine. I asked what punishment the officer received, and I noticed the plural pronoun as he icily replied, "We didn't enter any complaint."

I said with genuine warmth that if he would give me that man's name—etc.

He waited on the threshold with his dropsical back to me for my last word, and then, still in the same attitude, droned, "O-oh, he's dead. And anyhow," he finished out of sight in the hall, "that's not our way."

I sat on the edge of the bed, in the moonlight, wish-ing I knew what their way was. I considered my

The Cavalier

small stock of facts. The one that appalled me most was the inward guilt which I brought with me to this ordeal. I wanted to say my childhood prayers and I could not. For I could not repent; at least the *emotion* of repentance would not come. Moreover, every now and then there leapt across this blackness of guilt a forked lightning of fright, as I realized that I could no more plan than I could pray. No doubt Coralie Rothvelt, by this time in Fayette, was telling some Federal commander that a certain Confederate courier, now asleep at the house of Lucius Oliver, had let slip to her the fact that his despatches were written to be captured, and that, read with that knowledge, they would be of guiding value. What mine host himself might have in view for me I could not guess, but most likely those three rapscallions down at the quarters were already plotting my murder. So now for a counterplot—alas! the counterplot would not unfold for me!

I rallied all my wits. Here was an open window. Through it the moonlight poured in upon the lower half of the bed. If I should lie with my eyes in the shadow of the headboard no one entering by the door opposite could see that I was looking. Good! but what to do when the time should come—ah me!—and "Oh, God!" and "Oh, God!" again. Ought I, now, to let the enemy get the despatch, or must I not rather keep it from him at whatever risk of death or disgrace? Ah! if I might only fight, and let the outcome decide for me! And why not? Yes, I would fight! And oh! how I would fight! If by fighting too well I should keep the despatch, why, that, as matters now stood, was likely to be the very best for my country's cause. On the other hand, should I fight till I fell dead or senseless and only then lose it, surely then it would be counted genuine and retain all its value to mislead. Oh, yes,—I could contrive nothing better—I would fight!

I drew the counterpane aside, lay down under it revolver in hand, and then, for the first time since I had put on the glorious gray, found I could not face the thought of death. I grew steadily, penetratingly, excruciatingly cold, and presently—to the singular satisfaction of my conscience—began to shake from head to foot with a nervous chill. It was agonizing, but it was so much better than the spiritual chill of which it took the place! I felt as though I should never be warm again. Yet the attack slowly passed away, and with my finger once more close to the trigger, I lay trying to use my brain, when, without prayer or plan, I solved the riddle, what I should do, by doing the only thing I knew I ought not to do. I slept.

XX

CHARLOTTE OLIVER

AN envelope sealed with sealing-wax, unless it has also a wrapping of twine or tape whose only knot is under the seal, can be opened without breaking the seal. Gholson had once told me this. Hold a thin, sharp knife-blade to the spout of a boiling tea-kettle;

then press the blade's edge under the edge of the seal. Repeat this operation many times. The wax will yield but a hair's-breadth each time, but a hair's-breadth counts, and in a few minutes the seal will be lifted entire. A touch of glue or paste will fasten it down again, and a seal so tampered with need betray the fact only to an eye already suspicious.

As I say, I slept. The door between me and the hall had a lock, but no key; another door, letting from my room to the room in front of it, had no lock, but was bolted. I slept heavily and for an hour or more. Then I was aware of something being moved—slowly—slyly—by littles—under my pillow. The pillow was in a case of new unbleached cotton. When I first lay down, the cotton had so smelt of its newness that I thought it was enough, of itself, to keep me awake. Now this odor was veiled by another; a delicate perfume; a perfume I knew, and which brought again to me all the incidents of the night, and all their woe. I looked, and there, so close to the bedside that she could see my eyes as plainly as I saw hers, stood Coralie Rothvelt. In the door that opened into the hall were two young officers, staff swells, in the handsomest Federal blue. The moonlight lay in a broad flood between them and me. It silvered Miss Rothvelt from the crown of her hat to the floor, and brightened the earnest animation of her lovely face as she daintily tiptoed backward with one hand delicately poised in the air behind her, and the other still in the last pose of withdrawing from under the pillow—empty!

My problem was indeed simplified. The despatch

had been stolen, opened, read, re-sealed and returned. All I now had to do was to lie here till daybreak and then get away if I could, deliver the despatch to Ned Ferry, and tell him—ah! what?—how much? Oh, my bemired soul, how much must I tell? My shame I might bear; I might wash it out in blood at the battle's front; but my perfidy! how much was it perfidy to withhold; how much was it perfidy to confess?

The heaviness of my soul, by reacting upon my frame and counterfeiting sleep better than I could have done it in cold blood, saved me, I fancy, from death or a northern prison. When I guessed my three visitors were gone I stirred, as in slumber, a trifle nearer the window, and for some minutes lay with my face half buried in the pillow. So lying, there stole to my ear a footfall. My finger felt the trigger, my lids lifted alertly, and as alertly reclosed. Outside the window one of the officers, rising by some slender foothold, had been looking in upon me, and in sinking down again and turning away had snapped a twig. He glanced back just as I opened my eyes, but once more my head was in shadow and the moonlight between us. When I peeped again he was moving away.

Five, ten, fifteen minutes dragged by. Counting them helped me to lie still. Then I caught another pregnant sound, a mumbling of male voices in the adjoining front room. I waited a bit, hearkening laboriously, and then ever so gradually I slid from the bed, put on everything except my boots, and moved by inches to the door between the two rooms. It was very thin; "a good sounding-board," thought I as I

The Cavalier

listened for life or death and hoped my ear was the only one against it.

The discussion warmed and I began to catch words and meanings. Oftenest they were old Lucius Oliver's, whose bad temper made him incautious. While his son and the other two jayhawkers obstinately pressed their scheme he kept saying, sourly, "That's—not—our—wa-ay!"

At length he lost all prudence. "Nn—o!—Nnno—o, sir! Not in this house you don't; and not on this place! Wait till he's off my land; I'm not goin' to have the infernal rebels a-turpentinin' my house and a-burnin' it over my head. What *air* you three skunks in such a sweat to git found out for, like a pack o' daymn' fools! I've swone to heaven and hell to git even ef revenge can ever git me even, and this ain't the way to git even. It's not—our—wa-ay!"

His son's attitude exasperated him. "*You* know this ain't ever been our way; you'd say so, yourself, ef you wa'n't skin full o' china-ball whiskey! What in all hell is the reason we can't do him as we've always done the others?"

"Oh, shut your dirty face!" replied the son, while one of his cronies warned both against being overheard. But when this one added something further the old man snarled:

"What's that about the horse?—The horse might git away and be evidence ag'inst us?—What?—Oh, now give the true reason; you want the horse, that's all! You two lickskillets air in this thing pyo'ly for the stealin's. Me and my son ain't bushwhackers,

Charlotte Oliver

we're gentlemen! At least I'm one. Our game's revenge!"

Not because of this speech, but of a soft rubbing sound on the window-sill behind me, my heart turned cold. Yet there I saw a most welcome sight. Against the outer edge of the sill an unseen hand was moving a forked stick to and fro. The tip of one of its tines was slit, in the slit was a white paper, and in the fork hung the bridle of my horse. I glided to the window. But there bethinking me how many a man had put his head out at just such a place and never got it back, I made a long sidewise reach, secured the paper, and read it.

It was the envelope which had contained Coralie Rothvelt's pass. Its four flaps were spread open, and on the inside was scrawled in a large black writing the following:

Yankees gone, completely fooled. Do not stir till day, then ride for your life. We're not thwarting Lieutenant Ferry's plan, we're only improving upon it. When you report to him don't let blame fall upon the father and son whose roof this night saves you from a bloody death. Do this for the sake of her who is risking her life to save yours. We serve one cause; be wary—be brave—be true.

I stood equally amazed and alert. The voices still growled in the next room, and my horse's bridle still hung before the window. I peered out; there stood the priceless beast. I came a sly step nearer, and lo! in his shadow, flattened against the house, face outward, was Coralie Rothvelt comically holding the forked stick at a present-arms. Throbbing with a grateful, craving allegiance, I seized the rein. Then I bent low out the window and with my free hand touched her face as it turned upward into a beam of moonlight. She pressed my fingers to her lips, and then let me draw her hand as far as it could come and cover it with kisses. Then she drew me down and whispered " You'll do what I've asked? "

When I said I would try she looked distressfully unassured and I added " I'll do whatever risks no life but mine."

Her face spoke passionate thanks. " That's all I can ask ! " she said, whispered " When you go—*keep the plain road*,"—and vanished.

I sat by the window, capped, booted, belted, my bridle in one hand, revolver in the other. In all the house, now, there was no sound, and without there was a stillness only more vast. I could not tell whether certain sensations in my ear were given by insects in the grass and trees or merely by my overwrought nerves and tired neck. The moon sailed high, the air was at last comfortably cool, my horse stood and slept. I thought it must be half-past two.

" Now it must be three." Miss Rothvelt's writing lay in my bosom beside my despatch. At each half-hour I re-read it. At three-and-a-half I happened to glance at the original superscription. A thought flashed upon me. I stared at her name, and began to mark off its letters one by one and to arrange them in a new order. I took C from Coralie and h from Rothvelt; after them I wrote a from Coralie and r from Roth-

Charlotte Oliver

velt, l and o from Coralie and two t's and an e from
Rothvelt, and behold, Charlotte! while the remaining
letters gave me Oliver.

Ah! where had my wits been? Yet without a suspicion that she was Charlotte Oliver one might have
let the anagram go unsuspected for a lifetime. Evidently it concealed nothing from General Austin or
Ned Ferry; most likely it was only the name she used
in passing through the lines. At any rate I was convinced she was a good Confederate, and my heart rose.

But why, then, this ardent zeal to save the necks of
the two traitors "whose roof this night—" etc.?
Manifestly she was moved by passion, not duty; love
drove her on; but surely not love for them. "No,"
I guessed in a reverent whisper, "but love for Ned
Ferry." It must have been through grace of some
of her nobility and his, caught in my heart even before
I was quite sure of it in theirs, that I sat and framed
the following theory: Ned Ferry, loving Charlotte
Oliver, yet coerced by his sense of a soldier's duty, had
put passion's dictates wholly aside and had set about
to bring these murderers to justice; doing this though
he knew that she could never with honor or happiness
to either of them become the wife of a man who had
made her a widow, while she, aware of his love, a love
so true that he would not breathe it to her while this
hideous marriage held her, had ridden perilously in the
dead of night to circumvent his plans if, with honor to
both of them, it could be done.

The half-hour dragged round to four. My horse
roused up but kept as quiet as a clever dog. I heard

85

a light sound in the hall; first a step and then a slide, then a step again and then a slide; Lucius Oliver was coming toward my door. The cords gathered in my throat and my finger stole to the trigger; Heaven only knew what noiseless feet might be following behind that loathsome shuffle. It reached the door and was still. And now the door opened, softly, slowly, and the paralytic stood looking in. The moonlight had swung almost out of the room, but a band of it fell glittering upon the revolver lying in my lap with my fingers on it, each exactly in place. Also it lighted my other hand, on the window-sill, with the bridle in it. Old Lucius was alone. In the gloom I could not see his venom gathering, but I could almost smell it.

XXI

THE FIGHT ON THE BRIDGE

"GOOD-MORNING," I murmured.

"Good-morning," he responded, tardily and grimly. "Well, you *air* in a hurry."

"Not at all, sir. I'm sorry to seem so; it's not the tip-top of courtesy,—"

"No, it ain't too stinkin' polite."

"True; but neither are the enemy, and they're early risers, you know."

"Well, good Lord! don't hang back for my sake!"

I put on an offended esteem. "My dear sir, you've no call to take offence at me. I'm waiting because my business is too—well, if I must explain, it's—it's too

The Fight on the Bridge

important to be risked except by good safe daylight; that's all."

Oh, he wasn't taking offence. His reptile temper crawled into hiding, and when I said day was breaking, he said he would show me my way.

"Why, I keep the plain road, don't I?"

No, he would not; only wagons went that way, to cross the creek by a small bridge. I could cut off nearly two miles by taking the bridle-path that turned sharply down into the thick woods of the creek-bottom about a quarter of a mile from the house and crossed the stream at a sandy ford. "Ride round," he said, "and I'll show you from the front of the house."

Thence he pointed out a distant sycamore looming high against the soft dawn. There was the fence-corner at which the bridle-path left the road. He icily declined pay for my lodging. "We never charge a Confederate soldier for anything; that's not our way."

Day came swiftly. By the time I could trot down to the sycamore it was perfectly light even in the shade of an old cotton-gin house close inside the corner of the small field around which I was to turn. The vast arms of its horse-power press, spreading rigidly downward, offered the only weird aspect that lingered in the lovely morning. I have a later and shuddering memory of it, but now the dewy air was full of sweet odors, the squirrel barked from the woods, the woodpecker tapped, and the lark, the cardinal and the mocking-bird were singing all around. The lint-box of the old cotton-press was covered with wet morning-glories. I took the bridle-path between the woods and the field and very soon was down in the dense forest beyond them. But the moment I was hid from house and clearing I turned my horse square to the left, stooped to his neck, and made straight through the pathless tangle.

Silence was silver this time, speed was golden. But every step met its obstacle; there were low boughs, festoons of long-moss, bushes, briers, brake-cane, mossy logs, snaky pools, and things half fallen and held dead. If at any point on the bridle-path, near the stream, some cowpath, footpath, any trail whatever, led across to the road, my liers-in-wait were certainly guarding it and would rush to the road by that way as soon as they found I was flanking them. And so I strove on at the best speed I could make, and burst into the road with a crackle and crash that might have been heard a hundred yards away. One glance up the embowered alley, one glance down it, and I whirled to the right, drove in the spur, and flew for the bridge. A wild minute so—a turn in the road—no one in sight! Two minutes—another turn—no one yet! Three—three—another turn—no one in front, no one behind—

> The thunder of our own hoofs
> Was all the sound we heard.

A fourth turn and no one yet! A fifth—more abrupt than the others—and there—here—yonder now behind—was the path I had feared, but no one was in it, and the next instant the bridge flashed into view. With a great clatter I burst upon it, reached the mid-

The Fight on the Bridge

dle, glanced back, and dropped complacently into a trot. Tame ending if—but as I looked forward again, what did I see? A mounted man. At the other end of the bridge, in the shade of overhanging trees, he moved into view, and well I knew the neat fit of that butternut homespun. He flourished a revolver above his head and in a drunken voice bade me halt.

I halted; not making a point of valor or discretion, but because he was Charlotte Oliver's husband. I read his purpose and listened behind me as we parleyed. "Don't halt me, sir, I'm a courier and in a hurry."

He hiccoughed. "Let's—s'—see y' orders."

I took my weapon into my bridle-hand by the barrel and began to draw from my bosom the empty envelope addressed Coralie Rothvelt. At the same time I let my horse move forward again, while I still listened backward with my brain as busy as a mill. Was there here no hidden succor? Was that no part of Ned Ferry's plan—if the plan was his? Were those villains waiting yet, up at the ford? I could hear nothing at my back but the singing of innumerable birds.

"Halt!" the drunkard growled again, and again I halted, wearing a look of timid awe, but as full of guile as a weasel. I reined in abruptly so as to make the reach between us the fullest length of my outstretched arm with the paper in two fingers as I leaned over the saddle-bow. He bent and reached unsteadily, and took the envelope; but hardly could his eye light upon the superscription before it met the muzzle of my weapon.

"Don't move." My tone was affectionate. "Don't holla, or I'll give you to the crows. Back. Back off

The Cavalier

this bridge—quick! or I'll—" I pushed the pistol nearer; the danger was no less to him because I was thoroughly frightened. He backed; but he glared a devilish elation, for behind me beat the hoofs of both his horsemen. I had to change my tactics.

"Halt! Turn as I turn, and keep your eye on *this*."

Glad was I then to be on a true cavalryman's horse that answered the closing of my left leg and moved steadily around till I could see down the bridge. Oliver, after a step or two, stopped. "Turn!" I yelled, and swelled. "One, two,—"

He turned. There was not a second to spare. The two long-haired fellows came nip and tuck. I see yet their long deer-hunters' rifles. But I remembered my pledge to this man's wife, and proudly found I had the nerve to hold the trigger still unpressed when at the apron of the bridge the rascals caught their first full sight of us as we sat humpshouldered, eye to eye, like one gray tomcat and one yellow one. They dragged their horses back upon their haunches. One leaped to the ground, the other aimed from the saddle; but the first shot that woke the echoes was neither theirs nor mine, but Sergeant Jim Langley's, though that, of course, I did not know. It came from a tree on our side of the water, some forty yards downstream. The man in the saddle fired wild, and as his horse wheeled and ran, the rider slowly toppled over backward out of saddle and stirrups and went slamming to the ground.

His companion had no time to fire. Instantly after these two shots came a third, and some willows up-

The Fight on the Bridge

stream filled with its white smoke. The second long rifle fell upon the bridge and its owner sank to his knees heaving out long cries of agony that swelled in a tremor of echoes up and down the stream. Another voice, stalwart, elated, cut through it like a sword. "Don't shoot, Smith, we're coming; save that hound for the halter!"

The groans of the wounded man closed in behind it, a flood of agony, and my own outcry increased the din as I called "Come quick, come quick! the wounded fellow's remounting!"

The wretch had lifted himself to his feet by a stirrup. Then, giving out, he had sunk prone, and now, still torturing the air with his horrid cries, was crawling for his rifle. Oliver saw I had a new inspiration. All the drunkenness left his eyes and they became the eyes of a snake, but too quickly for him to guess my purpose I turned my weapon from his face and fired. His revolver flew from his bleeding hand, a stream of curses started from his lips, and as I thrust my pistol into his face again and snatched his bridle he screamed to the crawling woodman "Shoot! shoot! Kill one or the other of us! Oh! shoot! shoot!"

The rifle cracked, but its ball sang over us; a shot answered it behind me; the howling man's voice died in a gurgle, and Sergeant Jim ran by me, leaped upon the horse that had stayed beside his fallen rider, and was off hot-footed after the other. "Turn your prisoner over to Kendall, Smith," he cried, "and put out like hell for Clifton!"

I gave no assent, and I believe Oliver guessed my

purpose to save him, though his eyes were as venomous as ever. I flirted the rein off his horse's neck and said, savagely "Come! quick! trot! gallop!" The sergeant's young companion of the morning before dashed out of the bushes on his horse with Jim's horse in lead.

"I've got him safe, Kendall," I cried, and my captive and I sped by him at a gallop on our way to Ned Ferry's command.

XXII

WE SPEED A PARTING GUEST

Rising to higher ground, we turned into the Natchez, and Port Gibson road where a farm-house and country "store" constituted Clifton. Still at a gallop we left these behind and entered a broad lane between fields of tasselling corn, where we saw a gallant sight. In the early sunlight and in the pink dust of their own feet, down the red clay road at an easy trot in column by fours, the blue-gray of their dress flashing with the glint of the carbines at their backs, came Ferry's scouts with Ned Ferry at their head. There was his beautiful brown horse under him, too. My captive and I dropped to a walk, the column did the same, and Ferry trotted forward, beckoning us to halt. His face showed triumph and commendation, but no joy. Oliver answered his scrutiny with a blaze of defiance.

"Good-morning, Smith, who is your prisoner?"

"His name is Oliver."

Ferry looked behind to the halted column. "Lieu-

We Speed a Parting Guest

tenant Quinn, send two men to guard this one. Smith, where's Sergeant Langley; where's Kendall?"

While I told of the scrimmage, the guard relieved me of Oliver, and as I finished, three men galloped up and reined in. "All right," said one, saluting.

"South?" asked our leader.

"Before day," replied the new-comer, glowing with elation, and I grasped the fact that the enemy had taken our bait and I had not betrayed my country. The three men went to the column, and Ferry, looking up from the despatch which I had delivered to him, said—

"Of course no one has seen this despatch, eh?— Oh!"—a smile—"yes? who?"

"Two Federal officers."

"Two—what?" His smile broadened. "You *know* that?"

"I saw them, Lieutenant, looking in at the door to see the despatch put back under my pillow. Yes, sir, by the same hand that had shown it to them."

"Whose hand was it; that fellow's, yonder?" Oliver was several paces away.

"No, Lieutenant, I don't believe he had anything to do with it; and I've no absolute proof, either, that he was at the bridge to rob or kill me. I threatened his life first, sir. At any rate that hand under my pillow was neither his nor his father's."

"But they were present, eh?"

"They were neither of them present, Lieutenant; that hand was Miss Coralie Rothvelt's."

"Oh, no!" he murmured, "that cannot be!"

The Cavalier

"I saw her face, Lieutenant, nearer to mine than yours is now. But she did it to help us—oh, but I know that, sir! She came under my window and told me she had done it! She told me to tell you she hadn't thwarted your plan, but only improved on it, and I believe—Lieutenant, if you will hear me patiently through a confession which—" I choked with emotion.

He lighted up with happy relief. "No, you need not make it. And you need not turn so pale." Whereat I turned red. "She saw the despatch was a trap for the Yankees, and used it so, you think? Ah, yes, Smith, I see it all, now; she pumped you dry."

I could not speak, I shook my head, and for evidence in rebuttal I showed in my eyes two fountains of standing tears.

"How, then, did she know?"

"Lieutenant, she guessed! She must have just put two and two together and guessed! Or else, Lieutenant,—"

"She must have pumped others before she pumped you, eh?" There was confession in his good humor. "But tell me; did she not see also this other trap, for this man and his father, and try to save them out of it?—oh, if you don't want—never mind." He laid a leg over the front of his saddle and sat thinking. So I see him to-day: his chestnut locks, his goodly limbs and shoulders, the graceful boots, cut-away jacket, faded sash, straight sword, and that look of care on his features which intensified the charm of their spiritual cleanness; behind him his band of picked heroes, and for background the June sky. Whenever I smell dewy corn-fields smitten with the sun that picture comes back to me.

"No," he said again, "you need not tell me." By a placid light in his face I saw he understood. He drew his watch, put it back, thought on, and smiled at my uniform. "It has not the blue of the others," he said, "but indeed they are not all alike, and it will match the most of them—after a rain or two—and some dust. You have been trading horses?"

I explained. While doing so I saw one of the guard reaching the prisoner's bridle to the other. Hah! Oliver had slapped the bridle free. In went his spurs! By a great buffet on the horse's neck he wheeled him, and with the rein dangling under the bits went over the fence like a deer. "Bang! bang! bang!"

It was idle; a magic seems to shield a captive's leap for life. Away across the corn he went to the edge of a tangled wood, over the fence there again, and into the brush. "Halt! bang!" and "Halt! bang!" it was, at every bound, but now the pursuers came back empty-handed, some contemptuously silent, some laughing. Ferry glanced again at the time, and I was having within me a quarrel with him for his indifference at the prisoner's escape, when with cold severity he asked—

"Why did you not fire?"

I flushed with indignation, and my eye retorted to his that I had only followed his example. His answer was a smile. "You, also, have been guessing, eh?" he said, and when I glowed with gratitude he added,

The Cavalier

"Never mind, we must have a long talk. At present there is a verbal message for me; what is it?"

"Verbal message? No, Lieutenant, she didn't—oh! —from the General! Yes! the General says—'Rodney.'"

He turned and moved to the head of the column. I followed. There, "Left into line wheel—march!" chanted our second in command. "Backwards— march!" and then "Right dress!" and the line, that had been a column, dressed along the western edge of the road with the morning sun in their faces. Then Ferry called "Fours from the right, to march to the left—march!" and he and Quinn passed up the middle of the road along the front of the line, with yours truly close at their heels, while behind us the command broke into column again by fours from the right and set the pink dust afloat as they followed back northward over their own tracks with Sergeant Jim beside the first four as squadron right guide. I had got where I was by some mistake which I did not know how to correct,— I was no drill-master's pride,—and there was much suppressed amusement at my expense along the front as we rode down it. At every few steps until the whole line was a column Ned Ferry dropped some word of cheer, and each time there would come back an equally quiet and hearty reply. Near the middle he said "Brisk work ahead of us to-day, boys," and I heard the reiteration of his words run among the ranks. I also heard one man bid another warm some milk for the baby. Trotting by a grove where the company had passed the night, we presently took the walk to break

He cleared it at a bound, and away over the fence like a deer.

by twos, and as we resumed the trot and turned west-ward into a by-road, Lieutenant Quinn dropped back to the column and sent me forward to the side of Ned Ferry. I went with cold shivers.

XXIII

FERRY TALKS OF CHARLOTTE

" You have no carbine," said my commander. " And you have but one revolver; here is another."

I knew it at a glance. " It's Oliver's," I said.

" We'll call it yours now," he replied. " Kendall picked it up, but he has no need of it."

I remarked irrelevantly that I had not noticed when Sergeant Jim and Kendall rejoined us, but Ferry stuck to the subject of the captured weapon. " Take it," he insisted; " if you are not fully armed you will find your-self holding horses every time we dismount to fight. And now, Smith, I shall not report to the General this matter of the Olivers; you shall tell him the whole of it, yourself; you are my scout, but you are his courier."

" Lieutenant, I—I wish I knew the whole of it."

" Tell him all you know."

" Even things *she* doesn't want told?"

" Ah! "—he gave a Creole shrug—" that you must decide, on the honor of a good soldier. She has taken you into her confidence?"

" Only into her service," I said, but he raised his brows.

"That is more; certainly you are honored. What is it you would rather not tell the General and yet you must; do I know that already?"

"Yes, for one thing, I've got to tell him that old Lucius Oliver can't be hung too high or too soon. For months he has been—"

Ferry showed pain. " I know ; save that for the General. And what else?"

"Why, the other one—the son. Lieutenant, is she that monster's wife?"

Ferry stroked his horse's neck and said very softly, "She is his wife." I had to wait long for him to say more, but at length, with the same measured mildness, he spoke on. This amazing Charlotte, bereft of father, brother and mother, ward of a light-headed married sister, and in these distracted times lacking any friend with the courage, wisdom and kind activity to probe the pretensions of her suitor, had been literally snared into marriage by this human spider, this Oliver, a man of just the measure to simulate with cunning and patient labor the character, bearing and antecedents of a true and exceptional gentleman for the sake of devouring a glorious woman.

"But, oh!" I exclaimed, "how could ever such as she mistake him for—"

"Ah, he is, I doubt not, but the burnt-out ruin of what he was half a year ago. You perceive, he has not succeeded; he has not devoured her; actually she has turned his fangs upon himself and has defeated his designs toward her as if by magic. And yet the only magic has been her vigilance, her courage, her sagacity.

Smith,"—again he stroked the mane of his charger—" if I tell you—"

I gave him no pledge but a look.

" Since the hour of her marriage she has never gone into her chamber without locking the door; she has never come out of it unarmed."

I remarked that had I been in her place I should either have sunk into the mire, so to speak, or thrown myself, literally, into the river.

" Yes," he responded, " but not she! Her life is still hers; she will neither give it away nor throw it away. She wants it, and she wants it whole."

" Did she say that to you? "

He looked at me in wide surprise. " Ah! could you think she would speak with me on that subject? No, I have learned what I know from a man we shall meet to-day; the brother of Major Harper; and he, he has it from—" my companion smiled—" somebody you have known a pretty long time, I think, eh? "

" I see; I see; you mean my mother! "

He let me ponder the fact a long time. " Lieutenant," I asked at length, " did you know your plot against the two Olivers would cross her wishes? "

" Ah! " was his quick response, " it crossed mine, like-*wise*. But, you know, this life we have to live, it is never for two people only."

" No," I replied, with my eagerness to moralize, " no two persons, and above all no one man and one woman, can ever be sure of their duty, or even of their happiness, till they consider at least one third person,—"

" Hoh! " interrupted Ferry, in the manner of one to

The Cavalier

whom the fact was somehow of the most immediate and lively practical interest, " and to consider a thousand is better." Then, after a pause, " Yes," he said, " I know she could not like that move, but you remember our talk of yesterday, where we first met? "

Indeed I did. Between young men, to whom the principles of living were still unproved weapons, there was, to my taste, just one sort of talk better than table-talk, and that was saddle-talk; I remembered vividly. " You mean when we were saying that on whatever road a man's journey lies, if he will, first of all, stick to that road, and then every time it divides take the— I see! you came to where the road divided! "

" Yes, and of course I had to take the upper fork. I am glad you said that yesterday morning; it came as sometimes the artillery, eh?—just at the right moment."

" I didn't say it, Lieutenant; you said it."

" No, I think you said it;—sounds like you."

" It was you who said it! and anyhow, it was you who had the strength to do it! "

He laughed. " Oh!—a little strength, a little vanity, —pride—self-love—we have to use them all—as a good politician uses men."

I looked him squarely in the eyes and began to burn. At every new unfolding of his confidence I had let my own vanity, pride, self-love be more and more flattered, and here at length was getting ready to esteem him less for showing such lack of reserve as to use *me* as an escape-valve for his pent-up thoughts, when all at once I fancied I saw what he was trying to do. I believed he had guessed my temptations of the night and was making use of himself to warn me how to fight them. "I understand," said I, humbly.

But this only pleasantly mystified him. He glanced all over me with a playful eye and said, "You must have a carbine the first time our ordnance-wagon finds us. Drop back, now, into the ranks."

I did so; but I felt sure I should ride beside him again as soon as he could make an opportunity; for it was plain that by a subtle unconfessed accord he and *she* had chosen me to be a true friend between them.

About noon, while taking a brief rest to give our horses a bite, we were joined by an ambulance carrying Major Harper's brother and some freight which certainly was not hospital stores. When we remounted, this vehicle moved on with us, in the middle of the column, and I was called to ride beside it and tell all about the arrival of Miss Harper and her nieces at Hazlehurst, and their journey from Brookhaven to camp. Ned Ferry rode on the side opposite me and I noticed that all the fellows nearest the ambulance were choice men; Sergeant Jim was not there, but Kendall was one, and a young chap on a large white-footed pacer was another. Having finished my task I had gathered my horse to fall back to my place at the rear, when my distinguished auditor said, "I'm acquainted with your mother, you know."

He was not so handsome as his brother, though younger. His affability came by gleams. I asked how that good fortune had come to my mother, and he replied that there was hardly time now for another story;

The Cavalier

we might be interrupted—by the Yankees. "Ask the young lady you met yesterday evening," he added, with a knowing gleam, and smiled me away; and when by and by the enemy did interrupt, I had forgiven him. Whoever failed to answer my questions, in those days, incurred my forgiveness.

XXIV

A MILLION AND A HALF

ABOUT mid-afternoon I awoke from deep sleep on a bed of sand in the roasting shade of a cottonwood jungle. A corporal was shaking me and whispering "Make no noise; mount and fall in."

Round about in the stifling thicket a score of men were doing so. Lieutenant Quinn stood by, and at his side Sergeant Jim seemed to have just come among us. The place was pathless; only in two directions could one see farther than a few yards. Through one narrow opening came an intolerable glare of sunlight from a broad sheet of gliding water, while by another break in the motionless foliage could be seen in milder light, filling nearly the whole northern view, the tawny flood of the Mississippi. A stretch of the farther shore was open fields lying very low and hidden by a levee.

As we noiselessly fell into line, counting off in a whisper and rubbing from ourselves and our tortured horses the flies we were forbidden to slap, I noticed rising from close under that farther levee and some two miles upstream, a small cloud of dust coming rapidly down the hidden levee road. It seemed to be raised entirely by one or two vehicles. Behind us our own main shore was wholly concealed by this mass of cottonwoods on the sands between it and the stream, on a spit of which we stood ambushed. On the water, a hundred and fifty yards or so from the jungle, pointed obliquely across the vast current, was a large skiff with six men in it. Four were rowing with all their power, a fifth sat in the bow and the other in the stern. Quinn, in the saddle, watched through his glass the cottonwoods from which the skiff had emerged at the bottom of a sheltered bay. Now he shifted his gaze to the little whirl of dust across the river, and now he turned to smile at Jim, but his eye lighted on me instead. I risked a knowing look and motioned with my lips, " Just in time ! "

" No," he murmured, " they're late ; we've been waiting for them."

The sergeant's low order broke the platoon into column by file, Quinn rode toward its head with his blade drawn, and as he passed me he handed me his glass. " Here, you with no carbine, stay and watch that boat till I send for you. If there's firing, look sharp to see if any one there is hit, and who, and how hard. Watch the boat, nothing else."

He moved straight landward through the cottonwoods, followed by the men in single file, but halted them while the rear was still discernible in the green tangle. Presently they unslung carbines, and I distinctly heard galloping. It was not far beyond the cottonwoods. The Yankees were after us. Suddenly it ceased. Over yonder, shoreward in the thicket, came a sharp command and then a second, and then, right on the front of the jungle, at the water's edge, the shots began to puff and crack, and the yellow river out here around the boat to spit!—spit!—in wicked white splashes. Every second their number grew. Behind me Quinn and his men stole away. But orders are orders and I had no choice but to watch the boat. The man in the stern had his back to me, and no face among the other five did I know. They were fast getting away, but the splashes came thick and close and presently one ball found its mark. The man at the stern hurriedly changed places with an oarsman; and as the relieved rower took his new seat he turned slowly upon his face as if in mortal pain, and I saw that the fresh hand at the oar was the brother of Major Harper. Just as I made the discovery "Boom!" said my small dust-cloud across the river, and "hurry-hurry-hurry-hurry-hurry-hurry-hurry—" like a train on a trestle-work—"boom!"—a shell left its gray track in the still air over the skiff and burst in the tops of the cotton-woods. The green thicket grew pale with the bomb's white smoke, yet "crack! crack!" and "spit! spit!" persisted the blue-coats' rifles. "Boom!" said again the field-piece on yonder side the water. Its shell came rattling through the air to burst on this side, out of the flashing and cracking of rifles and the sulphurous bomb smoke arose cries of men getting mangled, and I whimpered and gnawed my lips for joy, and I watched the boat, but no second shot came aboard, and— "Boom!—hurry-hurry-hurry-hurry"—ah! the frightful skill of it! a third shell tore the cottonwoods, its

A Million and a Half

smoke slowly broadened out, a Federal bugle beyond
the thicket sounded the Rally, and the cracking of carbines ceased.

Now Major Harper's brother passes a word to the
man at the boat's bow, whereupon this man springs
up and a Confederate officer's braids flash on his sleeve
as he waves to the western shore to cease firing. I
still watch the boat, but I listen behind me. I hear
voices of command, the Federal sergeants hurrying
the troop out of the jungle and back to their horses.
Then there comes a single voice, the commander's evidently; but before it can cease it is swallowed up in
a low thunder of hoofs and then in a burst of cries and
cheers which themselves the next moment are drowned
in a rattle of carbine and pistol shots—Ferry is down
on them out of hiding. Thick and silent above the din
rises the dust of the turmoil, and out of all the hubbub
under it I can single out the voice of the Federal captain yelling curses and orders at his panic-stricken
men. And now the mêlée rolls southward, the crackle
of shots grows less and then more again, and then all
at once comes the crash of Quinn's platoon out of ambush, their cheer, their charge, the crackle of pistols
again, and then another cheer and charge—what is
that! Ferry re-formed and down on them afresh? No,
it was the hard-used but gallant foe cutting their way
out and getting off after all.

The skiff was touching the farther shore and the
three oarsmen lifting their stricken comrade out and
bearing him to the top of the levee, when Kendall came
to recall me. On our way back he told me of the fight,

The Cavalier

beginning with the results: none of our own men killed outright, but four badly wounded and already started eastward in the ambulance left us by the Major's brother; some others more slightly hurt. My questions were headlong and his answers quiet; he was a slow-spoken daredevil; I wish he came more than he does into this story.

Not slow-spoken did we find the command when we reached the road where they were falling into line. After a brief but vain pursuit, here were almost the haste and tumult of the onset; the sweat of it still reeked on everyone; the ground was strewn with its wreckage and its brute and human dead, and the pools of their blood were still warm. Squarely across the middle of the road, begrimed with dust, and with a dead Federal under him and another on top, lay the big white-footed pacer. At one side the enemy's fallen wounded were being laid in the shade to be left behind. In our ranks, here was a man with an arm in a bloody handkerchief, there one with his head so bound, and yonder a young fellow jesting wildly while he let his garments be cut and a flesh-wound in his side be rudely stanched. Here there was laughter at one who had been saved by his belt-buckle, and here at one who had dropped like dead from his horse, but had caught another horse and charged on. But these details imply a delay where in fact there was none; the moment Ferry spied me he asked "Did he get across?" and while I answered he motioned me into the line. Then he changed it into a column, commanded silence, and led us across country eastward.

A Million and a Half

For those few wounded who would not give up their places in the ranks it was a weary ten miles that brought us swiftly back to a point within five miles of that Clifton which we had left in the morning. And yet a lovely ten miles it was, withal. You would hardly have known this tousled crowd for the same dandy crew that had smiled so flippantly upon me at sunrise, though they smiled as flippantly now with faces powder-blackened, hair and eyelashes matted and gummed with sweat and dust, and shoulders and thighs caked with grime. Yet to Ned Ferry as well as to me —I saw it in his eye every time he looked at them—these grimy fellows did more to beautify those ten miles than did June woods beflowered and perfumed with magnolia, bay and muscadine, or than slant sunlight in glade or grove.

In a stretch of timber where we broke ranks for a short rest, unbitting but not unsaddling, a lot of fellows pressed me to tell them about the boat on the river. " You heard what was in it, didn't you? " asked one nearly as young as I.

" Besides the men? No. Same that was in the ambulance, I suppose; what was it? "

" Don't you know? Oh, I remember, you were asleep when Quinn told us. Well, sir,"—he tried to speak calmly but he had to speak somehow or explode—" it was soldiers' pay—for Dick Taylor's army, over in the Trans-Mississippi; a million and a half dollars! " He was as proud to tell the news as he would have been to own the money.

The Cavalier

XXV

A QUIET RIDE

WHERE Ferry's scouts camped that night I do not know, for we had gone only two or three miles beyond our first momentary halting-place when their leader left them to Quinn and sprang away southward over fence, hedge, road, ditch—whatever lay across his bee-line, and by his order I followed at his heels.

In a secluded north-and-south road he looked back and beckoned me to his side: " You saw Major Harper's brother land safe and sound, you say? He told you this morning he is acquainted with your mother, eh; but not how? "

" No, except that it was through—"

" Yes, I know. But you don't know even how your mother is acquainted with her."

" No, though of course if she lived in the city, common sympathies might easily bring them together."

" She did not live in the city; she lived across the river from the city. 'Tis but a year ago her father died. He was an owner of steamboats. She made many river trips with him, and I suppose that explains how she knows the country about Baton Rouge, Natchez, Grand Gulf, Rodney, better than she knows the city. But the boats are gone now; some turned into gunboats, one burnt when the city fell, another confiscated. I think they didn't manage her bringing-up very well."

" Maybe not," I replied, being nothing if not dis-

A Quiet Ride

putatious, " and she does strike me as one thrown upon her own intuitions for everything; but if she's the lady she is entirely by her own personal quality, Lieutenant, she's a wonder! "

" Ah, but she is a wonder. In a state of society more finished—"

" She would be incredible," I said for him, and he accepted the clause by a gesture, and after a meditative pause went on with her history. The subject of our conversation had first met Oliver, it seemed, when by reason of some daring performance in the military field —near Milliken's Bend, in the previous autumn—he was the hero of the moment. Even so it was strange enough that he should capture her; one would as soon look to see Vicksburg fall; but the world was upside down, everything was happening as if in a tornado, and he cast his net of lies; lies of his own, and lies of two or three match-making friends who chose to believe, at no cost to themselves, that war, with one puff of its breath, had cleansed him of his vices and that marriage would complete the happy change. This was in Natchez, Ferry went on to say. Most fortunately for the bride one of the bridegroom's wedding gifts was a certain young slave girl; before the wedding was an hour past—before the orange-blossoms were out of the bride's hair—this slave maid had told her what he was, " And you know what that is."

We rode in silence while I tried to think what it must be to a woman of her warmth—of her impulsive energies—to be, week in, week out, month after month, besieged by that man's law-protected blandishments

The Cavalier

and stratagems. "I wish you would use me in her service every time there is a chance," I said.

"The chances are few," he answered; "even to General Austin she laughs and says we must let the story work itself out; that she is the fool in it, but there is a chance for the fool to win if not too much burdened with help."

"How did you make her acquaintance?" I ventured to ask.

"You remember the last time the brigade was in this piece of country?" he rejoined.

I did; it had been only some five weeks earlier; Grant had driven us through Port Gibson, General Bowen had retired across the north fork of Bayou Pierre, and we had been cut off and forced to come down here.

"Yes; well, she came to us that night, round the enemy's right, with a letter from Major Harper's brother —he was then in New Orleans—and with information of her own that saved the brigade. I had just got my company. I took it off next morning on my first scout, whilst the brigade went to Raymond. She was my guide all that day; six times she was my guide before the end of May. Yet the most I have learned about her has come to me in the last few days."

"She has a fearful game to play."

"Oh!—yes, that is what she would call it; but me, I say—though not as Gholson would mean it, you know,—she has a soul to save. If it is a game, it is a very delicate one; let her play it as nearly alone as she can."

A Quiet Ride

" Yes," said I, " a man's hand in it would be only his foot in it;" and Ferry was pleased. He scanned me all over in the same bright way he had done it in the morning, and remarked " This time I see they have given you a carbine."

We went down into some low lands, crossed a creek or two, and in one of them gave our horses and ourselves a good scrubbing. On a dim path in thick woods we paused at a worm fence lying squarely across our way. It was staked and ridered and its zig-zags were crowded with brambles and wild-plum. A hundred yards to our left, still overhung by the woods, it turned south. Beyond it in our front lay a series of open fields, in which, except this one just at hand, the crops were standing high. The nearer half of this one, a breadth of maybe a hundred yards, though planted in corn, was now given up to grass, and live-stock, getting into it at some unseen point, had eaten and trampled everywhere. The farther half was thinly covered with a poor stand of cotton, and between the corn and the cotton a small, trench-like watercourse crossed our line of view at right angles and vanished in the woods at the field's eastern edge. The farther border of this run was densely masked by a growth of brake-cane entirely lacking on the side next us. Between the cotton and the next field beyond, a double line of rail fence indicated the Fayette and Union Church road. Suddenly Ferry looked through his field-glasses, and my glance followed the direction in which they were pointed. Dust again; one can get tired of dust! Some two miles off, a little southward of the setting sun, a golden haze of it floated across a low background of trees.

" 'Tis the enemy, I think," he said, " but only scouts, I suppose."

XXVI

A SALUTE ACROSS THE DEAD-LINE

I WAS not seeking enemies just then and was not pleased. " Didn't the Yankees fall back this morning before day and move southward ? " I asked.

" For what would they do that ? " inquired my leader, still using the glass, but before I could reply he gave a soft hiss, dropped the glass, and turned his unaided eye upon a point close beyond our field, in the road. Now again he lifted the glass, and I saw over there two small, black, moving objects. They passed behind some fence-row foliage, reappeared nearer, and suddenly bobbed smartly up to the roadside fence—the dusty hats of two Federal horsemen. The wearers sat looking over into the field between them and us. I asked Ferry if he wasn't afraid they would see us.

" That is what we want," was his reply ; " only, they must not know we want it. Keep very still ; don't move." At that word they espied us and galloped back.

We turned to our left and hurried along our own fence-line, first eastward, then south, and reined up behind some live brush at the edge of the public road. " Soon know how many they are, now," he said, smiling back at me.

A Salute Across the Dead-Line

"Are you going to count them?" It seemed so much easier to let them count us.

"Yes," he replied. "Wish we had our boys here," he added, and did not need to tell me how he would have posted them; the place was so favorable for an ambush that those Yankees had no doubt been looking for us before they saw us. Half of us would be in the locks of these highroad fences to lure them on, and half in the little gully masked with canes to take them in the flank. "We would count many times our own number before they should pass," he added.

"Can't we make them *think* our men are here?" I suggested. "Couldn't I go back to where this fence crosses the gully and let them see me opening a gap in it?"

He was amused. "Go if you want; but be quick; here they come already, a small bunch of them."

By the time I reached the spot they were in plain view, six men and an officer. I leaped to the ground, tugged at a rail and threw one end off. I thought I had never handled rails so heavy and slippery in my life. As I got a second one down I looked across to the road. The officer was distributing his men. Barely a mile behind was the dust of their column. The third rail stuck and the sweat began to pour down into my eyes and collar. Two of the blue-coats easily let down a panel of fence on the far side of the road and pushed into the tall corn; three others came galloping across the thin cotton to reconnoitre the fringe of canes; the officer and the remaining man cantered on up the road toward the spot where I could see Ferry observing everything from the saddle behind his mask of leaves. Of a sudden the Federal commander descried me wildly at work. He paused and pointed me out to the man at his back, but had no glass and seemed puzzled. At his word the man pricked up to the fence to come over it, but his horse was of another mind, and the impatient officer, crowding him away, cleared the fence himself and came across the furrows at a nimble trot. Still I tussled with the rails, and grew peevish. The enemy was counted, closely enough! one troop. Their dust showed it, the small advance guard proved it.

" Hello! " called the Federal officer, " who are you, over there? "

He might have known by looking a trifle more narrowly; I saw plainly, thrillingly, who he was; but his attention was diverted by some signal from the men he had sent to the fringe of cane; they had found the tracks of horses leading through the canes into the corn. But now he hailed me again. " Here, you! what are you doing at that fence? Who are you? "

He was within easy range and was still trotting nearer. I snatched up my carbine, aimed, and then recovered, looking sharply to my left as if restrained by the command of some one behind the canes. The Federal's cool daring filled me with admiration. Had the foes he was looking for been actually in hiding here they could have picked him out of his saddle like a bird off a bush. His only chance was that they would not let themselves be teased into firing prematurely on any one man or six. Ferry beckoned me. I mounted and trotted down the woods side of the fence, at the same time the Federal's six men approached from three directions, and down the road the main column entered upon the scene.

The officer halted with revolver drawn and sent a man back with some order to the main body. And then Ferry's beautiful brown horse, as though of his own choice, reared straight up where he stood, dropped his forelegs upon his breast, rose, over the fence, master and all, as unlaboriously as a kite, trotted out from the brush and halted in the open field. His rider's outdrawn sword flashed to the setting sun. The Federal, pointing here and there was deploying his remaining five men toward the spot I had left, but glancing round and seeing Ferry he trotted toward him. Thereupon Ferry advanced at a walk, and I—for I had followed him—moved at the same gait a few paces behind. " Halt him," said my leader.

" Halt! " I yelled with carbine at a ready, and the Federal halted. In fact he had come to a small hollow full of bushes and grapevines and had no choice but to halt or go round it.

" Don't swallow him," said Ferry, smilingly, " this isn't your private war."

" He's on my private horse! " I retorted.

" Well, you're on his," replied my commander. The giant before us, mounted on Cricket, was my prisoner of the previous day.

" Who are you? " he was calling imperiously.

" Captain Jewett ought to know," Ferry called back, and on that the questioner recognized us both. He became very stately.

The Cavalier

"Lieutenant Durand, I believe."

"At times," said Lieutenant Durand.

"And at other times——?"

"Lieutenant Ferry—Ferry's scouts."

The Federal expanded with surprise and then with austere pleasure. He glanced toward his five men galloping back to him having found no enemy, and then at his column, which had just halted. Frowning, he motioned the advance guard to the road again and once more hailed Ferry while he pointed at me. He straightened and swelled still more as he began his question, but as he finished it a smile went all over him. "Is that your entire present force?"

"It is."

"Then what the devil do you want?" he thundered.

"We have what we wanted," said Ferry, "only now we desire to cross the road."

"You're not asking my permission?"

"I am afraid not."

"I admit you are quite able to cross without."

"Thank you," said Ferry; "will you pardon me for passing in front of you?"

The Federal's pistol slid into its holster and his sabre flashed out. He threw its curved point up in a splendid salute. Ferry saluted with his straight blade. Then both swords rang back into their scabbards, and Jewett whirled away toward his column. For a moment we lingered, then faced to the left, trotted, galloped. Over the fence and into the road went he—went I. Down it, as we crossed, the blue column was just moving again. Then the woods on the south swallowed us up.

Ferry saluted with his straight blade.

Some Fall, Some Plunge

"If Captain Jewett will only go on to Union Church," said Ferry, "Quinn will see that he never gets back."

"But you think he will not go on?"

"Ah, now he is discovered, surely not. I think he will turn back at Wiggins."

"Why Wiggins? does he know Coralie Rothvelt?"

"Yes, he does; and if since last night he has maybe found out she is Charlotte Oliver,——"

"Oh! Lieutenant Ferry, oh! would such a man as that come hunting down a woman, with a troop of cavalry?"

"He is not hunting her; yet, should he find her, I have the fear he would do his duty as a soldier, any-how. No, he *was* looking, I think, for Ferry's scouts."

"But if she should be at Wiggins——"

My leader smiled at my simplicity. "She is not at Wiggins."

"Where is she?"

"I do not know."

XXVII

SOME FALL, SOME PLUNGE

AT a farm-house well hidden in the woods of a creek we got a brave supper for the asking and had our uniforms wonderfully cleaned and pressed, and at ten that evening we dismounted before the three brightly illumined tents of General Austin, Major Harper and that amiable cipher our Adjutant-general. On the front of the last the shadow of a deeply absorbed writer showed through the canvas, and Ferry murmured to me " The ever toiling." It was Scott Gholson. I had heard the same name for him the evening before, from her whose own lovely shadow fell so visibly and so often upon the bright curtain of Ned Ferry's thought.

My leader went in while I held our horses. Then he and Gholson came out and entered the General's tent; from which Gholson soon emerged again and sent an orderly away into the gloom of the sleeping camp, and I heard a small body of men mount and set off northward. Presently Ferry came out and sent me in, and to my delight I found, on standing before the General, that I did not need to tell what Charlotte Oliver wanted kept back.

" No, never mind that," he said, " Miss Rothvelt was here and saw me this afternoon, herself." Up to the point of my arrival at the bridge I had merely to fumble my cap and answer his crisp questions. But there he lighted a fresh cigar and said " Now, go on."

Gholson dropped in with something to be signed, and the General waved him to wait and hear. For Gholson, despite the sappy fetor of his mental temperament, had abilities that made him almost a private secretary to the General. Who, nevertheless, knew him thoroughly. When I had described Oliver's escape and would have hurried on to later details, General Austin raised a hand.

" Hold on; you say nearly everybody fired at Oliver; who did not? "

Some Fall, Some Plunge

" I did not, General."

" Did Lieutenant Ferry fire ? "

I said he did not. The General turned his **strong** eyes to Gholson's and kept them there while he took three luxurious puffs at his cigar. Then he took the waiting paper, and as he wrote his name on it he said, smiling, " I wish you had been in Lieutenant Ferry's place, Mr. Gholson; you would have done your duty."

The flattered Gholson received the signed paper and passed out, and the General smiled again, at his back. I hope no one has ever smiled the same way at mine.

Ferry and I slept side by side that night, and he told me two companies of our Louisianians were gone to cut off Jewett and his band. " Still, I think they will be much too late," he said, and when I rather violently turned the conversation aside to the subject of Scott Gholson, saying, to begin with, that Gholson had wonderful working powers, he replied, " 'Tis true. Yet he says the brigade surgeon told him to-day he is on the verge of a nervous break-*down*." But on my inquiring as to the cause of our friend's condition, my bedmate pretended to be asleep.

We rose at dawn and rode eastward, he and I alone, some fourteen miles, to the Sessions's, where the dance had been two nights earlier. On entering the stable to put up our horses we suddenly looked at each other very straight, while Ferry's countenance confessed more pleasure than surprise, though a touch of care showed with it. " I did not know this," he said, " and I did not expect it."

What we saw was the leather-curtained spring-wagon and its little striped-legged mules. The old negro in charge of them bowed gravely to me and smiled affectionately upon Ferry. About an hour later Gholson appeared. He took such hurried pains to explain his coming that any fool could have seen the real reason. The brigade surgeon had warned him— Oh! had I heard?—Oh! from Ned Ferry, yes. The cause of his threatened breakdown, he said, was the perpetual and fearful grind of work into which of late he had—fallen.

" Did the doctor say ' fallen ' ? " I shrewdly asked.

" No, the doctor said ' plunged,' but—did Ned Fer' —who put that into your head ? "

" Nobody; some fall, you know, some plunge." I did not ask the cause of the plunge; the two little mules told me that. He would never have come, Gholson hurried on to say, had not Major Harper kindly suggested that a Sabbath spent with certain four ladies would be a timely preventive.

" What ! " I cried, " are they here t'—too? Why,— where's their carryall? 'Tisn't in the stable; I've looked ! "

" No, it was here, but yesterday, when the fighting threatened to be heavy, it was sent to the front. Smith, I didn't know Charlie Tolliver was here ! "

I believed him. But I saw he was not in search of a preventive. Ah, no! he was ill of that old, old malady which more than any other abhors a preventive. Waking in the summer dawn and finding Ned Ferry risen and vanished hitherward, a rival's instinct had moved him to follow, as the seeker for wild honey follows the bee. He had come not for the cure of his honey-sickness, but for more—more—more—all he could find—of the honey. "Smith," he said, with a painful screw of his features, "I'm mightily troubled about Ned Ferry!"

"Yes," I dishonestly responded, "his polished irreligion—"

"Oh, no! No," he groaned, "it isn't that so much just now, though I know that to a true religionist like you the society of such a mere romanticist—"

We were interrupted.

XXVIII

OLDEST GAME ON EARTH

THE cause of our interruption was Camille Harper. We had been pacing the side veranda and she came out upon it with an unconscious song on her lips, and on one finger a tiny basket.

Her gentle irruption found me standing almost on the spot where she had stood two evenings before and said good-bye to me. From this point a path led to the rear of the house, where within a light paling fence bloomed a garden. She gave us a blithe good-morning as she passed, descended the two or three side steps, and tripped toward the garden gate, a wee affair which she might have lifted off its hinges with one thumb. I saw her try its latch two or three times and then turn back discomfited because the loose frame had sagged a trifle and needed to be raised half an inch. I did not

The Cavalier

understand the helplessness of girls as well then as I
do now; I ran and opened the gate; and when I shut
it again she and I were alone inside.

She let me cut the flowers. "You know who's
here?" she asked.

"Yes," I guilefully replied, "I came with him."

"I don't mean Lieutenant Ferry," she responded,
"nor anybody you'd ever guess if you don't know;
but you do, don't you?"

I said I knew and went on gathering sweet-pea blossoms.

"Did you ever see her?"

"Yes," I replied, stepping away for some roses, "I
—saw her—by chance—for a moment—she was in the
wagon she's got here—last—eh,—Thursday—morn'
—" I came back trimming the roses, and as she
reached for them and our glances met, she laughed
and replied, with a roguish droop of the head—

"She told us about it. And you needn't look so
disturbed; she only praised you."

Still I frowned. "How does it come that she's here,
anyhow?"

"Why! she's got to be everywhere! She's a war-
correspondent! She was at the front yesterday nearly
the whole time, near enough to see some of the fighting, and to hear it all! she calls it 'only a skirmish'!"

"When did she get here?"

"About five in the morning. But we didn't see her
then; she shut herself up and wrote and wrote and
wrote! They say she runs the most daring risks! And
they say she's so wise in finding out what the Yankees

are going to do and why they're going to do it, that they'd be nearly as glad to catch her as to catch Lieutenant Ferry! Didn't you know? Ah, you knew!" She attempted a reproachful glance, but exhaled happiness like a fragrance. I asked how she had heard these things.

"How did I hear them? Let me see. Oh, yes! from—from Harry."

I flinched angrily. "From what?"

She looked into her basket and fingered its flowers. "That's what he asked me to call him."

I stiffened up as though I heard a thief picking the lock of my lawful treasure. She threw me, sidewise, a bantering smile and then a more winsome glance, but I refused to see either. I burned with so many feelings at once that I could no more have told them than I could have raised a tune. "Don't you like him?" she asked, and tried to be very arch.

"Like whom?"

"You know perfectly well," she replied.

"No, I do not like him. Do you?"

"Why,—yes,—I do. I—I thought everybody did." She averted her face and toyed with the sweet-pea vines. Suddenly she gulped, faced me, blinked rapidly, and said "If I oughtn't to call him—that,—then I oughtn't to have called—" she dropped her eyes and bit her lip.

"*That*," I replied, "is a very different matter! At least I had hoped it was!"

Her rejoinder came in a low, grieved monotone: "Did you say *had* hoped?"

The Cavalier

It was the sweetest question my ear had ever caught, and I asked her, I scarce know how, if I might still say " do hope ".

" Why, I—I didn't know you ever did say it. I don't see that I have any right to forbid you saying things —to—to yourself."

So we played the game—oldest game on earth—and loveliest. Bungling moves we made, as you see, and sometimes did not know whose move it was. At length she admitted that this *is* a very unsafe world in which to be kind to soldiers. I told how *fickle* some of them were. She would not say she would—or wouldn't— make my case a permanent exception or a solitary one; yet with me she blissfully pooh-poohed the idea that our acquaintance was new, she being so wonderfully like my mother, and I being so wonderfully ditto, ditto. And when I burst into a blazing eulogy of my mother, my listener gave me kinder looks than I ever deserved of any woman alive. On my trying to reciprocate, she asked me for more flowers and hurried back to our earlier theme.

" And really, you know, they say she's almost as truly a scout as Ned Fer'—as Lieutenant Ferry-Durand. She's from New Orleans, you know, and she's like us, half-Creole; but her other half is Highland Scotch—isn't that romantic! When she told us about it she laughed and said it explained some things in her which nothing else could excuse! Wasn't that funny! —oh, pshaw! it doesn't sound a bit funny as I tell it, but she said it in such a droll way! She was so full of fun and frolic that day! You can't conceive how full

"Don't you like him?" she asked, and tried to be very arch.

Oldest Game on Earth

of them she is—sometimes; how soberly she *can* say the funniest things, and how *funnily* she can say the soberest things!"

"You say she was so full of fun that day; what day?"

The young thing gaped at me, gasped, and melted half to the ground: "O—oh—I've let it out!"

"Yes, you may as well go right on, now."

She straightened to her toes, covered her open mouth an instant, and then said "Yes, we knew her—at our house—in New Orleans—poor New Orleans! Your mother—oh, your splendid, lovely little mother is such a brave Confederate!"

"My mother brought her to your house?"

"Yes, oh, yes! and that's why it isn't wrong to tell *you*. Charlotte's been three times through the lines, to and from the city; once by way of Natchez and twice through Baton Rouge. And oh, the things she's brought out to our poor boys in the hospitals!"

"Generals' uniforms, for example?"

"Oh, now you're real mean! No! what she's brought the most of is—guess! You'll never guess it in the world!"

"Hindoo grammars!—No? Well, then,—perfumery!"

"Ah, you! No, I'll tell you." She spoke prudently; I had to bow my ear so close that it tingled: "Dolls!"

My amazement was genuine. "For our sick soldiers!" I sighed.

Her eyes danced; she leaned away and nodded. Then she drew nearer than before: "Dolls!" she

The Cavalier

murmured again;—" and pincushions!—and emeries!
—and 'rats'! you know, for ladies' hair—and chig-
non-cushions!"

" For our sick soldiers!"

" Yes!—stuffed with quinine!" She laughed in her
handkerchief till the smell of the sweet-peas was lost
in the odor of frangipani, and she staggered almost into
my arms. But that sobered her. " And when we speak
of the risk she runs of being sent to Ship Island she
laughs and says, ' Life is strife.' She says she'd like
it long, but she's got to have it broad."

" Life is strife indeed to her," I said.

" Oh! do you know that too?—and another reason
she gives for taking those awful risks is that ' it's the
best use she can make of her silly streak '—as if she
had any such thing!"

" Why did my mother bring her to you?"

" Oh! she had letters from uncle to aunt Martha!
He thinks she's wonderful!"

" Does your father think so, too?"

" My father? no; but he's prejudiced! That's one
of the things I can never understand—why nearly all
the girls I know have such prejudiced fathers."

A Gnawing in the Dark

XXIX

A GNAWING IN THE DARK

On our return to the veranda, Camille and I, we found on its front the house's entire company except only the children of the family. Mrs. Sessions, Estelle and Cécile formed one group, Squire Sessions and Charlotte Oliver made a pair, and Ferry and Miss Harper another. Our posies created a lively demonstration; Camille yielded them to Estelle, and Estelle took them into the house to arrange them in water. Gholson went with her; it was painful to see her zest for his society.

Miss Harper "knocked me down," as we boys used to say, to Charlotte Oliver; "Charlotte, my dear, you already know Mr. Smith, I believe?"

I had expected to see again, and to feel, as well, the starry charms of Coralie Rothvelt; but what I confronted was far different. The charms were here, unquenched by this stare of daylight, but from them shone a lustre of womanliness wholly new. It seemed to grow on even when a tricksy gleam shot through it as she replied, "Yes, our acquaintance dates from Gallatin."

With a spasm of eagerness I said it did: "Our acquai'—hh—Gallatin—hh—" But my soul cried like a culprit, "No, no, it begins only now!" and my whole being stood under arrest before the accusing truth that

The Cavalier

from Gallatin till now my acquaintance had been solely
with that false phase of her which I knew as Coralie
Rothvelt. At the same her kind eyes sweetly granted
me a stripling's acquittal—oh! why did it have to be
a stripling's?

Wonderful eyes she had; deep blue, as I have said,
in color; black, in spirit; never so wonderful as when
having sparkled black they quieted to blue again. Always then there came the slightest of contractions at
the outer corners of the delicate lids, that gave a four-
fold expression of thought, passion, tenderness and in-
trepidity. I never saw that silent meaning in but one
other pair of eyes; wherever it turned it said—at the
same time saying many other things but saying this
always plainest—"I see both out and in; I know myself—and thee." Never but in one other pair of eyes?
no; and whose were those? Ned Ferry's.

"Don't you love to see Charlotte and him look at
each other in that steady way when they're talking
together?" Camille asked me later. But rather coldly
I inquired why I should; I felt acutely enough without admitting it to Camille, that Charlotte and Ferry
were meeting on ground far above me; and when Gholson, in his turn, called to my notice, in Charlotte's case,
this unique gaze, and contrasted it with her beautiful
yet strangely childish mouth, I asked a second time why
she was here, anyhow.

"She's here," murmured Gholson, "because she has
to live! To live she must have means, Smith, and to
have means she must either get them herself or she
must—" and again he poised his hand horizontally

A Gnawing in the Dark

across his mouth and whispered — "live with her hus'—"

I jerked my head away—"Yes, yes." Scott Gholson was the only one of us who could give that wretch that title. "Gholson," I said, for I kept him plied with questions to prevent his questioning me, "how did that man ever get her?"

The rest of the company were going into the house; he glanced furtively after them and grabbed my arm; you would have thought he was about to lay bare the whole tragedy in five words: "Smith, — nobody knows!"

"Do you believe she has told Ned Ferry anything?"

"Never! About herself? no, sir!" He bent and whispered: "She despises him; she keeps in with him, but it's to get the news, that's all; that's positively all." On our way to the stable to saddle up—for we were all going to church—he told me what he knew of her story. I had heard it all and more, but I listened with unfeigned interest, for he recited it with flashes of heat and rancor that betrayed a cruel infatuation eating into his very bone and brain, the guilt of which was only intensified by the sour legality of his moral sense.

The church we went to was in Franklin, but the preacher was a man of note, a Vicksburg refugee. On the way back Gholson and I rode for a time near enough to Squire Sessions and Ned Ferry to know the sermon was being discussed by them, and something they said gave my companion occasion to murmur to

The Cavalier

me in a tone of eager censure that Ned Ferry's morals were better than his religion.

I said I wished mine were.

"Ah, Smith, be not deceived! Whenever you see a man bringing forth the fruits of the Spirit while he neglects the regularly appointed means of grace, you *know* there's something wrong, don't you? He went to church this morning—*of course;* but how often does he go? What's wrong with our dear friend—I don't like to say it, for I admire him so; I don't like to say it, and I never have said it, but, Smith,—Ned Ferry's a romanticist. We are relig'—what?"

"O—oh, nothing!"

At one point our way sloped down to a ramshackle wooden bridge that spanned a narrow bit of running water at the edge of a wood. Beyond it the road led out between two fields whose high worm-fences made it a broad lane. The farther limit of this sea of sunlight was the grove that hid the Sessions house on the left; on the right it was the woods-pasture in which lay concealed a lily-pond. As Gholson and I crossed the bridge we came upon a most enlivening view of our own procession out in the noonday blaze before us; the Sessions buggy; then Charlotte' little wagon; next the Sessions family carriage full of youngsters; and lastly, on their horses, Squire Sessions—tall, fleshy, clean-shaven, silver-haired—and Ned Ferry. Mrs. Sessions and Miss Harper, in the buggy, were just going by a big white gate in the right-hand fence, through which a private way led eastward to the lily-pond. A happy sight they were, the children in the rear vehicle

A Gnawing in the Dark

waving handkerchiefs back at us, and nothing in the
scene made the faintest confession that my pet song,
which I was again humming, was pat to the hour:

" To the lairds o' Convention 'twas Claverhouse spoke,
    Ere the sun shall go down there are heads to be broke."

" Gholson, if it isn't Ned Ferry's religion that's wor-
rying you just now about him, what is it? "

My companion looked at me as if what he must say
was too large for his throat. He made a gesture of
lament toward Ferry and broke out, " O—oh Smith,"
—nearly all Gholson's oh's were groans—" why is he
here? The scout is ' the eyes of the army '! a man
whose perpetual vigilance at the very foremost front—"

" Why, what do you mean? You know we're here
to rejoin the company as it comes down from Union
Church to camp here to-night. *That's* what we're here
for."

" Yes,—yes,—but, oh, don't you *see,* Smith? For
you, yourself, that's all right; you've got to stay with
him, and I'm glad you have. But he—oh why did he
not go on hours ago, to meet them? "

" Why should he? Isn't it good to leave one's lieutenant sometimes in command; isn't it bad not to? "

Gholson's eyes turned green. " Does Ned Ferry
give that as his reason? "

" I haven't asked his reason; I've asked you a
question."

" Well, I'll answer it. Do you think Jewett has run
back into his own lines? "

" Of course I do, and Ned Ferry does; don't you? "

The Cavalier

"No! Smith, there ain't a braver man in Grant's army than that one right now a-straddle of your horse. Why, just the way he got your horse night before—"

"Oh, hang him and the horse! you've told me that three times; what of it?"

"Smith, he's out here to make a new record for himself, at whatever cost!"

"And do you imagine Ned Ferry hasn't thought of that?"

"Ah-h, there are times when a man hasn't got his thinking powers; you ought to know that, Smith,—"

"Mr. Gholson, what do you mean by that?"

"Oh! I certainly didn't mean anything against you, Smith. Why is your manner so strange to me to-day? Oh, Smith, if you knew what—if I could speak to you in sacred confidence—I—I wouldn't injure Ned Ferry in your eyes, nor in anybody's; I only tell you what I do tell so you may help me to help him. But he's staying here, Smith, and keeping you here, to be near one whose name—without her a-dreaming of it —is already coupled with—why,—why, what made you start that a-way again, Smith?"

"Nothing; I didn't start. 'Coupled with some-body's name,' you say. With whose? Go on."

"With his, Smith, and most injuriously. He's here to tempt her to forget she's not—" He faltered.

"Free?" said I, and he nodded with tragic solemnity.

"You know who I mean, of course?"

"Certainly; you mean Mrs. Sessions."

He shook his head bitterly.

A Gnawing in the Dark

"Oh, well, then, of course I know. How am I to help you to help him; help him to do what?"

"O—oh! to tear himself away from her, Smith. I want you to appeal to him. He's taken a great shine to you. You can appeal to his feeling for romance— poetry—whatever he calls his hell-fired—I mean his unfortunate impiety. You know how, and I don't. And there you reach the foundations of his character, as far as it's got any; there's his conscience if it's any- where!"

I find myself giving but a faint impression of the spirit in which Gholson spoke; it went away beyond a mere backbiting mood and became a temper so vindictive and so venomously purposeful that I was startled; his condition seemed so fearfully like that of the old paralytic when he whined "That's not our way."

"Smith," my companion went on, "we ought to protect Ned Ferry from himself!" The words came through his clenched teeth. "And even more we ought to protect her. Who's to do it if we don't? Smith, I believe Provi-*dence* has been a-preparing you to do this, all through these last three nights and days!"

He looked at me for an answer until I became fright- ened. Was my late folly known to this crawling ma- ligner after all? A sweet-scented preparation I've had, thought I, but aloud I said only, "If Ned Ferry clears out, I suppose we must clear out, too."

"Why, eh,—I—I don't know that my move-*ments* need have anything to do with his. Yours, of course,—"

"Yes," I interrupted, beginning to boil.

The Cavalier

" I know," he said, " that comes hard; you'll have to tear *yourself* away—"

He stared at me and hushed. A panic was surging through me; must I be brought to book by such as he? "Mr. Gholson," I cried, all scorn without, all terror within; "Mr. Gholson, I—Mr. Gholson, sir!—" and set my jaws and heaved for breath.

"Why, Smith,—" He extended a soothing hand.

"No explanation, sir, if you please! I can get away from here without tearing myself, which is more than you can boast. Any fool can see why *you* are here. Stop, I take that back, sir! I don't play tit-for-tat with my tongue."

Gholson turned red on the brow and ashen about the lips. " I don't call that tit-for-tat, Mr. Smith. I remind you of an innocent attachment for a young girl; you accuse me of harboring a guilty passion for—" All at once he ceased with open lips, and then said as he drew a long breath of relief, " Smith, I beg your pardon! We've each misunderstood the other; I see, now, who you meant; you meant Miss Estelle Harper!"

"Whom else could I mean?" Disdain was in my voice, but he ought to have seen the falsehood in my eye, for I could feel it there.

" *Of* course!" he said; " of course! But, Smith, my mind was so full—just for the moment, you know,—of her we were speaking of in connection with Ned Ferry — Do you know? she's so unprotected and tagged after and talked about that it seems to me sometimes, in this nervous condition of mine, that if I could catch the entire gang of her pursuers in one hole I'd—I'd *end 'em* like so many rats. That sort of feeling is mere impulse, of course," he went on, " and only shows how near I am to that nervous breakdown. Yes, the Harper ladies are mighty lovely and hard enough to leave, but that's all I meant to you, and I'm sorry I touched your feelings. I'm *tchagrined*. Anyhow, all this is between us, you know. I wouldn't ever have confessed such feelings as I did just now except to a friend who knows as well as you do that if I ever should do a man a mortal injury I wouldn't do it in a spirit of resent-*ment*. You know that, don't you? No, that's not my way —Why, Smith, what gives you those starts? That's the third time you've done that this morning."

I said that entering the cool shade of the Sessions grove after the blazing heat of that long lane gave any one the right to a little shudder, and as we turned toward the house Gholson murmured " If you say you'll speak to Ned as I've asked you, I'll sort o' toll Squire Sessions off with me so's to give you the chance. It's for his own sake, you know, and you're the only one can do it."

XXX

DIGNITY AND IMPUDENCE

I KNEW Ned Ferry was having that inner strife with which we ought always to credit even Gholson's sort, and I had a loving ambition to help him " take the upper fork." So doing, I might help Charlotte Oliver fulfil the same principle, win the same victory. When, therefore, Gholson put the question to me squarely, Would I speak to Ferry? I consented, and as the four of us, horsemen, left our beasts in the stable munching corn, Gholson began a surprisingly animated talk with our host, and Ferry, with a quizzical smile, said to me " Talk with you?—shall be happy to; we'll just make a slight *détour* on this side the grove and woods-pasture, eh?"

He meant the north side, opposite that one by which we had come from church. Here the landscape was much the same as there; wide fields on each side the fenced highway that still ran north and south, and woods for the sky-line everywhere. We chose an easy footpath along the northern fence of the grove, crossed the highway, and passed on a few steps alongside the woods-pasture fence. We talked as we went, he giving the kindest heed to my every word though I could see that, like any good soldier, he was scanning all the ground for its fighting values, and, not to be outdone, I, myself, pointed out, a short way up the public road, a fence-gap on the left, made by our camping soldiers two nights before. It was at another such gap, in the woods-pasture fence, that we turned back by a path through it which led into the wood and so again toward the highway and the house-grove. The evening General Austin sent me to Wiggins it was at this gap that I saw old Dismukes sitting cross-legged on the ground, playing poker; and here, now, I summoned the desperation to speak directly to my point.

I had already tried hard to get something said, but had found myself at every turn entangled in generali-

Dignity and Impudence

ties. Now, stammering and gagging I remarked that our experiences of the morning, both in church and out, had in some way combined with an earlier word of his own to me, and given me a valuable thought. "You remember, when I wanted to shoot that Yankee off my horse?"

"Yes; and I said—what?"

"You said 'This isn't your private war.' Lieutenant, I hope those words may last in my memory forever and come to me in every moral situation in which I may find myself."

"Yes? Well, I think that's good."

"It seems to me, Lieutenant Ferry, that in every problem of moral conduct we confront we really hold in trust an interest of all mankind. To solve that problem bravely and faithfully is to make life just so much easier for everybody; and to fail to do so is to make it just so much harder to solve by whoever has next to face it." Whurroo! my blood was up now, let him look to himself!

"Yes?" said Ferry, picking at the underbrush as we sauntered, and for some time he said no more. Then he asked, "You want me to apply that to myself, in—in the present case?" and to my tender amazement, while his eyes seemed to count his slackening steps, he laid his arm across my shoulders.

An hour of avowal could not have told me more; could not have filled me half so full of sympathy, admiration and love, as did that one slight motion. It befitted the day, a day outwardly so quiescent, yet in which so much was going on. A realization of this

The Cavalier

quiet activity kept us silent until we had come through the woods-pasture to its southern border, and so through the big white field-gate into the public road; now we turned up toward the grove-gate, and here I spoke again. "Do you still think we ought to wait here for the command?"

That from a private soldier to his captain! Yet all my leader answered was "You think there's cause to change our mind?"

"I don't know, Lieutenant; do you think Jewett has run back into his own lines?"

"Yes, I think so; and you?"

"Why, eh,—Lieutenant, I don't believe there's a braver man in Grant's army than that one a-straddle of my horse to-day! Why, just the way he got him, night before last,—you've heard that, haven't you?"

"Yes, the General told me. And so you think—"

"Lieutenant, I can't help believing he's out here to make a new record for himself, at whatever cost!"

We went on some steps in silence and entered the gate of the house-grove; and just as Ferry would have replied we discovered before us in the mottled shade of the driveway, with her arm on Cécile's shoulders as his lay on mine, and with *her* eyes counting *her* slackening steps, Charlotte Oliver. They must have espied us already out in the highway, for they also were turned toward the house, and as we neared them Charlotte faced round with a cheery absence of surprise and said "Mr. Smith, don't we owe each other a better acquaintance? Suppose we settle up."

The Red Star's Warning

XXXI

THE RED STAR'S WARNING

IT seemed quite as undeniable, as we stood there, that Ned Ferry owed Cécile a better acquaintance. Every new hour enhanced her graces, and were I, here, less engrossed with her companion, I could pitch the praises of Cécile upon almost as high and brilliant a key—there may be room for that yet. Ferry moved on at her side. Charlotte stayed a moment to laugh at a squirrel, and then turned to walk, saying with eyes on the earth—

"If I tell you something, will you never tell?"

I looked down too. "Suppose I should feel sure it ought to be told."

"If you wait till you do you may tell it; that will suit me well enough."

"I will always suit you the best I can."

"I don't know why you should," she said.

"You risked your life to save mine; and you risked it when I did not deserve so much as your respect."

"Oh!—we must never talk about that again, Richard; you saw me in the evilest guise I ever wore, and that is saying much."

"But," I responded, "you put it on for a better reason than you could tell me then or can tell me now, though now I know your story."

"Please don't forget," she murmured, "that you know too much."

The Cavalier

" No, no! I don't know half enough; I know only
what Miss Camille and—and—Gholson could tell me,"
was my tricky reply, and I tried to look straight into
her eyes, but they took that faint introspective con-
traction of which I have spoken, and gazed through
me like sunlight through glass. Then again she bent
her glance upon her steps, saying—

" Ah, Richard, you have found out all you could,
and I am glad of it, except of what I, myself, have had
to betray to you; for *that* was more than one would
want to tell her twin brother. But I had to create you
my scout, and I had only two or three hours for my
whole work of creation."

" Well, you completed it." We went on some steps,
and then she said—

" You tell me I risked my life to save yours; I
risked more than life, and I risked it for more than
to save yours. Yet I did not save your life; you saved
it, yourself, and—" here her low tone thrilled like a
harp-string — " you risked it — frightfully — at that
bridge—merely to save the promise you made me that
you need not have made at all—oh, you needn't shake
your head; I *know*."

" Ah, how you gild my base metal! "

" No, no, I have the story exactly, and from one
who has no mind to praise you."

" From Gholson? "

" Gholson! no! I have it from Lucius Oliver, who
had it from his son. He told me carefully, quietly and
entirely, in pure spleen, so that I might know that they
know—think they know, that is,—why you and—he—

in front of us yonder—would not shoot his son when—"

"When as soldiers it was our simple du'—"

"Yes; and also that I may understand that he—the son—has sworn by that right hand you mutilated that the 'pair of you' shall die before he does."

"I ought not to have shown him that envelope addressed to you."

"Ah, but if it saved your life!"

"And this is what you don't want me to tell? Ah, I see; for me to know it is enough; I can put it to him as a theory. I can say Oliver is not a man to be put upon the defensive, and that he is more than likely to be hunting 'the pair of us'—" All at once I thought of something.

"What made you give that sudden start?" she asked as we faced about in the driveway to make our walk a moment longer; "that's a bad habit you've got; why do you do it?"

I fancied the thrilling freshness of the question I was about to put would be explanation enough. "Do you believe Jewett has gone back into his own lines?"

"I don't know; hasn't he?"

"Oh, I don't *know*, either, but—well, I don't believe there's a braver man in Grant's army than that one a-straddle of my horse to-day! Why, just the way he got him, night before last,—you've heard that, have you not?"

"Yes, I've heard it; he is a very daring man; what of it?"

The Cavalier

"Why, I can't help thinking he's out here to make a new record for himself, at whatever cost!"

A note of distress hung on my hearer's stifled voice; her head went lower and she laid her fingers pensively to her lips. "It would be like him," I heard her murmur, and when I asked if she meant Jewett she shook her head.

"No," I said, "you mean it would be like Oliver to join him," and with that the sudden start was hers. "He wouldn't have to touch Ned Ferry or me," I went on, heartlessly, "nor to come near us, to make us rue the hour we let ourselves forget this wasn't our private war."

She whispered something to herself in horrified dismay; but then she looked at me with her eyes very blue and said "You'll see him about it, won't you? You must help unravel this tangle, Richard; and if you do I'll—I'll dance at your wedding; yours and—somebody's we know!" Her eyes began forewith.

A light footfall sounded behind us, and Camille gave both her hands to my companion. "I was in the hall," she said, "telling Cécile she was like a white star that had come out by day, when I saw you here looking like a great red one; and you're still more like a red, red rose, and I've come to get some of your fragrance."

"I'd exchange for yours any day, and thank you, dear," responded Charlotte; "you're a bunch of sweet-peas. Isn't she, Mr. Smith?"

The bunch beamed an ecstatic bliss. What was the explanation; had her father arrived, or—or somebody else? The question went through me like an arrow.

A Martyr's Wrath

Was the cause of this heavenly radiance somebody else?—that was the barb; or was it I?—that was the soothing feather.

In gratitude for Charlotte's word she sank backward in a long obeisance. " May it please your ladyship, dinner is served. Oh, Mr. Smith, I've been listening to Mr. Gholson talking with aunt Martha and Estelle; I don't wonder you and he are friends; I think his ideas of religion are perfectly beautiful! "

At our two-o'clock dinner I found that our company had been reinforced. On one side of Camille sat I; but on the other side sat " Harry."

XXXII

A MARTYR'S WRATH

GREAT news the aide-de-camp brought us; from Lee, from Longstreet, Bragg and Johnston. Johnston was about to fall upon Grant's rear. Across the Mississippi Dick Taylor was expected this very day to deal the same adversary a crippling blow, and it was partly to mask this movement that we had made our feint upon the Federals near Natchez. Now these had fallen back, and our force had cunningly slipped away southward. Only General Austin and his staff had not gone when Lieutenant Helm left the front, and they were about to go.

Toward the end of the meal Mrs. Sessions, in her amiable plantation drawl, said she hoped the bearer of so much good tidings had not come to take away

The Cavalier

Lieutenant Ferry; and when Harry, flushing, asked what had given her such a thought, the simple soul replied that Mr. Gholson had told her he " suspicioned as much."

At once there arose the prettiest clamor all round the board, in which Charlotte and Cécile joined for the obvious purpose of making confusion. Gholson turned yellow and spoke things nobody heard, and Ferry tried to drown Harry's loud declarations that the word he had brought to Ferry was for him to stay, and that he had found him saddling up to go in search of his company. " Isn't that so, Ned?—Now,—now,—isn't that so?"

We left the table all laughing but Gholson. He tried to say something to Harry, which the latter waved away with mock gaiety until on the side veranda we got beyond view of the ladies, when the aide-de-camp reddened angrily and turned his back. As the two lieutenants were lighting cigarettes together, Harry, thinking Gholson had left us, blurted out, " Oh, that's all very well for you to say, Ned, but, damn him, he's not the sort of man that has the right to ' suspicion ' me of anything; slang-whanging, backbiting sneak, I know what *he's* here for."

On that the blood surged to Ferry's brow, but he set his mouth firmly, locked arms with the speaker and led him down the veranda. Gholson took on an uglier pallor than before and went back into the house. I followed him. He moved slowly up the two flights of hall stairs and into a room close under the roof, called the " soldiers' room ". It had three double beds, one

A Martyr's Wrath

of them ours. Without a fault in the dreary rhythm of his motions he went to the bedpost where hung his revolver, and turning to me buckled the weapon at his waist with hands that kept the same unbroken measure though they trembled and were as pallid as his face. In the same slow beat he shook his head.

"Smith, I rejoice! O—oh! I rejoice and am glad when I'm reviled and persecuted by the hounds of hell, and spoken evil against falsely for my religion's sake."

"Now, Gholson, that's nonsense!"

"O—oh! that's what it's for! that's what he meant by 'slang-whanging.' That's what it's for from first to last, no matter what it's for in between; and I know what it's for in between, too, and Ned Ferry knows. Did you see Ned Ferry take him under his protection? O—oh! they're two of one hell-scorched kind!" My companion stood gripping the bedpost and fumbling at his holster. I sank to the bed, facing him, expecting his rage to burn itself out in words, but when he began again his teeth were clenched. "You heard him tell Ned Ferry he knows why I'm here. It's true! he does know! he knows I'm here to protect a certain person from him and—"

"From whom? from Harry Helm? Oh, Gholson, that's too fantastical!"

"From him and the likes of him! Not that he loves her; that's the difference between them two cotton-mouth moccasins; Ned Ferry, hell grind him! does—or thinks he does; that other whelp *don't,* and knows he don't; he's only enam'—"

"HUSH!" He ceased. "I swear, Scott Gholson,

145

you must choose your words better when you allude— Lieutenant Helm is the last man in the brigade to be under *my* protection, but—oh, you're crazy, man, and blind besides. Harry Helm is not in love, but he thinks he is, though with quite another person!"

"O—oh! whether he loves or not, or whoever he loves, I know who he hates; he hates me and my religion; our religion, Smith, mine and yours; because it's put me between him and her. What was that the preacher said this morning? 'The carnal mind, being enmity against God, is enmity against them that serve God.' O—oh, I accept his enmity! it proves my religion isn't vain! I'm glad to get it!"

All this from his oscillating head, through his set teeth, in one malign monotone. As he quoted the preacher he mechanically drew his revolver. There was no bravado in this; he might lie, but he did not know how to sham; did not know, now, that his face was drawn with pain. Holding the weapon in one hand, under his absent gaze he turned it from side to side on the palm of the other. I put out my hand for it, but he dropped it into the holster and tried to return my smile.

"Do you propose to call him out?" I asked. "You can't call out an officer; you'll be sent to the water-batteries at Mobile."

"I've thought of all that," he droned.

"Then why do you put that thing on?"

"Why do I put it on? Why, I—you know what I told you about that Yankee—"

"Gholson," I exclaimed, for I saw that murder, even

A Martyr's Wrath

double murder, was hatching in his heart, with Charlotte Oliver for its cause, and looked hard into his evil eyes until they overmatched mine; whereupon I made as if suddenly convinced. "You're right!" I turned, whipped on my own belt with its two "persuaders," and blandly smoothing my ribs, added "Now! here are two ready, Yankees or no Yankees."

I never saw a face so unconsciously marked with misery as Gholson's was when we started downstairs. I stopped him on a landing. "Understand, you and I are friends,—hmm? I think Lieutenant Helm owes you an apology, and if you'll keep away from him I'll try to bring it to you."

The reply began with a vindictive gleam. "You needn't; I ain't got any more use for it than for him. I never apologized to a man in my life, Smith, nor I never accepted an apology from one; that's not my way."

Near the bottom of the second flight we met Charlotte, who, to make bad worse, would have passed with no more than a smile, but the look of Gholson startled her and she noticed our arms. With an arresting eye I offered a sprightly comment on the heat of the day, and while she was replying with the same gaiety I whispered "Take him with you."

How nimbly her mind moved! "Oh Mr. Gholson!" she said, and laughed to gain an instant for invention. "Mr. Gholson, can *you* tell me the first line of the last hymn we sang this morning?" Her beam was irresistible, and they went to the large parlor. I turned into the smaller one, opposite, where Squire Sessions

The Cavalier

started from a stolen doze and, having heard of my feeling for books, thrust into my hands, and left me with, the "Bible Defense of Slavery."

As I moved to a window which let out upon the side veranda the two lieutenants came around from the front and stood almost against it, outside; and as I intended to begin upon Harry as soon as Squire Sessions was safely upstairs, this suited me well enough. But the moment they came to the spot I heard Ned Ferry doing precisely what I had planned to do. At the same time, from across the hall came the sound of the piano and of Charlotte's voice, now a few bars, then an interval of lively speech, again a few bars, then more speech, and then a sustained melody as she lent herself to the kind flattery of Gholson's songless soul.

"But he is!" I overheard the aide-de-camp say; "he *is* a backbiting sneak, and I tell you again he's backbitten nobody more than he has you!"

"And I tell you again, Harry, that is my business."

"If he wants to fight me he can; I'll waive my rank."

"No, you will not, you have no right; our poor little rank, it doesn't belong to us, Harry, 'tis we belong to it. 'If he wants to fight!'—Do you take him for a rabbit? He is a brave man, you know that, old fellow. Of course he wants to fight. But he cannot! For the court-martial he would not care so much; I would not, you would not; 'tis his religion forbids him."

"O—oh!" groaned Harry in Gholson's exact tone, "'Hark from the tombs'!"

A Martyr's Wrath

"Ah!" said Ferry, "he does not live up to it? Well, of course! who does? But we will pass that; the main question is, Will you express the regret, and so forth, as I have suggested, and do yourself credit, Harry, as an officer and a gentleman, or—will you fight?"

"But you say his religion, so called, won't let him fight!"

"That's what I think; but if it forbids him, and if consequently he will not, well,—Harry,—I will."

"You will what!"

"I will have to fight you in his place."

"Why, Ned!—Ned!—you—you astound me! Wha'—what do you mean?"

"That is what I mean, Harry. You know—many times you have heard me say—I don't believe in that kind of thing; I find that worse than the religion of Gholson; yet still,—what shall I say?—we are but soldiers any-*how*—this time I make an exception in your favor. And of course this is confidential, on both sides; but you must make peace with Gholson, or you must fight with me."

"Oh, good Lord!—Ned!—Good Lord A'mighty! but this is too absurd. Why, Ned, don't you see that the bottom cause of this trouble isn't—"

"I know what is the bottom cause of this trouble very well, Harry; you can hear her in yonder, now, singing. Wherever Gholson is he hears her, too, like-*wise*. Perchance 'tis to him she is singing. If she can sing to him, are you too good to apolo-*gize?*"

"Oh, I'll give him the benefit of the doubt, Ned,

The Cavalier

damned if I don't! George! I'll apologize! Rather than lose your friendship I'd apologize to the devil!"

Ferry's thanks came eagerly. "Well, anyhow, old boy," he added, "in such a case to back down is braver than to fight; but to apologize to the devil—that is not hard; on the contrary, to keep *from* apologizing to the devil—ah! I wish I could always do that!—I wonder where is Dick Smith."

I stealthily laid down the "Bible Defense of Slavery" and was going upstairs three steps at a stride, when I came upon Camille and Estelle. My aim was to get Harry's revolver to him before he should have the exasperating surprise of finding Gholson armed, and to contrive a pretext for so doing; and happily a word from the two sisters gave me my cue. With the fire-arms of both officers I came downstairs and out upon the veranda loud-footed, humming—

' To the lairds o' Convention 'twas Claverhouse spoke,
  Ere the sun shall go down there are heads to be ——

Gentlemen, I hope I'm not too officious; they say we're all going for a walk in the lily-pond woods, and I reckon you'd rather not leave these things behind."

Both thanked me and buckled on their belongings, but Ferry's look was peculiarly intelligent; "I was in the small parlor, looking for you," he said; "I thought you would be near the music." And so he had seen Gholson with his revolver on him, and must have understood it!

"Smith," said Harry, "will you be so kind as to

150

say to Gholson—oh, Lord! Ned, this is heavy drags on a sandy road! I—"

"That's all right, Harry, I withdraw the request."

"Well, you needn't; I was in the wrong. Smith, will you say to Gholson—" His voice dropped to a strictly private rumble.

"Yes, Lieutenant, I'll do so with pleasure, and I'm sure what you say will have the proper—here are the ladies."

XXXIII

TORCH AND SWORD

"Now give me your hand, Miss Camille; now jump!" So twice and once again the rivulet was passed which ran from the lily-pond, she and I leading all the others on the return from the woodland afternoon walk. We turned and faced away from the declining sun and across the clear pool to where its upper end, dotted with lily-pads, lay in a deep recess of the woods. There were green and purple garlands of wild passion-flower around her hat and about the white and blue fabrics at her waist. At the head of the pond, with Ferry beside her, stood black-haired Cécile canopied by overhanging boughs, her hat bedecked with the red spikes of the Indian-shot and wound with orange masses of love-vine. Nearer to us around the shore was Estelle of the red-brown hair and red-brown eyes and brows and lashes, whose cheek seemed always to glow with ever rising but never con-

The Cavalier

fessed emotion; and with her walked Gholson. Near the waterside also, but farthest up the path, came Miss Harper and Charlotte Oliver.

Harry was not with us. The settlement of his trouble with Gholson awaited his return out of the region north of us, whither Ferry had suggested his riding on an easy reconnaissance. Camille and I were just turning again, when there came abruptly into our scene the last gallant show of martial finery any of us ever saw until the war was over and there was nothing for our side to make itself fine for. On the road from the house we heard a sound of galloping, and the next moment General Austin and his entire staff (less only Harry) reined up at the edge of the pond, ablaze with all the good clothes they could muster and betraying just enough hard usage to give a stirring show of the war's heroic reality. The General, on a beautiful cream-colored horse, wore long yellow gauntlets and a yellow sash; from throat to waist the sunlight glistened upon the over-abundant gold lace of his new uniform, his legs were knee-deep in shining boots, and his soft gray hat was looped up on one side and plumed according to Regulations with one drooping ostrich feather. Behind halted in pleasing confusion captains and captains, flashing with braids, bars, buckles, buttons, bands, sword-knots, swords and brave eyes, and gaily lifting hats and caps, twice, and twice again, and once more, to the ladies—God bless them! Major Harper, the oldest, most refined and most soldierly of them all, was also the handsomest. Old Dismukes was with them; burly, bushy, dingy, on a huge roan charger.

Torch and Sword

Camille asked me who he was, and I was about to reply that he was a bloodthirsty brute without a redeeming trait, when he lifted his shaggy brows at me and smiled, and as I smiled back I told her he was our senior colonel, rough at times, but the bravest of the brave. Meantime the General rode forward over a stretch of shallow water, Ned Ferry ran back along the margin to meet him, and at the saddlebow they spoke a moment together privately, while at more distance but openly to us all Major Harper informed his sister that with one night's camp and another day's dust the brigade would be down in Louisiana. Camille turned upon me and hurrahed, the Arkansas colonel smiled upon her approvingly, the ladies all waved, the General lifted his plumed hat, faced about, passed through his turning cavalcade and drew it after him at a gallop.

Our promenaders hurried into close order and with quick step and eager converse we moved toward the house. In raptures scintillant with their own beauty the three Harper girls inflated each item of the day's news and the morrow's outlook, and it was almost as pretty to see Miss Harper's keen black eyes and loving-tolerant smile go back and forth from Camille to Estelle, from Estelle to Cécile, and round again, as each maiden added some new extravagance to the glad vaunting of the last, and looked, for confirmation, to the gallant who toiled to keep her under her parasol. Suddenly the three girls broke into song with an adaptation of "Oh, carry me back" which substituted "Louisiana" for "Virginia," but whose absurd quaverings I will not betray in words to a generation that never knew the frantic times to which they belonged. I felt a shamefacedness for them even then, yet when I glanced behind, Miss Harper was singing with us in the most exalted earnest. We had nearly reached the field-gate, the big white one on the highway, and were noting that the dust of the General and his retinue had barely vanished from the southern stretch of the road, when one feminine voice said "What's that?" another exclaimed "See yonder!" and Miss Harper cried "Why, gentlemen, somebody's house is burning!"

Beyond the grove and the fields north of it, and beyond their farther bound of trees, in the northwest, was rising and unfolding into the peaceful Sabbath heavens a massive black column of the peculiar heavy smoke made by the burning of baled and stored cotton. We ran, two and two, into the road and up toward the grove-gate. "Don't stumble," I warned Camille as she looked back to see if any one besides me was holding his partner's hand. Inside the gate we paused, we two, still hand in hand. Her brown hair had shaken low upon her temples in two voluptuous masses between which she lifted her eyes to mine, my hand tightened on hers, and hers gave a little spasm of its own.

"Oh, Dick!" she whispered; but before I could rally from the blissful shock of it to reply, her face changed distressfully, and pointing beyond me, she drank a great breath, and cried, "Look!"

Sure enough, out there on the sky-line, in the northeast this time, another column of smoke was lifting its first billow over the tree-tops. "Oh, Dick!" she exclaimed, in beautiful alarm, "what does it mean?"

"It means the Yankees,—love," I said, and when she gasped her dismay without letting on to have heard the last word, I felt that fires were cheap at any price.

"There are others there besides Yankees," said Gholson to the general company as they joined us; "Yankees have got more sense than to start fires ahead of their march." On the same instant with Ned Ferry I sprang half-way to the top of the grove fence and peered out across road and fields upon the farthest point in line with the second fire. There we saw two horsemen reconnoitring, one a very commanding figure, the other mean enough. Ferry used his glass, but no glass was needed to tell either of us that Gholson's reckoning was true; those two were not Federals.

The ladies flew to the house and the rest of us to the stable. In its door Ferry stopped to look back upon the road while Gholson and I darted in, but now he, too, sprang to his horse's side. "How many, Lieutenant?" I cried, as the three of us saddled up.

"About a hundred; same we saw yesterday; captain at the rear; that means our fellows are close behind them."

For a moment more I could hear the thunder of their speeding column; then the grove seemed to swallow it up, and the stillness was grim. "Come on!" cried Ferry, swinging up, and after him we sprang. "They've dismounted on the far edge of the grove," said Gholson to me as we rode abreast, with Ferry a

The Cavalier

length ahead; "they'll form line on each side the road at right angles to it!" and again he was right. Ferry led northeastward, but hardly had we made half a dozen leaps when he waved me to a near corner of the flower-garden palings and I saw Miss Harper beckoning and Charlotte holding up my carbine and his sword. Miss Harper was drawn up as straight as a dart, her black eyes flashing and her lips charged with practical information that began to flow the moment I was near enough to hear her guarded voice. "They've all put their horses in the locks of the road fence, just beyond the big white gate—"

"We know," I interrupted, leaning and snatching the weapons from Charlotte's hands. She kissed them good-bye.

"Ah, yes, yes!" she said, "they know all we can tell them and all we can't!"

The only response I could give was the shower of loose earth thrown upon both women by my horse's heels as I whirled and sped after my leader. He and Gholson were half a broad field ahead of me, but I followed only at their speed, designing to hand over the sword so nearly at the moment of going into action that I might stay by its owner's side unrebuked; and my plan was not in vain. Up the highway our Louisianians burst into view in column at full speed; I knew them by their captain, a man noted throughout the brigade for the showiness of his dress; and the next instant, away across the fields beyond the highroad, Quinn and his scouts broke out of the woods, heading for the gap in the woods-pasture fence. As each friend-

The Charge in the Lane

ly column caught sight of the other, long cheers rang across the narrowing interval between them. Through that other gap which I had noted in my walk with Ferry he and Gholson reached the road, sped forward on it to a rise that overlooked the fields, and halted. Ferry rose on tiptoe in the stirrups, lifted his cap in air, pointed triumphantly backward to the grove, and was recognized by both columns at once. Again they cheered; at a full run I reached his side and threw his sword into his hand. Both columns saw him belt it on and flash it out, their cheers swelled again, the Louisianians hurtled down upon us, and we turned and were at the front of the onset.

XXXIV

THE CHARGE IN THE LANE

The instant Ferry wheeled at the flaming captain's side you could see he was unwelcome. I heard him tell what we knew of the foe and the ground; I saw him glance back at the blown condition of the speeding column and then say " You've got them any-*how,* Captain; you'll get every man of them without a scratch, only if you will take your time."

But the Captain answered headily; " No, sir! I've tried that twice already; this time I'll cut them in two and be in their rear at one dash! Bring in your company behind mine, if you choose."

Ferry drew back a few ranks but stayed with the column; Quinn had had the toil of the chase, he should have also the glory of the fight. So Ferry sent Gholson—whose horsemanship won a cheer from the passing Louisianians as he cleared the roadside fence—across to Quinn, bidding the Lieutenant slacken speed and count himself a reserve. And then into the broad lane between grove and woods-pasture, with the charging yell, the Louisianians thundered. Ah! but my Creole gentleman was a sight, with his straight blade lifted in air and his face turned back on us aglow with the joy of battle! I was huzzaing back at him and we were passing the front gate of the grove avenue, when down through it came from the house, with a tremor of echoes, the first shot; a shot and then a woman's scream, and his blazing eyes said to me, "He is there! That was Oliver!"

There was no time for speech. The shot was not a signal, yet on the instant and in our very teeth, on our right and our left, the cross-fire of the hidden and waiting foe flashed and pealed, and left and right, a life for a life, our carbines answered from the saddle. For a moment the odds against us were awful. In an instant the road was so full of fallen horses and dismounted men that the jaded column faltered in confusion. Our cunning enemy, seeing us charge in column, had swung the two extremes of their line forward and inward. So, crouching and firing upon us mounted, each half could fire toward the other with impunity, and what bullets missed their mark buzzed and whined about our ears and pecked the top rails of either fence like hail on a window. A wounded horse drove mine back upon his haunches and caused him to plant a hoof full on the breast of one of our Louisianians stretched dead on his back as though he had lain there for an hour. Another man, pale, dazed, unhurt, stood on the ground, unaware that he was under point-blank fire, holding by the bits his beautiful horse, that pawed the earth majestically and at every second or third breath blew from his flapping nostrils a cloud of scarlet spray. They blocked up half the road. As we swerved round them the horse of the company's first lieutenant slid forward and downward with knees and nose in the dust, hurling his rider into a lock of the fence, and the rider rose and rushed to the road again barely in time to catch a glittering form that dropped rein and sword and reeled backward from the saddle. It was his captain, shot through the breast. An instant later our tangled column parted to right and left, dashed into the locks of the two fences, sprang to the ground, and began to repay the enemy in the coin of their own issue. Only a dozen or so did otherwise, and it was my luck to be one of these. Espying Ned Ferry at the very front, in the road, standing in his stirrups and shouting back for followers to carry the charge on through, we spurred toward him and he turned and led. Then what was my next fortune but to see, astride of my stolen horse, the towering leader of the foe, Captain Jewett.

He came into the road a few rods ahead of us through a gap his men had earlier made opposite the big white gate. He answered our fierce halloo, as he crossed, by a pistol-shot at Ferry, but Ferry only glanced around at me and pointed after him with his sword. A number of blue-coats afoot followed him to

the gap but at our onset scattered backward, sturdily
returning our fire. Into the gap and into the enemy's
left rear went Ferry and his horsemen, but I turned
the other way and spurred through the woods-pasture
gate after the Federal leader, he on my horse and I
on his. Down the highway, on either side, stood his
brave men's horses in the angles of the worm-fence,
and two or three horse-holders took a shot at me as I
sped in after the man who was bent on reaching the
right of his divided force before Quinn should strike
it, as I was bent on foiling him. Twice I fired at his
shapely back, and twice, while he kept his speed among
the tree-trunks, he looked back at me as coolly as at
an odd passer-by and sent me a ball from his revolver.
A few more bounds carried him near enough to his
force to shout his commands, but half a hundred cheers
suddenly resounded in the depth of the woods-pasture,
and Quinn and his men charged upon the foe's right
and rear. I joined the shout and the shouters; in a
moment the enemy were throwing down their arms, and
I turned to regain the road to the pond. For I had
marked Jewett burst through Quinn's line and with a
score of shots ringing after him make one last brave
dash—for escape. Others, pursuing him, bent northward, but my instinct was right, his last hope was for
his horse-holders, and at a sharp angle of the by-road,
where it reached the pond, exactly where Camille
and I had stood not an hour before, I came abruptly
upon Cricket—riderless. I seized his rein, and as I
bent and snapped the halter of one horse on the snaf-
fle of the other I saw the missing horseman. Leaping

from the saddle I ran to him. He was lying on his face in the shallow water where General Austin and his staff had so gaily halted a short while before, and as I caught sight of him he rolled upon his back and tried to lift his bemired head.

XXXV

FALLEN HEROES

I DROPPED to my knee in the reddening pool and passed my arm under his head.

"Thank you," he said, and repeated the word as I wet my handkerchief and wiped the mire from his face; "thank you;—no, no,"—I was opening his shirt —"that's useless; get me where you can turn me over; you've hit me in the back, my lad."

"I?—I hit you? Oh, Captain Jewett, thank God, I didn't hit you at all!"

"What's the difference, boy; you didn't aim to miss, did you? I didn't. It's not my only hurt; I think I broke something inside when I fell from the sad'—ah! that's *your* bugle, isn't it? It's my last fight—oh, the devil! my good boy, don't begin to cry again; war's war; give me some water. . . . Thank you! And now, if you don't want me to bleed to death get me out of this slop, and—yes,—easy!—that's it—*easy*—oh, God! oh, let me down, boy, let me *down, you're killing me!* Oh!—" he fainted away.

With his unconscious head still on my arm I faced

toward the hundred after-sounds of the fray and hallooed for help. To my surprise it promptly came. Three blundering boys we were who lifted him into the saddle and bore him to the house reeling and moaning astride of Cricket, the poor beast half dead with hard going. The sinking sun was as red as October when we issued into the highroad and moved up it to the grove gate through the bloody wreckage of the fray. The Louisianians were camping in the woods-pasture, Ferry's scouts in the grove, and the captive Federals were in the road between, shut in by heavy guards. At our appearance they crowded around us, greeting their undone commander with proud words of sympathy and love, and he thanked them as proudly and lovingly, though he could scarcely speak, more than to ask every moment for water. A number of our Sessions house group crowded out to meet us at the veranda steps; Camille; Harry Helm with his right hand bandaged; Cécile, attended by two or three Sessions children; and behind all Miss Harper exclaiming " Ah, my boy, you're a welcome sight—Oh! is that Captain Jewett! "

Two or three bystanders helped us bear him upstairs, where, turning from the bedside, I pressed Camille with eager questions.

"Lieutenant Ferry? he's unhurt—and so is Mr. Gholson! Mr. Gholson's gone to Franklin for doctors; Lieutenant Ferry sent him; he's been sending everybody everywhere faster than anybody else could think of anything! "

I asked where Ferry was now. Her eyes refilled—they were red from earlier distresses—and she motioned across the hall: "The captain of the Louisianians, you know, has sent for him!"

"Yes," I said, "the Captain's hit hard. I saw him when he was struck."

"Oh, Dick! then you were at the very front!"

"Did you think I was at the rear?"

She looked down. "I couldn't help hoping it."

"Then you were thinking of me."

"I prayed for you."

Such news seemed but ill-gotten gains, to come before I had gathered courage to inquire after Charlotte Oliver. "Wh'—where is—where are the others?"

"They're all about the house, tending the wounded; Mrs. Sessions is with the Squire, of course,—dear, brave old gentleman! we thought he was killed, but Charlotte found the ball had glanced."

I asked if it was Oliver who shot him, and she nodded. "It was down at the front door; the Squire said he'd shoot him if he shot Charlotte, and Charlotte declared she'd shoot him if he shot the Squire, and all at once he shot at her and struck him."

"Who was it that screamed; was it she?"

My informant's head drooped low and she murmured, "It was I."

"Then *you* were at the front."

"Did you think I was at the rear?"

I fear I answered evasively. I added that I must go to Lieutenant Ferry, and started toward the door, but she touched my arm. "Oh, Dick, you should have heard him praise you to her!—and when he said you had chased Captain Jewett and was missing, she cried;

but now I'll tell her you're here." She started away but returned. " Oh, Dick, isn't it wonderful how we're always victorious! why don't those poor Yankees give up the struggle? they must see that God is on our side!"

As she left me, Ned Ferry came out with a sad face, but smiled gladly on me and caught me fondly by the arm. On hearing my brief report he saddened more than ever, and when I said I had promised Jewett he should hand his sword to none but him, " Oh!"— he smiled tenderly—" I don't want to refuse it; go in and hang it at the head of his bed as he would do in his own tent; I'll wait here."

I pointed to the door he had softly closed behind him: " How is it in there?"

" Ah, Richard, in there the war is all over."

" Dead?"

" So called."

XXXVI

" SAYS QUINN, S'E "

LIEUTENANT HELM came out as I went in, and I paused an instant to ask him in fierce suspicion if he had bandaged his hand himself. " No," he whispered, " Miss Camille." It was a lie, but I did not learn that until months after. " Come downstairs as soon as you can," he added, " there's a hot supper down there; first come first served." We parted.

I found Miss Harper fanning the wounded giant

and bathing his brows, and my smiles were ample explanation of my act as I hung the sword up. Then I brought in my leader. "Captain Jewett," he said after a nearly silent exchange of greetings, "I wish we had you uninjured."

"Ah, no, Lieutenant, this is bad enough. Lieutenant, there is one matter—"

"Yes, Captain, what is that?"

"The villain who set those fires—you know who he is, I hope."

"Yes, Captain, I know."

"He didn't begin that until after he left me. I had some private reasons for not killing him when I might have done it."

"Yes, Captain, I know that, too."

"Yet if I had caught him again I would have strung him up to the first limb."

"I have sent some picked men to catch him if they can," said Ferry, and the racked sufferer lifted a hand in approval. Camille came to her aunt and whispered "Mr. Gholson with two doctors." The wounded captive heard her.

"Lieutenant," he panted, "I hope you'll—do me the favor—to let my turn with those gentlemen—come last,—after my boys,—will you?"

"Ah! Captain, even our boys wouldn't allow that; no, here's a doctor, now."

I went down to the supper-table. Camille was there, dispensing its promiscuous hospitality to men who ate like pigs. I would as leave have found her behind a French-market coffee-stand. Harry Helm, nursing his

The Cavalier

bandaged hand, was lolling back from the board and quizzing her with compliments while she cut up his food. A fellow in the chair next mine said he had seen me with Ferry when we joined the Louisianians' charge. "Your aide-de-campp friend over yonder's a-gitt'n' lots o' sweetenin' with his grub; well, he deserves it."

I asked how he deserved it. "Why, we wouldn't 'a' got here in time if he hadn't 'a' met-up with us. That man Gholson, he's another good one."

The latter remark seemed to me a feeler, and I ignored it, and inquired how Lieutenant Helm had got that furlough. (Furlough was our slang for a light wound.) "Oh, he got it mighty fair! Did you see that Yankee lieutenant with the big sabre-cut on his shoulder? Well, your friend yonder gave him that— and got the Yankee's pistol-shot in his hand. But that saved Gholson's life, for that shot was aimed to give Gholson a furlough to kingdom-come. Are they kinfolks?"

I mumbled that they were not even friends. "Well, now, I suspicioned that,—when I first see 'em meet at the head of our column! But the aide-de-campp he took it so good-natured that, thinks I,—"

Another of Ferry's men, seated opposite, swallowed hurriedly, and covertly put in— "Y' ought to hear what Quinn said to Gholson just now as they met-up out here in the hall. Quinn thought they were alone. Says Quinn, as cold as a fish, s's'e 'Mr. Gholson,' s'e, 'you're not a coward, sir, and that's why I'm curious to ask you a question,' s'e. And says Gholson, just as cold, s'e ' I'm prepared, Lieutenant Quinn, to answer it.' And says Quinn, s'e ' Why was it, that when Harry Helm struck that blow which saved your life, and which you knew was meant to save it, and you seen his sword shot out of his hand and three or four Yankees makin' a dead set to kill him, and nothin' else in any particular danger at all, why was it, Mr. Gholson, that you never turned a hand nor an eye to save him?' "

" Great Scott! wha'd Gholson say? "

" Gholson, s'e, ' I done as I done, sir, from my highest sense o' duty. This ain't Lieutenant Helm's own little private war, Lieutenant Quinn, nor mine, nor yours.' "

" Jo'! that to Quinn! wha'd Quinn answer? "

" Why, with that Quinn popped them big glass eyes o' his'n till the whites showed clear round the blue, and s'e ' I know it better than you do; that's just what it suited you to forget. Oh! I'd already seen through you in one flash, you sneak. It's good for you you're not in my command; I'd lift you to a higher sense of whose war this is, damn you, if I had to hang you up by the thumbs.' With that he started right on by, Gholson a-keepin' his face to him as he passed, when Ned Ferry and—her—came out o' the parlor, and Ned turned out on the rear gallery with Quinn while she sort o' smiled at Gholson to come to her and sent him off on some business or other. George! I never seen her so beautiful."

Thereupon occurred a brief exchange of comments which seemed to me to carry by implication as fine a praise as could possibly come from two rough fellows of the camp. Speaking the names of Ferry and Charlotte in undertone, of course, but with the unrestraint of soldiers, they said their say without a shadow of inuendo in word or smile. Her presence, they agreed, always made them feel as though something out of the common "was bound to happen pretty quick," while his, they said, assured them that "whatever did happen would happen right." I turned with a frown as Harry laughed irrelevantly, and saw Camille and him smiling at me with childish playfulness. Then suddenly their smile changed and went beyond me, two or three men softly said "Smith!" and I was out of my chair and standing when Charlotte Oliver, in a low voice, tenderly accosted me.

"Oh, Richard Thorndyke Smith!—alive and well! Lieutenant Ferry wants you; he has just gone to his camp-fire."

XXXVII

A HORSE! A HORSE!

NIGHT had fully come. A few bivouac fires burned low in the grove, and at one of them near the grove gate I found our young commander. On a bench made of a fence-rail and two forked stakes he sat between Quinn and the first-lieutenant of the Louisianians. The doctor whom I had seen before sat humped on his horse, facing the three young men and making clumsy excuses to Ferry for leaving. The other physician would stay for some time yet, he said, and he, himself, was leaving his instruments, such as they were, and would return in the morning. "Fact is, my son's a surgeon, and he taken all my best instru-*ments* with *him*."

"When; where is he?" eagerly asked Quinn, seeing Ferry was not going to ask.

"My son? Oh, he's in Virginia, with General Lee."

"Hell!" grunted Quinn, but the doctor pretended to listen to Ferry.

"Ah, but we move south at day-*light;* the prisoners and wounded we send east, to Hazlehurst," said our leader, with a restraining hand on Quinn's knee. The other lieutenant made some inquiry of him, and the doctor was ignored, but stayed on, and as I stood waiting to be noticed I gathered a number of facts. The lightly injured would go in a plantation wagon; for the few gravely hurt there was the Harpers' ambulance, which had just arrived to take the ladies back to Squire Wall's, near Brookhaven, alas! instead of to Louisiana. For the ladies Charlotte's spring-wagon was to be appropriated, one of them riding beside it on horseback, and there was to be sent with them, besides Charlotte's old black driver, "a reliable man well mounted." Whoever that was to be it was not Harry, for he was to go south with a small guard, bearing the body of the Louisiana captain to his home between the hostile lines behind Port Hudson.

"Good-night, gentle-*men,*" said the doctor at last. As he passed into the darkness Quinn bent a mock frown upon his young superior.

"Lieutenant Ferry, the next time I have to express

my disgust please to keep your hand off my knee, will you?"

Ferry's response was to lay it back again and there ensued a puerile tussle that put me in a precious pout, that I should be kept waiting by such things. But presently the three parted to resume their several cares, and the moment Ferry touched my arm to turn me back toward the house I was once more his worshipper. "Well!" he began, "you have now *two* fine horses, eh?"

"Oh, by Regulations, I suppose, I ought to turn one of them over to Major Harper. I wish it were to you, Lieutenant; I'd keep my own—he'll be all right in a day or two—and give you Captain Jewett's."

"Well,—just for a day or two,—do that, while I lend my horse to a friend."

I had already asked myself what was to become of Charlotte Oliver while the Harpers were preëmpting her little wagon, and now I took keen alarm. "Why, Lieutenant, I shall be glad! But why not lend Captain Jewett's horse and keep yours? Yours is right now the finest and freshest mount in the command."

"Yes, 'tis for that I lend him."

We went on in silence. Startled and distressed, I pondered. What was her new purpose, that she should ask, or even accept, such a favor as this from Ned Ferry; a favor which, within an hour, the whole command would know he had granted? Was this a trifle, which only the Gholson-like smallness of my soul made spectral? The first time I had ever seen Ferry with any of his followers about him, was he not on Char-

A Horse! A Horse!

lotte's gray, now, unluckily, beyond reach, at Wiggins? Ah, yes; but Beauty lending a horse to speed Valor was one thing; Valor unhorsing himself to speed Beauty—oh, how different! What was the all-subordinating need?

As we entered the hall I came to a conviction which lightened my heart; the all-subordinating need was—Oliver. I thought I could see why. The spring of all his devilish behavior lay in those relations to her for which I knew she counted herself chargeable through her past mistakes. Unless I guessed wrong her motives had risen. I believed her aim was now, at whatever self-hazard, to stop this hideous one-woman's war, and to speed her unfinished story to the fairest possible outcome for all God's creatures, however splendidly or miserably the " fool in it " should win or lose. We stopped and waited for Cécile and the remaining doctor, she with a lighted candle, to come down the stairs. From two rooms below, where most of the wounded lay, there came women's voices softly singing, and Charlotte's was among them. Their song was one listening to which many a boy in blue, many a lad in gray, has died: " Rock me to sleep, mother."

Cécile and the doctor had come from the bedside of the Union captain, where Miss Harper remained. " I've done all I can," he said to Ferry; " we old chill-and-fever doctors wa'n't made for war-times; he may get well and he may not."

" Smith," said Ferry, " go up and stay with him till further orders."

The Cavalier

XXXVIII

" BEAR A MESSAGE AND A TOKEN "

LATE in the night Gholson came to the Union captain's bedside for Miss Harper. Charlotte had sent him; the doctor had left word what to do if a certain patient's wound should re-open, and this had happened. The three had succeeded in stanching it, but Charlotte had prevailed upon Miss Harper to lie down, and the weary lady had, against all her intentions, fallen asleep. I was alone with the wounded captain. He did not really sleep, but under the weight of his narcotics drowsed, muttered, stirred, moaned, and now and then spoke out.

Sitting in the open window, I marked the few red points of dying firelight grow fewer in the bivouac under the grove. Out there by the gate Ned Ferry slept. Fireflies blinked, and beyond the hazy fields rose the wasted moon, by the regal slowness of whose march I measured the passage of time as I had done two nights before. My vigil was a sad one, but, in health, in love, in the last of my teens and in the silent company of such a moon, my straying thoughts lingered most about the maiden who had " prayed for me." My hopes grew mightily. Yet with them grew my sense of need to redouble a lover's diligence. I resolved never again to leave great gaps in my line of circumvallation about the city of my siege, as I had done in the past —two days. I should move to the final assault, now,

at the earliest favorable moment, and the next should
see the rose-red flag of surrender rise on her temples;
in war it is white, but in love it is red.

First favorable moment; ah! but when would that
be? Who was to convey the Harpers to Hazlehurst?
Well, thank Heaven! not Harry. Scott Gholson?
Gholson was due at headquarters. Poor Gholson!
much rest for racked nerves had he found here; what
with Ferry, and Harry, and the fight, and Quinn, I
wondered he did not lie down and die under the pure
suffocation of his " tchagrin." Even a crocodile, I believed, could suffer from chagrin, give him as many
good causes as Gholson had accumulated. But no, the
heaven of " Charlie Tolliver's " presence and commands—she seemed to have taken entire possession of
him—lifted and sustained him above the clouds of all
unkinder things.

A faint stir at the threshold caught my ear and I
discerned in the hall a young negro woman. The light
of an unseen candle made her known at a glance; she
had been here since the previous evening, as I knew,
though it chanced that I had not seen her; Oliver's
best wedding-gift, the slave maid whom I had seen
with Charlotte in the curtained wagon at Gallatin. I
stole out to her; she courtesied. " Miss Charlotte say
ef you want he'p you fine me a-sett'n' on de step o' de
stairs hafe-ways down."

I inquired if she was leaving us. " She a-gitt'n'
ready, suh; Misteh Goshen done gone to de sta-able
to git de hosses." The girl suddenly seemed pleased
with herself. " Mis' Charlotte would 'a' been done

The Cavalier

gone when de yethehs went—dem-ah two scouts what was sent ayfteh *him*—ef I hadn' spoke' up when I did."

"Indeed! how was that?"

"Why, I says, s' I, ' Mis' Charlotte, how we know he ain' gwine fo' to double on his huntehs? Betteh wait a spell, and den ef no word come back dat he a-doublin', you kin be sho' he done lit out fo' to jine de Yankees roun' Pote Hudsom.' "

"Why did you tell her that? You want him caught; so do I; but you know she doesn't want to catch him, and you don't want her to. Neither do I. Nor neither do we want Lieutenant Ferry to catch him."

"No, suh, dass so. But same time, while she no notion o' gitt'n' him cotch, she believe she dess djuty-bound to head-off his devil-*ment*. 'Tis dess like I heah' Mr. Goshen say to Miss Hahpeh, ' Dis ain't ow own li'l' pri'—' "

I waved her away and went back into the room; the Captain had called. He asked the time of night; I said it was well after two; he murmured, was quiet, and after a moment spoke my name. I answered, and he whispered " Coralie Rothvelt—she's here; I—recognized her voice—when they were singing. Did you know I knew her?"

"Yes, Captain."

"Daring game that was you fellows let her put up on us night before last, my boy,—and it hung by a thread. If our officers had only asked the old man his name—it would have been—a flash of light. If I had dreamed, when I saw—you and Ned Ferry—yesterday,—that Coralie Rothvelt was—Charlotte Oliver,

"Bear a Message and a Token"

—and could have known her then—as I've—learned to know her—to-day—from her—worst enemy,—you know,—"

"Yes, Captain."

"I should—have turned back, my boy." After a silence the hero said more to himself than to me "Ah, if my brother were here to-night—I might live!"

Many days afterward I thought myself dull not to have guessed what that speech meant, but now I was too distressed by the change I saw coming over him to do any surmising. He began to say things entirely to himself. "Home!" he murmured; "sweet, sweet home!—my home! my country!—My God, my country, my home!—Smith,—you know what that is you're—wiping off my brow,—don't you?"

"Yes, Captain."

"I—I didn't want you to be—taken too unpleasantly by surprise—just at the—end. You know what's—happening,—don't you?"

"Yes, Captain." As I wiped the brow again I heard the tread of two horses down in front of the house; they were Gholson's, and Ned Ferry's for Charlotte. "Captain, may I go and bring her—tell her what you say, and bring her?"

"Do you think she'd come? She'd have gone to Ship Island if I had caught her."

"I know she'll come."

"I wish she would; she could 'bear a message and a token,' as the song says."

She came. I met her outside the door, and for a moment I feared she would come no farther. "How can I, Richard! Oh, how can I?" she whispered; "this is my doing!" But presently she stood at the bedside calm and compassionate, in the dark dress and limp hat of two nights before. The dying man's eyes were lustrous with gratitude.

"I have one or two things," he said, after a few words of greeting, "that I'd like to send home—to my mother—and my wife; some trifles—and a message or two; if I—if—if I—"

"Will you let me take them?" Charlotte asked. I did not see or hear what they were; Gholson beckoned me into the hall. He did not whisper; there are some people, you know, who can never exercise enough self-suppression to whisper; he mumbled. He admitted the dying had some rights, but—he feared the delay might result unfortunately; wanted me to tell Charlotte so, and was sure I was ever so wrong to ask to have Ned Ferry awakened for the common incident of a prisoner's death; he would let him know the moment he awoke.

When I came back into the room the captive had asked Charlotte to pray. " Tisn't that I'm—the least bit afraid," he was saying.

"Oh, no," she responded, wiping his brow, "why should you be? Dying isn't nearly so fearful a thing as living. I'd rather, now, you'd pray for me; I'm such an unbeliever—in the beliefs, I mean, the beliefs the church people think we can't get on without. My religion is scarcely anything but longings and strivings"—she sadly smiled—"longings and strivings and hopes."

Charlotte Sings

"Yet you wouldn't—"

"Part with it? Oh, not for the world beside!"

"Neither would I—with mine." The soldier folded his hands in supplication. "Neither would I—though mine, O Lord—is only the—old-fashioned sort—for whose beliefs our fathers—used to kill one another; God have mercy—on them—and us."

There was a great stillness. Against the bedside Charlotte had sunk to her knees, and under the broad brim of her Leghorn hat leaned her brow upon her folded hands. Thus, presently, she spoke again.

XXXIX

CHARLOTTE SINGS

"I KNOW, Captain," she said, "that we can't have longings, strivings, or hopes, without beliefs; beliefs are what they live on. I believe in being strong and sweet and true for the pure sake of being so; and yet more for the world's sake; and as much more again for God's sake as God is greater than his works. I believe in beauty and in joy. I believe they are the goal of all goodness and of all God's work and wish. As to resurrection, punishment, and reward, I can't see what my noblest choice has to do with them; they seem to me to be God's part of the matter; mine is to love perfect beauty and perfect joy, both in and infinitely beyond myself, with the desiring love with which I rejoice to believe God loves them, and to pity the lack of them with the loving pity with which God pities it. And above all I believe that no beauty and no joy can be perfect apart from a love that loves the whole world's joy better than any separate joy of any separate soul."

"Thank you," was murmured from the pillow. Then, as Charlotte once more wiped the damp brow, the captive said, with much labor, "After that—war seems—an awful thing. I suppose it isn't half so much a crime—as it is a—penalty—for the crimes that bring it on. But anyhow—you know—being—" The bugle rang out the reveillé.

"Being a soldier," said Charlotte, "you want to die like one?"

"Yes, oh, yes!—the best I can. I'd like to sit half up—and hold my sword—if there's—no objection. I've loved it so! It would almost be like holding—the hand that's far away. Of course, it isn't really necessary, but—it would be more like—dying—for my country."

He would not have it in the scabbard, and when I laid it naked in his hand he kissed the hilt. Charlotte sent Gholson for Ned Ferry. Glancing from the window, I noticed that for some better convenience our scouts had left the grove, and the prisoners had been marched in and huddled close to the veranda-steps, under their heavy marching-guard of Louisianians. One of the blue-coats called up to me softly: "Dying —really?" He turned to his fellows—"Boys, Captain's dying."

Every Northern eye was lifted to the window and I

turned away. "Richard!" gently called Charlotte, and I saw the end was at hand; a new anguish was on the brow; yet the soldier was asking for a song; "a soldier's song, will you?"

"Why, Captain," she replied, "you know, we don't sing the same words to our soldier-songs that you do—except in the hymns. Shall I sing 'Am I a soldier of the cross?'"

He did not answer promptly; but when he did he said "Yes—sing that."

She sang it. As the second stanza was begun we heard a responsive swell grow softly to fuller and fuller volume beneath the windows; the prisoners were singing. I heard an austere voice forbid it, but it rose straight on from strength to strength:

> " Sure I must fight if I would win,
> Increase my courage, Lord.
> I'll bear the toil, endure the pain,
> Supported by thy word."

The dying man lifted a hand and Charlotte ceased. He had not heard the muffled chorus of his followers below; or it may be that he had, and that the degree of liberty they seemed to be enjoying prompted him to seek the new favor he now asked. I did not catch his words, but Charlotte heard, and answered tenderly, yet with a thrill of pain so keen she could not conceal it even from him.

"Oh! you wouldn't ask a rebel to sing that," she sighed, "would you?"

He made no rejoinder except that his eyes were insistent. She wiped his temples. " I hate to refuse you."

His gaze was grateful. She spoke again: " I suppose I oughtn't to mind it."

Miss Harper came in, and Charlotte, taking her hand without a glance, told the Captain's hard request under her voice. Miss Harper, too, in her turn, gave a start of pain, but when the dying eyes and smile turned pleadingly to her she said, " Why, if you can, Charlotte, dear, but oh! how can you? "

Charlotte addressed the wounded man: " Just a little bit of it, will that do? " and as he eagerly assented she added, to Miss Harper, " You know, dear, in its history it's no more theirs than ours."

" No, not so much," said Miss Harper, with a gleam of pride; and thereupon it was my amazement to hear Charlotte begin guardedly to sing:

" O say, can you see, by the dawn's early light,
What so proudly we hailed at the twilight's last gleaming? "

But guardedly as she began, the effect on the huddled crowd below was instant and electrical. They heard almost the first note; looking down anxiously, I saw the wonder and enthusiasm pass from man to man. They heard the first two lines in awed, ecstatic silence; but at the third, warily, first one, then three, then a dozen, then a score, bereft of arms, standard, and leader, little counting ever again to see freedom, flag, or home, they raised their voices, by the dawn's early light, in their song of songs.

Our main body were out in the highway, just facing

Charlotte Sings

into column, and the effect on them I could not see. The prisoners' guards, though instantly ablaze with indignation, were so taken by surprise that for two or three seconds, with carbines at a ready, they—and even their sergeant in command—only darted fierce looks here and there and up at me. The prisoners must have been used to singing in ordered chorus, for one of them strode into their middle, and smiling sturdily at the maddened guard and me, led the song evenly. "No, sir!" he cried, as I made an angry sign for them to desist, "one verse through, if every damned fool of us dies for it—let the Captain hear it boys—sing!

"'The rockets' red glare, the bombs bursting in air——'"

Charlotte had ceased, in consternation not for the conditions without more than for those within. With the first strong swell of the song from below, the dying leader strove to sit upright and to lift his blade, but failed and would have slammed back upon the pillows had not she and Miss Harper saved him. He lay in their arms gasping his last, yet clutching his sabre with a quivering hand and listening on with rapt face untroubled by the fiery tumult of cries that broke into and over the strain.

"Club that man over the head!" cried the sergeant of the guard, and one of his men swung a gun; but the Yankee sprang inside of its sweep, crying, "Sing her through, boys!" grappled his opponent, and hurled him back. In the same instant the sergeant called steadily, "Guard, ready—aim—"

There sounded a clean slap of levelled carbines, yet

The Cavalier

from the prisoners came the continued song in its closing couplet:

"The star-spangled banner! O, long may it wave!——"

and out of the midst of its swell the oaths and curses and defiant laughter of a dozen men crying, with tears in their eyes, "Shoot! shoot! why don't you shoot?"

But the command to fire did not come; suddenly there was a drumming of hoofs, then their abrupt stoppage, and the voice of a vigilant commander called, "Attention!"

With a few words to the sergeant, more brief than harsh, and while the indomitable singers pressed on to the very close of the stanza without a sign from him to desist, Ferry bade the subaltern resume his command, and turned toward me at the window. He lifted his sword and spoke in a lowered tone, the sullen guard stood to their arms, and every captive looked up for my reply.

"Shall I come?" he inquired; but I shook my head.

"What!—gone?" he asked again, and I nodded. He turned and trotted lightly after the departing column. I remember his pensive mien as he moved down the grove, and how a soft gleam flashed from his sword, above his head, as with the hand that held it he fingered his slender mustache, and how another gleam followed it as he reversed the blade and let it into its sheath. Then my eyes lost him; for Gholson had taken his place under the window and was beckoning for my attention.

"Is she coming?" he called up, and Charlotte, at my side, spoke downward:

Harry Laughs

" I shall be with you in a moment."

While he waited the second lieutenant of the Louisianians came, and as guard and prisoners started away she came out upon the veranda steps. Across her knee, as she and Gholson galloped off by a road across fields, lay in a wrapping of corn-husks the huge sabre of the dead northerner.

XL

HARRY LAUGHS

THE first hush of the deserted camp-ground was lost in the songs of returning birds. Captain Jewett, his majestic length blanket-bound from brow to heel as trimly as a bale, had been laid under ground, and the Harpers stood in prayer at the grave's head and foot with hats on for their journey. The burial squad, turned guard of honor to the dead captain of the Louisianians, were riding away on either side of a light wagon that bore his mortal part. I, after all, was to be the Harpers' guardian on their way.

Day widened into its first perfection as we moved down the highroad toward a near fork whose right was to lead Harry and his solemn cortége southward, while the left should be our eastward course. Camille and I rode horseback, side by side, with no one near enough to smile at my sentimental laudations of the morning's splendors, or at her for repaying my eloquence with looks so full of tender worship, personal acceptance and self-bestowal, that to tell of them here would make as poor a show as to lift a sea-flower out of the sea; they call for piccolo notes and I am no musician.

The familiar little leather-curtained wagon was just ahead of us, bearing the other three Harpers, the old negro driver and—to complete its overloading—his daughter, Charlotte's dark maid. Beside the wheels ambled and babbled Harry Helm. At the bridge he fell back to us and found us talking of Charlotte. Camille was telling me how well Charlotte knew the region south of us, and how her plan was to dine at mid-day with such a friend and to pass the night with such another; but the moment Harry came up she began to upbraid him in her mellowest flute-notes for not telling us that he had got his wound in saving—

"Now, you ladies—" cried the teased aide-de-camp, "I—I didn't save Gholson's life! I didn't try to save it! I only tried to split a Yankee's head and didn't even do that! Dick Smith, if you tell anybody else that I saved— Well, who did, then? Good Lordy! if I'd known that to save a man's life would make all this fuss I wouldn't 'a' done it! Why, Quinn and I had to sit and listen to Ned Ferry a solid half-hour last night, telling us the decent things he'd known Gholson to do, and the allowances we'd ought to make for a man with Gholson's sort of a conscience! And then, to cap —to clap—to clap the ki'—to cap—the *climax*—con—sound that word, I never did know what it meant—to clap the climax, Ned sends for Gholson and gets Quinn to speak to him civilly—aw, haw, haw!—Quinn showing all the time how he hated the job, like a cat when you make him jump over a stick! And then he led us

Harry Laughs

on, with just a word here and there, until we all agreed as smooth as glass, that all Quinn had said was my fault, and all I had done was Gholson's fault, and all Gholson had said or done or left undone was our fault, and the rest was partly Ned's fault, but mostly accident.

Camille declared she did not and would not believe there had been any fault with any one, anywhere, and especially with Mr. Gholson, and I liked Lieutenant Helm less than ever, noticing anew the unaccountable freedom with which Camille seemed to think herself entitled to rebuke him. "Oh, I'm in your power," he cried to her, "and I'll call him a spotless giraffe if you want me to! that's what he is; I've always thought so!" The spring-wagon was taking the left fork and he cantered ahead to begin his good-byes there and save her for the last. When he made his adieu to her he said, "Won't you let Mr. Smith halt here with me a few moments? I want to speak of one or two matters that—"

She resigned me almost with scorn; which privately amused me, and, I felt sure, hoodwinked the aide-de-camp.

"Say, Dick!" he began, as she moved away, "look here, I'm going to tell you something; Ned Ferry's in love with Charlotte Oliver!"

"You don't mean it!"

"Yes, I do, mean it! Smith, Ned's a grand fellow. I'm glad I came here yesterday."

"Yes, you've secured a furlough."

"Oh, this thing, yes; don't you wish you had it! No, I'm glad I came, for what I've learned. I'm glad for what Ned Ferry has taught me a man can do, and keep

The Cavalier

from doing, when he's got the upper hold of himself. And I'm glad for what she—you know who—by George! any man would know who ever saw her, for she draws every man who comes within her range, as naturally as a rose draws a bee. I'm glad for what she has taught me a woman can *be,* and can keep from being, so long as she knows there's one real man to live up to! just *up to,* mind you, I don't even say to live *for.*"

I stared with surprise. Was this the trivial Harry talking? Fact is, the pair we were talking about had by some psychical magic rarified the atmosphere for all of us until half our notes were above our normal pitch.

"Do you mean she loves him; what sign of such a thing did she show yesterday or last evening?"

"Not a sign of a sign! And yet I'll swear it! Do you know where she's gone?"

"To-day? I think I do."

"Where?"

"Well, Lieutenant, if I were she, *I* should go straight into the Yankee lines behind Port Hudson. She's got Jewett's messages and his sword, and the Yank's won't know her as a Confederate any better than they ever did; for it's only these men whom we've captured who have found out she's Charlotte Oliver, or that she had any knowing part in General Austin's ruse."

"If Oliver doesn't tell," said Harry, lifting his bad hand in pain.

"He will not dare! If she can only get her word in first and tell them, herself, that he's Charlotte Oliver's

Harry Laughs

husband and has just led the finest company of Federal scouts in the two States to destruction—"

" Hi! that ought to cook his dough!—with her face —and her voice! "

" Yes," I responded, " — and his breath."

" And why do you think she wants to do this? " asked Harry.

" She doesn't want to do it; but she feels she must, knowing that every blow he strikes from now on is struck on her account. I believe she's gone to warn the Yankees that his whole animus is personal revenge and that he will sacrifice anything or anybody, any principle or pledge or cause, at any moment, to wreak that private vengeance, in whole or in part."

" Dick Smith, yes! But don't you see, besides, what she *does* want? Why, she wants to keep Oliver and Ferry apart until somebody else for whom she doesn't care as she cares for Ned, say you, or I, or—or—"

" Gholson? "

" Gholson, no! she can't trust Gholson, Gholson's conscience is too vindictive; that's why she's keeping him with her as long as she can. No, but until some of us, I say, can give Oliver a thousand times better than he ought ever to get—except for her sake—"

" Yes, you mean a soldier's clean death; and what you want of me is for me to say that I, for one, will lose no honest chance to give it to him, isn't it? "

" What I want of you, Smith, is to tell you that *I* shall lose no such chance."

" Well, neither shall I."

" Bully for you, Dick; bully boy with the glass eye!

The Cavalier

You see, you're one of only half a dozen or so that know Oliver when they see him; so Ned will soon be sending you after him. Ned's got a conscience, too, you know, as squirmy as Gholson's. Oh, Lord! yes, yon don't often *see* it, but it's as big and hard as a conscript's ague-cake." The Lieutenant gathered his rein; "Smith, I want Ned and her to get one another; that's me!"

I was tempted to say it was me, too, but I forbore and only said it was I.

"All the same," said Harry, "I'm sorry for the little girl!"

"Little girl?"

"Oh, come, now, you know!" He leaned to me and whispered, "Miss Cécile!"

"Lieutenant," I replied, with a flush, realizing what I owed to the family as a prospective member of it, "you're mistaking a little patriotic ardor—"

"Pat who—oh? I tell you, my covey,—and of course, you understand, I wouldn't breathe it any further—"

"I'd rather you would not."

"Phew-ew! I don't know why in the devil *you'd* rather I would not, but—Smith,—she's so dead-gone in love with Ned Ferry, that if she doesn't get him—I George! it'll e'en a'most kill her!"

I guffawed in derision. "And she didn't even have to tell you so! She can't even hide its deadly intensity from the casual bystander! haw! haw! haw! And it's all the outcome of a *three-days acquaintance!* It beats Doctor Swiftgrow's Mustache Invigor'—aw, haw! haw!"

Harry Laughs

" Oh, you think so? Pity you couldn't get a few barrels of it—aw, haw! haw! " said Harry, and my laughter left off where his began. But, some way hurting his hand, he, too, stopped short. I drew my horse back.

" Is that all you've noticed? " I smilingly inquired. " Isn't anybody else mortally in love with anybody else? You can't make me believe that's all you know! "

" Well, then, I sha'n't try. I do know one thing more; heard it yesterday. Like to hear it? "

" Like! Why, I'm just that dead-gone with curiosity that if I don't hear it it'll e'en a'most kill me—aw, haw! haw! haw! "

" Well, I'm tired saving people's lives, but we won't count this one; you say you want to hear it—I can't give you all of it but it begins:

" ' Turn away thine eyes, maiden passing fair!
O maiden passing fair, turn away thine eyes ! ' ——

Haw! haw! haw! Good-bye, Smith,—aw, haw! haw! haw!—and it's all the outcome of a three-days acquaintance!—haw! haw! haw!—Oh, say!—Smith ! " —I was leaving him—" that's right, go back and begin over!—' Return! return! '—aw, haw! haw! haw! "

The Cavalier

XLI

UNIMPORTANT AND CONFIDENTIAL

On the second night after that morning of frantic
mortification I was riding at Ned Ferry's side, in Louisiana. The camp of the brigade was a few miles behind
us. Somewhere in front of us, fireless and close hid,
lay our company of scouts, ahead of whose march he
had pushed the day before to confer with the General,
and we were now on our way to rejoin them. Under
our horses' feet was that old Plank-road which every
" buttermilk ranger " must remember—whether dead or
not, I am tempted to say,—who rode under either flag
in the Felicianas in '63 and '64.

Late in the evening of the day on which I had conducted the Harpers to Squire Wall's I had received a
despatch ordering me to board the next morning's train
at Brookhaven with my horse. On it I should find a
number of cases of those shoes I had seen at Hazlehurst.
At Tangipahoa I was to transfer them to one or two
army-wagons which would by that time have reached
there, and bring them across to Clinton, where a guard
would meet and join me to conduct the wagons to camp.
And thus I had done, bearing with me a sad vision of
dear dark Miss Harper fluttering her handkerchief
above her three nieces' heads, one of whom refrained
until the opportunity had all but gone, to wave good-
bye to the visibly wretched author of " Maiden passing
fair, turn away thine eyes."

Unimportant and Confidential

My lucky Cricket had gone three nights and two whole days with no harness but his halter, and to-night, beside the Yankee's horse, that still bore Ned Ferry, he was as good as new. My leader and I talked of Charlotte. In the middle of this day's forenoon Gholson had come into camp reporting at the General's tent the long ride she had made on Monday; as good a fifty miles as Ferry's own. We called it, now, Ferry and I, a most clever achievement for a woman. "Many women," he said, "know how to ride, but she knows how to march."

"I think you must have taught her," I responded, and he enjoyed his inability to deny it. So I ventured farther and said she seemed to me actually to have reached, in the few days since I had first seen her, a finer spiritual stature.

"She?" he asked; "ah! she is of the kind that must grow or die. Yes, you may be right; but in that time she has kept me so occupied growing, myself, that I did not notice she was doing the same. But also, I think, the eyes with which we look at her have grown."

"She has outgrown this work," I insisted.

"Those letters—to the newspapers?"

"No, this other; this work which she has to do by craft and wiles and disguises. Lieutenant, I don't believe she can go on doing that now with her past skill, since life has become to her a nobler story than it promised to be."

My companion lifted higher in the saddle with delight. Then soberly he said, "We have got to lose her." I turned inquiringly and he continued: "She has done

me the honor to tell me—Miss Harper and me—that if
she succeeds in what she is now trying to do — you
know?—"

" I think I do. It's to prevent Oliver from making
himself useful to the enemy, isn't it? "

" Well—like that; and she says if she comes out
all right she will leave us; yes, for the hospital service."

" Hosp'—Oh—oh! gangrene, typhoid, lock-jaw, itch,
small-pox! Isn't she deep enough in the hospital service already, with her quinine dolls? "

" Ah! but she cannot continue to play dolls that way;
she must find something else. I see you have my
temptation; yes, the desire to see her always doing
something splendid. That is not ' real life,' as you call
it. And besides, was not that you said one time to me
' No splendor shines at last so far as a hidden splendor '? "

" No, sir! I suppose it's true, but I never want to see
her splendor shining through pock-marks." The reply
won from him a gesture of approval, and this gave me
a reckless tongue. " Why, if I were you, Lieutenant,
she simply shouldn't go! Good Heaven! isn't she far
enough away at the nearest? How can you tamely—
no, I don't mean tamely, but—how can you *endure* to
let this matter drift—how can you endure it? "

At the beginning of my question he straightened exactly as I had seen him do in the middle of the lane
when our recoiled column was staggering; but as my
extravagance flamed up he quieted rebukingly, and with
a quieter smile than ever asked " Is that a soldier's ques-

tion? Smith, is there not something wrong with you to-night?"

" There always is," I replied.

" No, but to-night I think you are taking that ' lower fork' you talk sometimes about. Of course, if you don't want to tell——"

" *May* I tell you?"

" Ah, certainly! Is it that little Harper girl?"

I nodded, all choked up. When I could speak I had to drop the words by ones and twos, and did not so much say them as let them bleed from my lips; and never while I live shall I forget the sweet, grave, perfect sympathy with which my friend listened and led me on, and listened and led me on. I said I had never believed in love at first sight until now when it had come upon me to darken and embitter my life henceforth.

He replied that certainly love sometimes *germinated* at first sight, and I interrupted greedily that that was all I claimed—except that love could also, at times, *grow to maturity* with amazing speed, a speed I never could have credited previous to these last four days. And he admitted as much, but thought time only could prove such love; whereto I rejoined that that was what she had answered.

He glanced at me suddenly, then smoothed his horse's mane, and said, gently, " That means you have declared yourself to her?"

I confessed I had, and told him how, on our journey to Squire Wall's, being stung to desperation by the infantile way in which she had drooled out to others what my love had sacredly confided to her alone, I had abruptly confronted her with the fact, and in the ensuing debate, carried away by the torrent of my emotions, had offered her my love, for life and all.

" And she—ah, yes. I see; and I see, too, that in all she ever said or did or seemed, before, she never made herself such a treasure to be longed for and fought and lived for as in the way in which she—" He paused.

" Refused me! Oh, it's so; it's so! Ah! if you could have witnessed her dignity, her wisdom, her grace, her compassionate immovableness, you'd never think of her as the little Harper girl again. She said that if the unpremeditated, headlong way in which I had told my passion were my only mistake, and if it were only for my sake, she would not, if she could, answer favorably, and that I, myself, at last, would not have a girl who would have a man who would offer his love in that way, and that she would not have a man who would have a girl who would have a man who should offer his love in that way."

I call it one of the sweetest kindnesses ever done me, that Ned Ferry heard me to the end of that speech and did not smile. Instead he asked " Did she say that as if a'—as if—amused? "

" No, Lieutenant, she nearly cried. Oh, I wish we were on some dangerous errand to-night, instead of just camp and bed! "

" Well, that's all right, Richard; we are."

"By Candle-Light?"

XLII

"CAN I GET THERE BY CANDLE-LIGHT?"

AFTER a few minutes we quitted the public way by an obscure path in the woods on our right. When we had followed this for two or three miles we turned to the left again and pressed as softly as we could into a low tangled ground where the air seemed stagnant and mosquitoes stung savagely. We wiped away the perspiration in streams. I pushed forward to Ferry's side and whispered my belief that at last we were to see rain.

"Yes," he said, "and with thunder and lightning; just what we want to-night."

I asked why. "Oh, they hate our thunder-storms, those Yankee patrols."

Presently we were in a very dark road, and at a point where it dropped suddenly between steep sides we halted in black shadow. A gleam of pale sand, a whisper of deep flowing waters, and a farther glimmer of more sands beyond them challenged our advance. We had come to a "grapevine ferry." The scow was on the other side, the water too shoal for the horses to swim, and the bottom, most likely, quicksand. Out of the blackness of the opposite shore came a soft, high-pitched, quavering, long-drawn, smothered moan of woe, the call of that snivelling little sinner the screech-owl. Ferry murmured to me to answer it and I sent the same faint horror-stricken tremolo back. Again it came to us, from not farther than one might toss his

cap, and I followed Ferry down to the water's edge.
The grapevine guy swayed at our side, we heard the
scow slide from the sands, and in a few moments,
moved by two videttes, it touched our shore. Soon we
were across, the two videttes riding with us, and beyond a sharp rise, in an old opening made by the swoop
of a hurricane, we entered the silent unlighted bivouac
of Ferry's scouts. Ferry got down and sat on the
earth talking with Quinn, while the sergeants quietly
roused the sleepers to horse.

Now we marched, and when we had gone a mile or
so Ned Ferry turned aside, taking with him only Sergeant Jim, Kendall, another private, and me. We went
at an alert walk single-file for the better part of an hour
and stopped at length in a narrow untilled "deaden-
ing." Beyond it at our left a faint redness shone just
above the tree-tops. At our right, in the northwest, a
similar glow was ruddier, the heavens being darker
there except when once or twice they paled with silent
lightnings. Sergeant Jim went forward alone and on
foot, and presently was back again, whispering to Ferry
and remounting.

Ferry led Kendall and me into the woods, the other
two remaining. We found rising ground, and had ridden but a few minutes when from its crest we looked
upon a startling sight. In front of us was a stretch of
specially well farmed land. Our woods swept round it
on both sides, crossed a highway, and gradually closed
in again so as to terminate the opening about half a
mile away. Always the same crops, bottom cause of
the war: from us to the road an admirable planting of

cotton, and from there to the farther woods as goodly a show of thick corn. The whole acreage swept downward to that terminus, at the same time sinking inward from the two sides. On the highway shone the lighted rear window of a roadside "store," and down the two sides of the whole tract stretched the hundred tent-fires of two brigade camps of the enemy's cavalry. Their new, white canvases were pitched in long, even alleys following the borders of the wood, from which the brush had been cut away far enough for half of them to stand under the trees. The men had quieted down to sleep, but at one tent very near us a group of regimental officers sat in the light of a torch-basket, and by them were planted their colors. A quartet of capital voices were singing, and one who joined the chorus, standing by the flag, absently yet caressingly spread it at such breadth that we easily read on it the name of the command. Let me leave that out.

As they sang, and as we sat in our saddles behind the low fence that ran quite round the opening, Ferry turned from looking across into the lighted window on the road and handed me his field-glass. "How many candles do you see in there?"

I saw two. "Yes," he said, dismounting and motioning me to do the same. Kendall took our bridles. Leaving him with the animals we went over the fence, through the cotton, across the road at a point terribly near the lighted and guarded shop, and on down the field of corn, to and over its farthest fence; stooping, gliding, halting, crouching, in the cotton-rows and corn-rows; taking every posture two upright gentlemen would rather not take; while nevertheless I swelled with pride, to be alone at the side—or even at the heels—of one who, for all this apparent skulking and grovelling, and in despite of all the hidden drawings of his passion for a fair woman at this hour somewhere in peril, kept his straight course in lion-hearted pursuit of his duty (as he saw it) to a whole world of loves and lovers, martyrs and fighters, hosts of whom had as good a right to their heart's desire as I to mine or he to his; and I remembered Charlotte Oliver saying, on her knees, " I believe no beauty and no joy can be perfect apart from a love that loves the whole world's joy better than any separate joy of any separate soul."

XLIII

" YES, AND BACK AGAIN "

ONE matter of surprise to me was that this whole property had escaped molestation. I wondered who could be so favored by the enemy and yet be so devoted to our cause as to signal us from his window with their sentinels at his doors; and as we passed beyond the cornfield's farther fence I ventured to ask Ferry.

" Aaron Goldschmidt," he whispered, as we descended into a dry, tangled swamp. In the depths of this wild, beside a roofed pen of logs stored with half a dozen bales of cotton, we were presently in the company of a very small man who tossed a hand in token of great amusement.

" Hello, Ned! " he whispered in antic irony; " what

an accident is dat, meeding so! Whoever is expecting someding like dis!"

"Well, I hope nobody, Isidore; I hardly expected it myself, your father set those candles so close the one behind the other."

Isidore doubled with mirth and as suddenly straightened. "Your horse is here since yesterday. *She* left him—by my father. She didn't t'ink t'e Yankees is going to push away out here to-night. But he is a pusher, t'at Grierson! You want him to-night, t'at horse? He is here by me, but I t'ink you best not take him, hmm? To cross t'e creek and go round t'e ot'er way take you more as all night; and to go back t'is same way you come, even if I wrap him up in piece paper you haven't got a lawch insite pocket you can carry him?" He laughed silently and the next instant was more in earnest than ever.

"*She* is in a tight place! She hires my mother's pony to ride in to headquarters." He called them hate-kvartuss, but we need not. "I t'ink she is not a pris-oner—*unless*—she wants to come back." He doubled again. "Anyhow, I wish you can see her to-night; she got another doll-baby for t'e gildren, and she give you waluable informations by de hatfull. . . . Find her? I tell you how you find her in finfty-nine minutes—vedder permitting, t'at is."

The last phrase was fitted to a listening pose, and the first mutter of the pending thunder-storm came out of the northwest. Then Isidore hastened through the practical details of his proposition. Ferry drew a breath of enthusiasm.

The Cavalier

"Can I have my horse, bridled and saddled, in three minutes?"

"I pring um in two!" said Isidore, and vanished. Ferry turned with an overmastering joy in every note of his whispered utterance. "After all!" he said, and I could have thrown my arms around him in pure delight to hear duty and heart's desire striking twelve together.

"Smith," he asked, "can you start back without me? Then go at once; I shall overtake you on my horse."

I stole through the cornfield safely; the frequent lightnings were still so well below the zenith as to hide me in a broad confusion of monstrous shadows. But when I came to cross the road no crouching or gliding would do. I must go erect and only at the speed of some ordinary official errand. So I did, at a point between two opposite fence-gaps, closely after an electric gleam, and I was rejoicing in the thick darkness that followed, when all at once the whole landscape shone like day and I stood in the middle of the road, in point-blank view of a small squad, a "visiting patrol". They were trotting toward me in the highway, hardly a hundred yards off. As the darkness came again and the thunder crashed like falling timbers, I started into the cotton-field at an easy double-quick. The hoofs of one horse quickened to a gallop. A strong wind swept over, big rain-drops tapped me on the shoulder and pattered on the cotton-plants, the sound of the horse's galloping ceased as he turned after me in the soft field, and presently came the quiet call "Halt, there, you on foot."

"Yes, and Back Again"

I went faster. I knew by my pursuer's coming alone that he did not take me for a Confederate, and that the worst I should get, to begin with, would be the flat of his sabre. Shrewdly loading my tongue with that hard northern *r* which I hated more than all unright-eousness, I called back " Oh, I'm under orders! go halt some fool who's got time to halt!"

I obliqued as if bound for the headquarters fire where we had seen the singers, the lightning branched over the black sky like tree-roots, the thunder crashed and pounded again, the wind stopped in mid-career, and the rain came straight down in sheets. "Halt!" yelled the horseman. He lifted his blade, but I darted aside and doubled, and as he whirled around after me, another rider, meeting him and reining in at such close quarters that the mud flew over all three of us, lifted his hand and said—

" He is right, sergeant, he is carrying out my or-ders." Ferry's black silk handkerchief about his neck covered his Confederate bars of rank, and the Federal may or may not have noted the absence of shoulder-straps; our arms remained undrawn; and so the ser-geant, catching a breath or two of disconcertion, caught nothing else. While Ferry spoke on for an-other instant I showed my heels; then he left the drip-ping Yankee mouthing an angry question and loped after me, and over the low fence went the two of us almost together.

Kendall was not there, the Federal camp-makers had tardily repaired their blunder by posting guards; but these were not looking for their enemies from the side of their own camp, and as we cleared the fence in the full blaze of a lightning flash, only two or three wild shots sang after us. In the black downpour Ferry reached me an invisible hand. I leapt astride his horse's croup, and trusting the good beast to pick his way among the trees himself, we sped away. Soon we came upon our three men waiting with the horses, and no great while afterward the five of us rejoined our command. The storm lulled to mild glimmerings and a gentle shower, and the whole company, in one long single file, began to sweep hurriedly, stealthily, and on a wide circuit of obscurest byways, deeper than ever into the enemy's lines.

XLIV

CHARLOTTE IN THE TENTS OF THE FOE

FROM certain rank signs of bad management in the Federal camp one could easily guess that our circuit was designed to bring us around to its rear. That a colonel's tent—the one where the singers were—was not where the colonel's tent belonged was a trifle, but the slovenliness with which the forest borders of the camp were guarded was a graver matter. Evidently those troops were at least momentarily in unworthy hands, and I was so remarking to Kendall when a murmured command came back from Ferry, to tell Dick Smith to stop that whispering. I was sorry, for I wanted to add that I knew we were not going to attack the camp itself.

Charlotte in the Tents of the Foe

That was on Wednesday night. Charlotte and Gholson had made their ride of fifty miles on Monday. The friends with whom she stopped at nightfall contrived to cram him into their crowded soldiers' room, and he had given the whole company of his room-mates, as they sat up in their beds, a full account of the fight at Sessions's, Charlotte's care of the sick and dying, and the singing, by her and the blue-coats, of their battle-song. Next morning Charlotte, without Gholson— who turned off to camp—rode on to Goldschmidt's store, just beyond which there was then still a Confederate picket. Here she hired Mrs. Goldschmidt's pony, rode to the picket, and presented the Coralie Rothvelt pass.

" Miss Coralie Rothvelt; yes, all right." said the officer, " the men that rode with you this morning told me all about you." He went with her as far as his videttes, and thence she rode alone to a picket of the Federal army and by her request was conducted under guard to the headquarters of a corps commander. To him and his chief-of-staff she told the fate of Jewett's scouts and delivered the messages of their dying leader; and then she tendered the hero's sword.

The staff-officer cut away its cornhusk wrapping and read aloud the owner's name on the hilt. The General laid the mighty weapon across his palm and sternly shut his lips. " How did you get through the enemy's pickets with this? "

" I had a Confederate general's pass."

" Ah! Is the Confederate general as nameless as yourself? "

The Cavalier

" I am not nameless; I only ask leave to withhold my name until I have told one or two other things."

" But you don't mind confessing you're an out-and-out rebel sympathizer?"

Under the broad-brimmed hat her smile grew to a sparkle. " No, I enjoy it."

The chief-of-staff smiled, but the General darkened and pressed his questions. At length he summed up. " So, then, you wish me to believe that you did all you did, and now have come into our lines at a most extraordinary and exhausting speed and running the ugliest kinds of risks, in mere human sympathy for a dying stranger, he being a Union officer and you a secessionist of "—a courtly bow—" the very elect; that's your meaning, is it not?"

" No, General; in the first place, I am not one of any elect."

A flattering glimmer of amusement came into the two men's faces, but some change in Charlotte's manner arrested it and brought an enhanced deference.

" In the second place, I am not here merely on this errand."

" Oh!"

" No, General. And in the last place, my motive in this errand is no mere sympathy for any one person; I am here from a sense of public duty—" The speaker seemed suddenly overtaken by emotions, dropped her words with pained evenness, and fingered the lace handkerchief in her lap.

" Pardon," interrupted the General, " the sunlight annoys you. Major, will you drop that curtain?"

Charlotte in the Tents of the Foe

" Thank you. One thing I am here for, General, is to tell you something, and I have to begin by asking that neither of you will ever say how you learned it."

The two men bowed.

" Thank you. Please understand, also, I have never uttered this but to one friend, a lady. There was no need; I have not wanted aid or counsel, even from friends. But I feel duty bound to tell it to you, now, because, for one thing, the brave soldier who wore that sword—" Her eyes rose to the weapon and fell again; she bit her lip.

" Yes—well—what of him?"

" He was lured to disaster and death by a man whose supreme purpose was, and is to-day, revenge upon me. That man drew him to his ruin purely in search of my life." Charlotte sat with her strange in-looking, out-looking gaze holding the gaze of her questioner until for relief he spoke.

" Why, young lady, it's hard to doubt anything you say, but really that sounds rather fanciful. Why should you think it?"

" I do not think it, I know it. He sends me his own assurance of it by his own father, so that his revenge may be fuller by my knowing daily and hourly that he is on my trail."

" And you appeal to me for protection?"

She smiled. " No. I am not seeking to divert his fury from myself, but to confine it to myself. Fancy yourself a human-hearted woman, General, and murder being done day by day because you are alive."

The Cavalier

"Oh, this is incredible! What is its occasion, its origin? How are you in any way responsible?"

"Why, largely I am not. Yet in degree I am, General, because of shortcomings of mine—faults—errors —that—oh—that have their bearing in the case, don't you see?"

"No, I don't; pray don't ask me to draw inferences; I might infer too much."

"Yes, you might, easily," said Charlotte; "for I only mean shortcomings of the kind we readily excuse in others though we never can or should pardon them in ourselves."

The General turned an arch smile of perplexity upon his chief-of-staff. "I don't think we're quite up to that line of perpetual snow, Walter, are we?"

The chief-of-staff "guessed they were not."

Charlotte resumed. "I have come to you in the common interest, to warn you against that man. I believe he is on his way here to offer his services as a guide. He is fearless, untiring, and knows all this region by heart."

"Union man, I take it, is he not?"

"No, he's Federal, Confederate or guerilla as it may suit his bloody ends."

"And you want me not to make use of him."

"Oh, more than that; I want him stopped!—stopped from killing and burning on his and my private account. But I want much more than that, too. I know how you commonly stop such men."

"We hang them to the first tree."

"Yes, our side does the same. If I wanted such a

Charlotte in the Tents of the Foe

fate to overtake him I should only have to let him alone. At risks too hideous to name I have saved him from it twice. I am here to-day chiefly to circumvent his purposes; but if I may do so in the way I wish to propose to you, I shall also save him once more. I am willing to save him—in that way—although by so doing I shall lose—fearfully." She dropped her glance and turned aside.

"How do you propose to circumvent and yet save him?"

"By getting you to send him so far to your own army's rear that he cannot get back; to compel him to leave the country; to go into your country, where law and order reign as they cannot here between the lines."

"And you consider that a reasonable request?"

"Oh, sir, I must make it! I can ask no less!"

"But you say if this scheme works you lose by it. What will you lose?"

"I may lose track of him! If I lose track of him I may have to go through a long life not knowing whether he is dead or alive."

"And suppose—why,—young lady, I thought you were unmarried. I—oh, what do you mean; is he—?"

Charlotte's head drooped and her hands trembled. "Yes, by law and church decree he is my husband."

"Good Heaven!" murmured the General, drew a breath, and folded his arms. "But, madam! if a man *abandons* his wife—"

"I abandoned him."

"Good for you!"

" It was vital for me. But I did it on evidence which our laws ignore, the testimony of slaves. Oh, General, don't try to untangle me ; only stop him ! "

" Ah ! madam, I'll do the little I can. How am I to know him ? "

" By a pistol-wound in his right hand, got last week. He would have got it in his brain but for my pleading. His name is Oliver."

" Oliver ; hmm ! any relation to Charlotte Oliver, your so called newspaper correspondent ? I'd like to stop her.—How ?—I don't quite hear you."

" I am Charlotte Oliver."

The two officers glanced sharply at each other. When the General turned again he flushed resentfully. " Have you never resumed your maiden name ? "

" Never."

" Then, madam, tell me this ! With a whole world of other people's names to choose from, why *have* you borrowed Charlotte Oliver's ? Have you come here determined to be sent to prison, Miss Coralie Rothvelt ? "

XLV

STAY TILL TO-MORROW

CHARLOTTE did not move an eyelash. Gradually a happy confidence lighted her face. " Freedom or prison is to me a secondary question. I came here determined to use only the truth. No wild creature loves to be free more than I do. I want to go back into our lines, and to go at once; but—I am Charlotte Oliver."

"Young lady, listen to me. I know your story is nearly all true. I know some good things about you which you have modestly left out; one of the rebels who stopped where you did last night and rode with you this morning was brought to me a prisoner half an hour ago. But he said your name was Rothvelt. How's that?"

"Unfortunately, General, my name is Charlotte Oliver. Two or three times I have had use for so much concealment as there was in the childish prank of turning my name wrong side out." The speaker made a sign to the chief-of-staff: "Write the two names side by side and see if they are not one."

He was already doing so, and nodded laughingly to his superior. Charlotte spoke on. "I tell you the truth only, gentlemen, though I tell you no more of it than I must. I have run many a risk to get the truth, and to get it early. If it is your suspicion that by so doing, or in any other way, I have forfeited a lady's liberty, let me hear and answer. If not—"

"Oh, I'll have to send you to the provost-martial at Baton Rouge and let you settle that with him."

"Ah, no, General! By the name of the lady you love best, I beg you to see my need and let me go. I promise you never henceforth to offend your cause except in that mere woman's sympathy with what you call rebellion, for which women are not so much as banished by you—or if they are, then banish me!

The Cavalier

Treat me no better, and no worse, than a 'registered enemy'!"

The General shook his head. "Your registration has been in the open field of military action; sometimes, I fear, between the lines. At least it has been with your pen."

"General, I have laid down the pen."

"Indeed! to take up what?"

"The spoon!" said Charlotte, with that smile which no man ever wholly resisted. "I leave the sword and its questions to my brother man, in the blue and in the gray—God save it!—and have pledged myself to the gray, to work from now on only under the yellow flag of mercy and healing."

"Yes, of course; mercy—and comfort—and every sort of unarmed aid—to rebels."

"To the men you call so, yes. Yet I pledge you, General, to deal as tenderly with every man in blue who comes within range of my care as I did with Captain Jewett."

"Oh, I know you did even better than you've told me, but I'd be a fool to send you back on the instant, so. Stay till to-morrow or next day." The captor smiled. "Major, I think we owe the lady that much hospitality."

The Major thought so, and that she must need a day's rest, more than she realized. She could be made in every way comfortable—under guard at "Mr. Gilmer's." The Gilmers were Unionists, whose fine character had been their only protection through two years of ostracism, yet he believed they would treat her well.

Stay Till To-Morrow

" Oh! not there, please," said Charlotte; " I hear they are to give some of your officers a dance to-morrow evening! " and there followed a parley that called forth all her playfullest tact. " Oh, no," she said, at one critical point, " I'm not so narrow or sour but I could dance with a blue uniform; but suppose—why, suppose one's friends in gray should catch one dancing with one's enemies in blue. Such things have happened, you know."

" It sha'n't happen to-morrow night," laughed the General.

She offered to nurse the Federal sick, instead, in the command's field-hospital, but no, the General rose to end the interview. " My dear young lady, the saintliest thing we can let you do is to dance at that merry-making."

She rose. " As a prisoner under guard, General, I can nurse the sick, but I will not dance."

The General smiled. " I'll take your parole."

" Oh! exact a parole from a woman? "

" Good gracious, why shouldn't I! As for you,—ha!—I'd as soon turn a commissioned rebel officer loose in my camp unparoled as you."

" Then take my parole! I give it! you have it! I'll take the chances."

" And the dances? " asked the Major.

" Very good," said the General, " you are now on parole. See the lady conducted to Squire Gilmer's, Major. And now, Miss—eh,—day after to-morrow morning I shall either pass you beyond my lines or else send you to Baton Rouge. Good-day."

The Cavalier

When Charlotte found herself alone in a room of the Gilmer house she lay down upon the bed staring and sighing with dismay; she was bound by a parole! If within its limit of time Oliver should appear, "It will mean Baton Rouge for me!" she cried under her breath, starting up and falling back again; "Baton Rouge, New Orleans, Ship Island!" She was in as feminine a fright as though she had never braved a danger. Suddenly a new distress overwhelmed her: if—if—someone to deliver her should come—"Oh Heaven! I am paroled!—bound hand and foot by my insane parole!"

Softly she sprang from the bed, paced the floor, went to the window, seemed to look out upon the landscape; but in truth she was looking in upon herself. There she saw a most unaccountable tendency for her judgment—after some long overstrain—momentarily, but all at once, to swoon, collapse, turn upside down like a boy's kite and dart to earth; an impulse—while fancying she was playing the supremely courageous or generous or clever part—suddenly to surrender the key of the situation, the vital point in whatever she might be striving for. "Ah me, ah me! why did I give my parole?"

At the close of the next day—"Walter," said the General as the chief-of-staff entered his tent glittering in blue and gold,—"oh, thud devil!—you going to that dance?"

The Dance at Gilmer's

XLVI

THE DANCE AT GILMER'S

ALL the while that I recount these scenes there come to me soft orchestrations of the old tunes that belonged with them. I am thinking of one just now; a mere potsherd of plantation-fiddler's folk-music which I heard first—and last—in the dance at Gilmer's. Indeed no other so widely recalls to me those whole years of disaster and chaos; the daily shock of their news, crashing in upon the brain like a shell into a roof; wail and huzza, camp-fire, litter and grave; battlefield stench; fiddle and flame; and ever in the midst these impromptu merrymakings to keep us from going stark mad, one and all,—as so many literally did.

The Gilmer daughters were fair, but they were only three, and the Gilmers were the sole Unionists in their neighborhood. "Still, a few girls will come," said Charlotte, sparkling first blue and then black at a sparkling captain who said that, after all, the chief-of-staff had decided he couldn't attend. I know she sparkled first blue and then black, for she always did so when she told of it in later days.

"They say," responded the captain, "that in this handy little world there are always a few to whom policy is the best honesty; is that the few who will come?"

"You are cynical," said Charlotte, "this is only their unarmed way of saving house and home for the brothers to come back to when you are purged out of the land."

When the time came there were partners for eight gallants, and the gallants numbered sixteen. They counted off by twos; the evens waited while the odds danced the half of each set, and then the odds waited and cooled, tried to cool, out on the veranda. But when a reel was called the whole twenty-four danced together, while the fiddler (from the contraband camp) improvised exultant words to his electrifying tunes.

> " O *ladies* ramble in,
> Whilst de *beaux* ramble out,
> For to *quile** dat golden *cha—ain.*
> My *Lawdy !* it's a sin
> Fo' a *fiddleh* not to shout !
> Miss *Charlotte's* a-comin' down de *la—ane !* "

Now the dance is off, but now it is on again, and again. The fiddler toils to finer and finer heights of enthusiasm; slippers twinkle, top-boots flash, the evens come in (to the waltz) and the odds, out on the veranda, tell one another confidentially how damp they are. Was ever an evening so smotheringly hot ! Through the house-grove, where the darkness grows blacker and blacker and the tepid air more and more breathless, they peer toward the hitching-rail crowded with their horses. Shall they take their saddles in, or shall they let them get wet for fear the rebels may come with the shower, as toads do ? [Laughter.] One or two, who grope out to the animals, report only a lovely

---

* Coil.

The Dance at Gilmer's

picture: the glowing windows; the waltzers circling by them; in the dining-room, and across the yard in the kitchen, the house-servants darting to and fro as busy as cannoneers; on their elbows at every window-sill, and on their haunches at every door, the squalid field-hands making grotesque silhouettes against the yellow glow that streamed out into the trees.

Now the lightning seems nearer. Hark, that was thunder; soft, but real. At last the air moves; there is a breeze, and the girls come out on the gallants' arms to drink it in. As they lift their brows and sigh their comfort the lightning grows brighter, the thunder comes more promptly and louder, and the maidens flinch and half scream, yet linger for one more draft of the blessed coolness. Suddenly an inverted tree of blinding light branches down the sky, and the thunder crashes in one's very ears; the couples recoil into a group at the door, the lightning again fills heaven and earth, it shows the bending trees far afield, and the thunders peal at each other as if here were all Vicksburg and Port Hudson, with Porter and Farragut going by. So for a space; then the wind drops to a zephyr, and though the sky still blazes and crashes, and flames and roars, the house purrs with content under the sweet strokings of the rain.

Let it pour! the dining-room is the centre of all things; the ladies sip the custards and nibble the cake the gallants cram the cake and gulp the punch. The fiddler-improvisator disappears, reappears, and with crumbs on his breast and pan-gravy and punch on his breath remounts his seat; and the couples are again

The Cavalier

on the floor. The departing thunders grumble as they go, the rain falls more and more sparingly, and now it is a waltz, and now a quadrille, and now it's a reel again, with Miss Sallie or Louise or Laura or Lucille or Miss Flora " a-comin' down de lane ! "

So come the stars again, one by one. In a pause between dances Charlotte and the staff captain go to the veranda's far end and stand against the rail. The night is still very dark, the air motionless. Charlotte is remarking how far they can hear the dripping of the grove, when she gives a start and the captain an amused grunt ; a soft, heart-broken, ear-searching quaver comes from just over yonder by the horses. " One of those pesky little screech-owls," he says. " Don't know as I ever heard one before under just these condi'—humph ! there's another, around on this side."

" I think I will go in," says Charlotte, with a pretence of languor. As they do so the same note sounds a third time ; her pace quickens, and in passing a bright window, with a woman's protecting impulse she changes from his left arm to his right so as to be on the side next the owls. A moment later she is alone in the middle of her room, a lighted candle in one hand, a regally dressed doll in the other, and in her heart the cry, " Oh, Edgard, Edgard, my parole, my parole ! "

Once more she is downstairs, in the lane which the dancers are making for their last reel. Two of the gallants have gone out to see the horses, and something keeps them, but there is no need to wait. The

The Dance at Gilmer's

fiddle rings a chord! the merry double line straightens down the hall from front door to rear, bang! says the fiddler's foot—"hands round!"—and hands round it is! In the first of the evening they had been obliged to tell the fiddler the names of the dancers, but now he knows them all and throws off his flattering personalities and his overworked rhymes with an impartial rotation and unflagging ardor. Once in a while some one privately gives him a new nickname for the next man "a-comin' down de lane," and as he yawps it out the whole dance gathers new mirth and speed.

Now the third couple clasp hands, arch arms, and let the whole countermarching train sweep through; and a beautiful arch they make, for they are the aforesaid captain and Charlotte Oliver. "Hands round!" —hurrah for the whirling ellipse; and now it's "right and left" and two ellipses glide opposite ways, "to quile dat golden chain." In the midst of the whirl, when every hand is in some other and men and girls are tossing their heads to get their locks out of their eyes, at the windows come unnoticed changes and two men loiter in by the front hall door, close to the fiddler. One has his sword on, and each his pistols, and their boots and mud-splashed uniforms of dubious blue are wet and steamy. The one without the sword gives the fiddler a fresh name to sing out when the spinning ring shall straighten into its two gay ranks again, and bids him—commandingly—to yell it; and with never a suspicion of what it stands for, the stamping and scraping fiddler shouts the name of a man who "loves a good story with a positive passion."

The Cavalier

" Come *a-left*, come a-right,
Come yo' *lily*-white hand,
Fo' to *quile* dat *golden cha—ain.*
O *ladies* caper light—
Sweetest *ladies* in de land—
NED FERRY 's a-comin' down de la—ane ! "

He's Dead.—Is She Alive?

XLVII

HE'S DEAD.—IS SHE ALIVE?

CRIES of masculine anger and feminine affright filled the hall, but one ringing order for silence hushed all, and the dance stood still with Ned Ferry in its centre. In his right hand, shoulder high, he held not his sword, but Charlotte's fingers lightly poised for the turn in the arrested dance. "Stand, gentlemen, every man is covered by two; look at the doors; look at the windows." The staff captain daringly sprang for the front door, but Ferry's quick boot caught his instep and he struck the floor full length. Like lightning Ferry's sword was out, but he only gave it a deferential sweep. "Sir! better luck next time!—Lieutenant Quinn, put the Captain in your front rank."

Quinn hustled the captives "down a lane," as the fiddler might have said, of Ferry's scouts, mounted them on their own horses at the door, and hurried them away. Charlotte had vanished but was back again in hat and riding-skirt. Ferry caught her hand and they ran to the front veranda steps just as the prisoners and guard rode swiftly from them. Kendall and I had the stirrup ready for her; the saddle was a man's, but she made a horn of its pommel, and in a flash the four of us were mounted. Nevertheless before we could move the grove resounded with shots, and Ferry, bidding us ride on after the fleeing guard, wheeled and galloped to where half our troop were holding back their assail-

The Cavalier

ants in the dark. But then, to our distraction, Charlotte would not fly. "Richard, I'm paroled!"—"Charlotte Oliver, you're my prisoner!" I reached for her bridle, but she avoided me and with a cry of recollection wheeled and was on her way back. "I forgot something! I can get it, I left the room lighted!"

I remember vividly yet the high purpose and girlish propitiation that rang together in her voice. Kendall dashed after her while I went against a wet bough that all but threw me; but before he could reach her she flew up the steps, crying "Hold my horse!"

"Mine, too!" I cried, springing up after her. How queerly the inner house stood alight and silent, its guests and inmates hidden, while outside pistols and carbines flashed and cracked. I came upon Charlotte, just recrossing her chamber to leave it, with her doll in her arms. "Come!" I cried, "our line is falling back behind the house!" Her head flinched aside, a bit of her hat flew from it, and a pistol-ball buried itself in the ceiling straight over my head. We ran downstairs together, pulling, pushing and imploring each other in the name of honor, duty and heaven to let him—let her—go out first through the bright hall door. Kendall was not in sight, but in a dim half-light a few yards off we saw Oliver. He was afoot, bending low, and gliding toward us with his revolver in his left hand. He fired as I did; her clutch spoiled my aim; with eager eyes she straightened to her finest height, cried "Richard! tell Lieutenant Ferry he—" and with a long sigh sank into my arms. A rush of hoofs sounded behind Oliver, he glanced up, and Ferry's blade fell across his brow and launched him face upward to the ground. I saw a bunch of horses, with mine, at the foot of the steps, and a bunch of men at the top; Ferry snatched Charlotte's limp form from me and said over his shoulder as he went down the steps, " Go get *him* and bring him along, dead or alive ! "

I called a man to my aid and was unlucky in not getting the cool-headed Kendall, for my own wits were gone. The next moment all had left us and I was down on the ground toiling frantically, with no help but one hand of my mounted companion, to heave the stalwart frame of Oliver up to my saddle.

" Why, he's dead ! " cried the lad, letting him slide half-way down when we had all but got him up; " don't you see he's dead ? His head's laid wide open ! He's as dead as a mackerel ! I'll *swear* we ain't got any right to get captured trying to save a dead Yankee."

I was in despair ; our horses had caught our frenzy and were plunging to be after their fellows, and a fresh body of the enemy were hurtling into the grove. Dropping my burden I vaulted up, and we scurried away, saved only by the enemy's healthy fear of an ambush. The first man we came up with was Quinn, with the rear-guard. " Is he dead ? " he growled.

" Dead as Adam ! " said I, and my comrade put in " Head laid wide open ! "

" Drop back into the ranks," said Quinn to him. " Smith, ride on to Lieutenant Ferry. Corporal,"— to a man near him—" you know the way so well, go with him."

The two of us sprang forward. How long or what

way we went I have now no clear idea, but at length we neared again the grapevine ferry. The stream was swollen, we swam our horses, and on the farther side we found Kendall waiting. To the corporal's inquiry he replied that Ferry had just passed on. "You know Roy's; two miles off the Plank Road by the first right? He expects to stop there."

"Is she alive, Kendall?" I interrupted. "Is she alive?"

"No," said he, to some further question of the corporal; "I'm to wait here for the command."

"Is she alive, Kendall?" I asked again.

"Hello, Smith." He scanned my dripping horse. "Your saddle's slipped, Smith. Yes, she's alive."

XLVIII

IN THE HOLLOW OF HIS RIGHT ARM

"THERE they are!" said the corporal and I at the same moment, when we had been but a few minutes on the Plank-road. Two men were ahead of us riding abreast, and a few rods in front of them was a third horseman, apparently alone. Two others had pushed on, one to the house, the other for surgical aid. The two in the rear knew us and let us come up unchallenged; the corporal stayed with them, and I rode on to my leader's side.

Charlotte lay in his double clasp balanced so lightly on the horse's crest as hardly to feel the jar of his

In the Hollow of His Right Arm

motion, though her head lay as nearly level with it as
Ferry's bending shoulders and the hollow of his lowered right arm would allow; from under his other arm
her relaxed figure, in its long riding-skirt, trailed down
over his knee and stirrup; her broad limp hat, as if it
had been so placed in sport, hung at his back with its
tie-ribbons round his throat, while the black masses
of her hair spread in ravishing desolation over and
under his supporting arm. Her face was fearfully pale,
the brows glistened with the damp of nervous shock,
and every few moments she feebly brought a handkerchief to her lips to wipe away the blood that rose
to them with every sigh. Steadfastly, except when her
eyes closed now and then in deathly exhaustion, her
gaze melted into his like a suffering babe's into its
mother's. From time to time a brief word passed between them, and with joy I noticed that it was always
in French; I hoped with my whole heart and soul that
they had already said things, and were saying things
yet, which no one else ought to hear. I waited some
time for his notice, and when he gave it it was only
by saying to her in a full voice and in English "Dick
Smith is here, alongside of us."

Her response was a question, which he repeated: "Is
he hurt? no, Richard never gets hurt. Shall he tell us
whatever he knows?"

He bent low for the faint reply, and when it came
he sparkled with pride. "'It matters little,' she says,
'to either of us, now.' Give your report; but *I* tell
you"—there came a tiger look in his eyes—"there is
now no turning back; we shall go on."

The Cavalier

I answered with soft elation: " My news needn't turn you back: Oliver is dead."

He drew a long breath, murmured " My God! " and then suddenly asked " You found him so, or—? "

" We found him so; had to leave him so; head laid wide open; we were about to be captured—thought the news would be better than nothing—"

" Certainly, yes, certainly. Now I want you to ride to the brigade camp and telegraph Miss Harper this: ' She needs you. Come instantly. Durand.' "—I repeated it to him.—" Right," he said. " Send that first; and after that—here is a military secret for you to tell to General Austin; I think you like that kind, eh? Tell him I would not send it verbally if I had my hands free. You know that regiment at whose headquarters we saw them singing; well, tell him they are to make a move to-day, a bad mistake, and I think if he will stay right there where he is till they make it, we can catch the whole lot of them. As soon as they move I shall report to him."

Two gasping words from Charlotte brought his ear down, and with a worshipping light in his eyes he said to her " Yes,—yes! " and then to me, " Yes, I shall report to him *in person*. Now, Smith, the top of your speed! "

Reveillé was sounding as I entered the camp. In the middle of my story to the General—" Saddle my horse," he said to an attendant, " and send Mr. Gholson to me. Yes, Smith, well, what then? "—I resumed, but in a minute—" Mr. Gholson, good-morning. My compliments to Major Harper, Mr. Gholson, and ask

In the Hollow of His Right Arm

him if he wouldn't like to take a ride with me; and let me have about four couriers; and send word to Colonel Dismukes that I shall call at his headquarters to see him a moment, on my way out of camp. Now, Smith, you've given me the gist of the matter, haven't you? Oh, I think you have; good-morning."

Gholson had helped me get the despatch off to Miss Harper, whose coming no one could be more eager to hasten. Before leaving camp I saw him again. He was strangely reticent; my news seemed to benumb and sicken him. But as I remounted he began without connection—"You see, she'll be absolutely alone until Miss Harper gets there; not a friend within call! *He* won't be there, she won't let him stay; she dislikes him too much; I *know* that, Smith. Why, Smith, she wouldn't ever 'a' let him carry her off the field if she'd been conscious; she'd sooner 'a' gone to Ship Island, or to death!" He looked as though he would rather she had. His tongue, now it had started, could not stop. "Ned Ferry can't stay by her; he mustn't! he hadn't ought to use around anywheres near her."

I gave a sort of assent—attended with nausea—and turned to my saddle, but he clung. "Why, how can he hang around that way, Smith, and he a suitor who's just killed her husband? Of course, now, he'd ought to know he can't ever be one henceforth. I'm sorry for him, but—"

"Good-morning," I interrupted, quite in the General's manner, and made a spirited exit, but it proved a false one; one thing had to be said, and I returned. "Gholson, if she should be worse hurt than—"

The Cavalier

"Ah! you're thinking of the chaplain; I've already sent him. Yonder he goes, now; you can show him the way."

"Understand," I said as I wheeled, "I fully expect her to recover."

"Yes, oh, yes!" replied my co-religionist, with feverish zest; "we must have faith—for her sake! But o—oh! Smith, what a chastening judg-*ment* this is against dancing!"

I moved away, looking back at him, and seeing by his starved look how he was racking his jaded brain for some excuse to go with me, I honestly believe I was sorry for him. The chaplain was a thick-set, clean-shaven, politic little fellow whose "*Good*-mawning, brothah?" had the heavy sweetness of perfumed lard. We conversed fluently on spiritual matters and also on Ned Ferry. He asked me if the Lieutenant was "a believer."

"Why," said I, "as to that, Lieutenant Ferry believes there's something right about everything that's beautiful, and something wrong about everything that isn't. Now, of course that's a very dangerous idea, and yet—" So I went on; ah me! the nightmare of it hangs over me yet, "religionist" though I am, after a fashion, unto this day. In Ferry's defence I maintained that only so much of any man's religion as fitted him, and fitted him not as his saddle or his clothes, but as his nervous system fitted him, was really his, or was really religion. I said I knew a man whose ready-made religion, small as it was, bagged all over him and made him as grotesque as a child in his father's trousers. The chaplain tittered so approvingly that I straightened to spout again, but just then we saw three distant figures that I knew at a glance.

"There he is, now!—Excuse me, sir—" I clapped in the spurs, but the chaplain clattered stoutly after me. The two horsemen moving from us were the General and Major Harper, and the one meeting them was Ned Ferry. Between the three and us rose out of a hollow the squad of couriers. And yonder came the sun.

XLIX

A CRUEL BOOK AND A FOOL OR TWO

I COULD see by Ferry's face that there was no worse news. He met me aside, and privately bade me go to Roy's (where Charlotte was). "Kendall is there," he said; "I leave you and him in charge. That will rest your horses. Kendall has your Yankee horse, his own is sick. You and Kendall get all the sleep you can, you may get none to-night."

"Lieutenant," I began eagerly as he was drawing away, "is—?"

"Yes! oh, yes, yes!" His eyes danced, and a soft laugh came, as happy as a child's. "The surgeon is yonder, he will tell you."

This person Kendall and I had the luck to meet at the Roy's breakfast-table. "Yes, left lung," he said. "No, hardly 'perforated,' but the top deeply grazed." The ball, he said, had passed on and out, and he went into particulars with me, while I wondered if Kendall knew, as I did, what parts of the body the pleura, the thorax, the clavicle and the pyemia were.

We lay down to sleep on some fodder in the Widow Roy's stable, while around three sides of the place, in a deep wooded hollow, Quinn and the company, well guarded by hidden videttes, drowsed in secret bivouac. I dreamed. I had feared I should, and it would have been a sort of bitter heart's-ease to tell Kendall of my own particular haunting trouble. For now, peril and darkness, storm, hard riding, the uproar and rage of man-killing, all past and gone, my special private wretchedness came back to me bigger than ever, like a neglected wound stiffened and swollen as it has grown cold. But Kendall would not talk, and when I dreamed, my dream was not of Camille. It seemed to me there was a hot fight on at the front, and that I, in a sweat of terror, was at the rear, hiding among the wagons and telling Gholson pale-faced lies as to why I was there. All at once Gholson became Oliver, alive, bloody-handed, glaring on me spectrally, cursing, threatening, and demanding his wife. His head seemed not " laid wide open," but to have only a streak of the skull bared by Ferry's glancing left-cut and a strip of the scalp turned inside out. Cécile drew his head down and showed it to me, in a transport of reproaches, as though my false report had wronged no one else so ruinously as her.

I awoke aghast. If Kendall had still been with me I might, in the first flush of my distress, have told my vision; but in the place where Kendall had lain lay Harry Helm. Kendall was gone; a long beam of after-

A Cruel Book and a Fool or Two

noon sunlight shone across my lair through a chink in the log stable. I sprang half up with an exclamation, and Harry awoke with a luxurious yawn and smile. Kendall, he said, had left with the company, which had marched. Quinn was in command and had told Harry that he was only going to show the enemy that there was no other hostile force in their front, and get himself chased away southeastward.

"I don't know whether he was telling me the truth or not," said Helm, as we led our saddled horses toward the house; "I reckon he didn't want me alongside of him with this arm in a sling." The hand was bad; lines of pain were on the aide's face. He had taken the dead Louisianian home, got back to camp, and ridden down here to get the latest news concerning Charlotte. Kendall had already given him our story of the night; I had to answer only one inquiry. "Oh, yes," was my reply, "head laid wide open!" But to think of my next meeting with Ned Ferry almost made me sick.

Harry was delighted. "That lays their way wide open—Ned's and hers! Smith, some God-forsaken fool brought a chaplain here to talk religion to her! He hasn't seen her—Doctor wouldn't let him; but he's here yet, and—George! if I was them I'd put him to a better use than what he came here for, and I'd do it so quick it would make his head swim!" He went on into all the arguments for it; the awkwardnesses of Charlotte's new situation, her lack of means for even a hand-to-mouth daily existence, and so on. Seeing an ambulance coming in through the front gate, and in

The Cavalier

order not to lose the chance for my rejoinder, I interrupted. "Lieutenant, she will not allow it! She will make him wait a proper time before he may as much as begin a courtship, and then he will have to begin at the beginning. She's not going to let Ned Ferry narrow or lower her life or his—no, neither of them is going to let the other do it—because a piece of luck has laid the way wide open!" I ended with a pomp of prophecy, yet I could hear Ned Ferry saying again, with Charlotte's assenting eyes in his, "There is no turning back."

The driver of the ambulance did not know why he had been ordered to report here, but when the Widow Roy came to the door she brought explanation enough. A courier had come to her and gone again, and the chaplain and the surgeon and every one else of any "army sort" except us two had "put out," and she was in a sad flurry. "The Lieutenant," she said, "writes in this-yeh note that this-yeh place won't be safe f'om the Yankees much longer'n to-day, and fo' us to send the wounded lady in the avalanch. Which she says, her own self, it'd go rough with her to fall into they hands again. My married daughter she's a-goin' with her, and the'd ought to be a Mr. Sm'—oh, my Lawdy! you ain't reg-lahly in the ahmy, air you?"

With some slave men to help us, Harry and I bore Charlotte out and laid her in the ambulance, mattress and all, on an under bedding of fodder. She had begged off from opiates, and was as full of the old starlight as if the day, still strong, were gone. I helped the married daughter up beside the driver, Harry and

A Cruel Book and a Fool or Two

I mounted, and we set forth for the brigade camp. Mrs. Roy's daughter had with her a new romance, which she had been reading to Charlotte. Now she was eager to resume it, and Charlotte consented. It was a work of some merit; I have the volume yet, inscribed to me on the fly-leaf " from C. O.," as I have once already stated, in my account of my friend " The Solitary." At the end of a mile we made a change; Harry rode a few yards ahead with an officer who happened to overtake us, I took the reins from the ambulance driver, and he followed on my horse; I thought I could drive more smoothly than he.

And so I began to hear the tale. I was startled by its strong reminder of Charlotte's own life; but Charlotte answered my anxious glance with a brow so unfretted that I let the reading go on, and so made a cruel mistake. At every turning-point in the story its reader would have paused to talk it over, but Charlotte, with a steadily darkling brow, murmured each time " Go on," and I was silent, hoping that farther along there would be a better place to stop for good. Not so; the story's whirling flood swept us forward to a juncture ever drawing nearer and clearer, clearer and crueler, where a certain man would have to choose between the woman he loved and that breadth and fruitfulness of life to which his splendid gifts imperiously pointed him. Oh, you story-tellers! Every next page put the question plainer, drove the iron deeper: must a man, or even may a man, wed his love, when she stands between him and his truest career, a drawback and drag upon his finest service to his race and

The Cavalier

day? And, oh, me! who let my eye quail when Charlotte searched it, as though her own case had brought that question to me before ever we had seen this book. And, oh, that impenetrable woman reading! Her husband was in Lee's army, out of which, she boasted, she would steal him in a minute if she could. She was with us, now, only because, at whatever cost to others, she was going where no advancement of the enemy's lines could shut her off from him; and so stop reading a moment she must, to declare her choice for Love as against all the careers on earth, and to put that choice fairly to shame by the unworthiness of her pleadings in its defence. I intervened; I put her grovelling arguments aside and thrust better ones in, for the same choice, and then, in the fear that they were not enough, stumbled into special pleading and protested that the book itself had put the question unfairly.

"Shut it," said Charlotte, with a sigh like that which had risen when the lead first struck her. "If I could be moved ever so little,—" she said.

I had the driver tie my horse behind the vehicle and resume the lines. Then the soldier's wife and I moved Charlotte, and when the reader began to handle the book again wishfully our patient said, with the kindest voice, "Read the rest of it to yourself; I know how it will end; it will end to please you, not as it ought; not as it ought."

For a while we went in silence, and she must have seen that my heart was in a rage, for with suffering on her brow, amusement on her lips, and a sweet desperation in her eyes, she murmured my name. "Richard:

A Cruel Book and a Fool or Two

—what fun it must have been to live in those old Dark Ages—when all you had to do—was to turn any one passion into—one splendid virtue—at the expense—of all the rest."

I could answer pleadingly that it were far better not to talk now. But she would go on, until in my helplessness I remarked how beautiful the day had been. Her eyes changed; she looked into mine with her calm inward-outward ken, and once more with smiling lips and suffering brow murmured, " Yes." I marvelled she should betray such wealth of meaning to such as I ; yet it was like her splendid bravery to do it.

At the brigade's picket, where I was angry that Ferry did not meet us, and had resumed the saddle and stretched all the curtains of the ambulance, who should appear but Scott Gholson. Harry and I were riding abreast in advance of the ambulance. Gholson and he barely said good-evening. I asked him where was Lieutenant Ferry, and scarcely noted his words, so promptly convinced was I by their mere tone that he had somehow contrived to get Ferry sent on a distant errand. " Is she better ? " he inquired ; " has the hemorrhage stopped ? "

" It's begun again," growled Harry, who wanted both of us to suffer all we could. Gholson led us through the camp. A large proportion of the men were sleeping when as yet it was hardly night.

" Has the brigade got marching orders ? " I asked, and he said the three regiments had, though not the battery. He passed over to me two pint bottles filled, corked, and dangling from his fingers by a stout double

233

twine on the neck of each. "Every man has them," he said; "hang one on each side of your belt in front of your pistol."

I held them up and scowled from them to Harry, and we both laughed, so transparent was Gholson's purpose to get every one away from our patient who yearned to be near her. "One in front of each pistol," I said, so tying them; "but use the pistols first, I suppose."

"Yes," replied Gholson, "pistols first, and then the turpentine." Whereat Harry and I exchanged glances again, it came so pat that Scott Gholson should be a dispenser of inflammables. At a house a mile behind the camp the surgeon stood waiting for us. He frowned at me the instant he saw Charlotte, and I heard him swear. As we bore her in with Gholson and me next her head she murmured to him:

"Mr. Gholson, when does the command move?"

"At twelve," he replied, and I bent and softly added "That's why——"

"Yes," she said, with a quick, understanding look, and wiped her lips as daintily as if it were with wine they were crimsoned.

The Bottom of the Whirlwind

L

THE BOTTOM OF THE WHIRLWIND

ON my way back through camp with Gholson I saw old Dismukes. He called me to him, quit his cards, and led me into his tent. There, very beguilingly, he questioned me at much length, evidently seeking to draw from the web of my replies the thread of Ferry's and Charlotte's story; and as I saw that he believed in both of them with all his brutal might, I let him win a certain success. "Head laid wide open!" he said gleefully, and boiled over with happy blasphemings.

I left him, found supper, and had been long asleep under a tree, when I grabbed savagely at some one for silently shaking me, and found it was Ned Ferry. His horse's bridle was in his hand; his face was more filled with the old pain than I had ever seen it; he spoke low and hurriedly. "Come, tell me what this means."

In an envelope addressed to him in the handwriting I had first seen at Lucius Oliver's I found a scripture-text, a heading torn from a tract which the chaplain may have sent in to Charlotte in the morning. I turned it to the light of my fire. Under this printed line she had pencilled her name.

I asked if he had seen her. "Ah, no! the Doctor has drugged her to sleep; but that woman who came with you was still in the parlor, reading a book, and she gave me this. What does it mean?"

"Lieutenant," I replied, choking with dismay, "why

The Cavalier

mind her meanings now? Ought you not rather to ignore them? She is fevered, dejected, overwrought.
Why, sir, she is the very woman to say and mean things
now which she would never say or mean at any other
time!" But my tone must have shown that I was only
groping in desperation after anything plausible, and he
waved my suggestions away.

"The Doctor says that woman has been reading her
an exciting story."

"Yes, and that helps to account—"

"Richard, it helps the wrong way; *I know that story.*
After hearing that story she is, yes! the one woman of
all women to send me *this.*"

I took it again. The signature was extended in full,
with the surname blackly underlined. The first clause
of the print, too, was so treated. "*Keep thy heart,*" it
read; "*Keep thy heart* with all diligence; for out of it
are the issues of life.—Charlotte *Oliver.*"

"Why, Lieutenant, that is just what you have
done—"

"You think so? But I *have done.* I will keep it no
longer! Ah, I never kept it; 'twas she! Without taking it from me she kept it—'with all diligence'; otherwise I should have lost it—and her, too—and all that
is finest and hardest to keep—long ago. Give me that
paper; come; saddle up; you may go with me if you
want, as my courier." No bugle had sounded, yet the
whole camp was softly and diligently astir. We rode
toward the staff tents; the pulse of enterprise enlivened
him once more, though he clung to the same theme.
"I have *her* heart now, Smith, and I will keep *that* with

The Bottom of the Whirlwind

all diligence, for out of *that* are the issues of *my* life—
if I live. And if I do live I will have her if I have to
steal her even from herself, as last night from the
Yankees."

Three hours later the stars still gleamed down
through the balmy night above the long westward-gal-
loping column of our brigade, that for those three hours
had not slackened from the one unmitigated speed. The
Federal regiment of whose plans Charlotte had apprised
Ferry had been camped well to southward of this course,
but in the day just past they had marched to the north,
intending a raid around our right and into our rear.
To-night they were resting in a wide natural meadow
through the middle of which ran this road we were on.
Around the southern edge of this inviting camp-ground
lay a considerable stream of water; the northern side
was on rising ground and skirted by woods, and in these
woods as day began to break stood our brigade, its
presence utterly unsuspected in all that beautiful
meadow whitened over with lane upon lane of the tents
of the regiment of Federal cavalry, whose pickets we
had already silently surprised and captured. Now, as
warily as quails, we moved along an unused, woodcut-
ters' road and began to trot up a gentle slope beyond
whose crest the forest sank to the meadow. We were
within a few yards of this crest, when a small mounted
patrol came up from the other side, stood an instant
profiled against the sky, bent low, gazed, wheeled and
vanished.

Over the crest we swept after them at a gallop and
saw them half-way down an even incline, going at a

The Cavalier

mad run and yelling "Saddle up! saddle up! the rebels are coming! saddle up!" The bugles had begun the reveillé; it ceased, and the next instant they were sounding the call To Arms. It was only a call to death; already we were half across the short decline and coming like a tornado; in the white camp the blue-coats were running hither and yon deaf to the brave shoutings of their captains; above the swelling thunder of our hoofs rose the mad yell of the onset; and now carbines peal and pistols crack, and here are the tents so close you may touch them, and yonder is one already in a light blaze, and at every hand and under every horse's foot is the crouching, quailing, falling foe, the air is one crash of huzzas and groans, screams, shots and commands, horses with riders and horses without plunge through the flames and smoke of the burning tents, and again and again I see Ned Ferry with the flat of his unstained sword strike pistol or carbine from hands too brave to cast them tamely down, and hear him cry "Throw down your arms! For God's sake throw down your arms and run to the road! run to the public road!"

And still every moment men fell, and what could we do but smite while the foe's bugles still rang out from beside his unfurled standard. Thitherward sprang a swarm of us and found a brave group massed on foot around the colors, men and officers shoulder to shoulder in sudden equality. I saw Ned Ferry make straight for their commander, who alone had out his sabre; the rest stood with cocked revolvers, and at twenty yards fired low. Ferry's horse was hit; he reared, but the

The Bottom of the Whirlwind

spur carried him on; his rider's sword flashed up and then down, the Federal's sabre turned it, the pistols cracked in our very faces, and down went my leader and his horse into the bottom of the whirlwind, right under the standard. I saw the standard-bearer bring down one of our men on top of Ferry, and as Ferry half regained his feet the Federal aimed point-blank against his breast. But it was I who fired and the Federal who fell. As he reeled I stretched out for the standard, and exactly together Ned Ferry and I seized it—the same standard we had seen the night before. But instantly, graciously, he thrust it from him. "'Tis yours!" he cried in the midst of a general huzza, smiling up at it and me as I swung the trophy over my head. Then he turned ghastly pale, his smile faded to an unmeaning stare, two or three men leaped to his side, and he sank lifelessly into their arms beside his dying horse.

I was swinging from the saddle to my leader's relief, when a familiar voice forbade it, and old Dismukes came by at a long trot, pointing forward with the reddest sabre I ever saw, and bellowing to right and left with oaths and curses "Fall in, every man, on yon line! Ride to yon line and fall in, there's more Yankees coming! Ride down yonder and fa'—*here*, you, Legs, there! follow me, and shoot down every man that stops to plunder!"

Now I saw the new firing-line, out on our left, and as the rattle of it quickened, the Colonel galloped, still roaring out his rallying-cries and wiping his reeking blade across his charger's mane. Throngs gathered after him; the high-road swarmed with prisoners doublequicking to the rear under mounted guards; here, thinly stretched across the road at right-angles, were our horse-holders, steadily, coolly falling back; farther forward, yet vividly near, was our skirmish-line, crackling and smoking, and beyond it the enemy's, in the edge of a wood, not yet quite venturing to fling itself upon us. We passed General Austin standing, mounted, at the top of the rise, with a number of his staff about him. Minie balls had begun to sing about them and us, and some officer was telling me rudely I had no business bringing that standard—when something struck like a sledge high up on my side, almost in the arm-pit; I told one of our men I was wounded and gave him the trophy, our horse-holders suddenly came forward, every man afoot rose into his saddle, and my horse wheeled and hurried rearward at a speed I strove in vain to check. Then the old messmate to whom I had said good-bye at this very hour just a week before, came and held me by the right arm, while I begged him like a drunk-and-disorderly to let me go and find Ned Ferry.

But he said Lieutenant Ferry was in a captured ambulance ahead of us and of our hundreds of prisoners, that a full creek and a burning bridge were between us and the foe, and that the fight was over.

Under the Room Where She Lay

LI

UNDER THE ROOM WHERE CHARLOTTE LAY

THE fight was over only in degree. Our brigade was drawing away into the north and the enemy were pressing revengefully after them. Our hundreds of prisoners and our few wounded were being taken back eastward over the road by which we had come in the night, and even after we had turned into it I saw a Yankee shell kill a wounded man and his horse not thirty yards from me.

Before we had gone another mile I met Harry Helm. The General had left him in camp with flat orders to remain, but at daylight he had ridden out to find us. He was in two tremendous moods at once; lifted to heaven on the glory of our deeds, yet heart-broken over the fate of Ned Ferry. "Surgeon's told him he can't live, Dick! And all the effect that's had—' No opiates, then, Doctor,' s'e, 'till I get off these two or three despatches.' So there he lies in that ambulance cross-questioning prisoners and making everybody bring him every scrap of information, as if he were General Austin and Major Harper rolled into one and they were wounded instead of him—By George! Dick, he knows you're hit and just how you're hit, and has sent me to find you!"

I said I thought I could gallop if Harry could, and in a few minutes we were up with the ambulance. It had stopped. There were several men about it, including Sergeant Jim and Kendall, which two had come from Quinn, and having just been in the ambulance, at Ferry's side, were now remounting, both of them openly in tears. "Hello, Kendall."

"Hello, Smith." He turned sharply from me, horse and all.

"Good - morning, sergeant, is Lieutenant Ferry—worse?"

The sergeant only jabbed in the spurs, and leapt away with Kendall, bearing despatches to the brigade. Harry, looking back to me from the ambulance, called softly, "All right again; it was only a bad swoon!"

"Hello, Smith," said some one whom I was too sick and dizzy to recognize, "one of those prisoners says he saw Oliver dead."

They say two or three men sprang to catch me, but the first thing I knew was that the ambulance was under way and I in it on my back within elbow-touch of Ferry, looking up into a surgeon's face. "How's the Lieutenant?" I asked.

"Oh—getting on, getting on," he replied. Doctors think patients are fools.

In a parlor under the room where Charlotte lay they made a bed for Ferry and one for me, and here, lapped in luxury and distinction, I promptly fell asleep, and when I reopened my eyes it was again afternoon. In the other bed Ferry was slumbering, and quite across the room, beside a closed door, sat Cécile and Camille. The latter tiptoed to me. Her whispers were as soft as breathing, and when I answered or questioned, her

Under the Room Where She Lay

ear sank as near as you would put a rose to smell it. "The Lieutenant, sleeping? yes, this hour past; surgeons surprised and more hopeful. Miss Estelle? in another room with other wounded. Her aunt? upstairs with Charlotte, who was—oh—getting on, getting on." That made me anxious.

"Does Charlotte," I asked, "know—everything?"

Camille allowed herself all the motions of a laugh, and said "No, not quite everything;" and then with solemn tenderness she added that Charlotte knew about Ferry. "And she knows about *you*," the whisperer went on; "they all know."

I thought she was alluding to the verses, and had an instant of terror and rage before I saw what she meant. She glided back to the door and the two opened it an inch or so to answer some inquirer without. I saw her no more until bedtime, when she stood at her aunt's elbow to hand and hold things, while Miss Harper, to my all but screaming embarrassment, bared the whole upper half of one side of me and washed and dressed my wound anew. Ferry it was imperative to let alone, but when I awoke the next morning there was a radiance of joy throughout all the house; for he had slept and improved. The next morning again he was ever so much stronger, and Harry Helm rode off in simulated disgust, not seeing "any fun in hanging round girls who were hanging round other fellows."

Another day arose. A courier brought passes for our three or four other wounded to go home as soon as they were fit to travel, and by night they were all gone. At early bedtime came two surgeons of high rank all

The Cavalier

the way from Johnston's army up in Mississippi. General Austin had asked this favor by telegraph. Harry had been gone thirty-six hours, and Ferry was just asking if he had not yet got back, when the surgeons came in to the room. A pleasantry or two consumed a few moments. Then the surgeon in charge of us told of a symptom or two, to which they responded only "hmm," and began the examination. Miss Harper sent her three nieces away. I lay and listened in the busy stillness. Presently one of the examiners murmured with a certain positiveness to the other, who after a moment's silence replied with conviction; Miss Harper touched our surgeon's arm inquiringly and he looked back in a glad way and nodded. Miss Harper nodded to me; they had located the ball! Now the conversation turned upon men and events of the day, while one of the visitors, with his back to the patient, opened a case of glittering knives. Presently the professional heads came so close together as quite to hide the patient; they spoke once or twice in a manly soothing tone. Miss Harper stroked my temples to keep me down, one of the busy ones spoke again, and lo! the thing was done, there was the ball in the basin. As the men of blood sped through their kind after-work the news flew to and fro; Camille wept,—since she could not hurrah,—Cécile told Charlotte, the heavenly-minded Estelle was confirmed in her faith, Miss Harper's black eyes, after a brief overflow, were keener and kindlier than ever, and as the surgeons spoke the word "done," Ferry asked again if Harry had not got back yet.

Same Book and Light-Head Harry

Pretty soon Harry did arrive, with news of great feats by our cavalry against our old enemy Grierson, in which Austin's brigade had covered themselves with glory, and in which he had had his own share; his hand was swelled as big as his heart. In all the Confederacy no houseful went to sleep that night in sweeter content. I sank into perfect bliss planning a double wedding.

LII

SAME BOOK AND LIGHT-HEAD HARRY

THE next day found me so robustly happy that I was allowed to dress and walk out to the front door. Three days later the surgeons were gone, all three, and at the approach of dew-fall Cécile and Harry, Camille and I, walked in a field-path, gathered hedge roses, and debated the problem of Mrs. Roy's daughter's book, which all of us were reading and none had finished.

" A woman," I remarked, " who, for very love of a man, can say to him, ' Go on up the hill without me, I have a ball and chain on my foot and you shall not carry them and me, you have a race to run,'—a woman so wonderfully good as to say that—"

" Ah, no! " interrupted Cécile, with her killing Creole accent, " not a woman so *good* to say that, only with the so-good *sanse* to say it."

Harry was openly vexed. " Well, either way! would any true man leave *that* woman behind? " and I tried to put in that that was what I had been leading up to;

The Cavalier

but it makes me smile yet, to recall how jauntily she discomfited us both. She triumphed with the airy ease of a king-bird routing a crow in the upper blue. Camille had more than once told me that Cécile was wise beyond the hope of her two cousins to emulate her; which had only increased my admiration for Camille; yet now I began to see how the sisters came by their belief. In the present discussion she was easily first among the four of us. At the same time her sensuous graces also took unquestionable preëminence; city-bred though she was, she had the guise of belonging to the landscape, or, rather, of the landscape's belonging, by some fairy prerogative, to her. She seemed just let loose into the world, yet as ready and swift to make right use of it as any humming-bird let into a garden; as untimorous as any such, and as elusive. In this sultry June air she had all the animation both of mind and of frame that might have been expected of her on a keen, clear winter day. Her face never bore the same expression at the beginning and middle, or at either of these and the close, of any of her speeches, yet every change was lovely, the sign of a happy play of feeling, and proof of a mercurial intelligence. No report of them by this untrained pen would fully bear me out, and the best tribute I can offer is to avoid the task.

It was a sweet mercy in her to change the subject, and tactful to change it to Charlotte, as if Charlotte were quite an unrelated theme. The cousins vied with each other ever so prettily in telling how beautiful the patient was on her couch of enfeeblement and pain, how her former loveliness had increased, and what new no-

bility it had taken on. That any such problem overhung her life as that which we had just been weighing,
seemed never to have entered their thought, and if
they had ever conceived of a passion already conscious
between Charlotte and Ferry, they veiled the fact with
charming feminine art.

When we got back to the house Harry detained me
on the veranda alone. Camille told me how long I
might tarry. It was heaven to have her bit in my
mouth, and I found it hard to be grum even when
Harry beat with his good hand the rhythm of " Maiden
passing fair, turn away thine eyes."

" Dick," he said, suddenly grave as he walked me
down the veranda, " her cousin Cécile! isn't it awful?
Now that poor girl's gone back to Ned's bedside; back
to her torture! Why *do* they let her? My George!
it's merciless! Has her aunt no eyes? "

" But, Lieutenant, you don't know she loves him;
there are signs, I admit; but proofs, no. She's lost
color, and her curves are more slender, but, my goodness! a dozen things might account for that."

" Dick Smith,"—my questioner worked himself up
over the rail and sat out on the shelf that held the
bucket of drinking-water and its gourd—" do you imagine she didn't know, when we were talking about that
book, that she was arguing against the union of Ned
Ferry and Charlotte Oliver? *Didn't* she do it bravely!
Richard, my friend, she couldn't have done it if she had
suspected us of suspecting her. It's a bleeding pity!
And yet you can't side with her, for I just swear Ned's
got to have Charlotte Ol'—what? No, he won't over-

The Cavalier

hear a blank word; here's his window shut, right here. He's got to have her, I say, and he's got to have her just as soon as the two of 'em can stand up together to be sworn in! Don't you say so?"

I replied that I was not aware of any one who did not say so.

"Well, I can name several! I don't call Scott Gholson anybody, but there's Major Harper—No, I'm not talking too loud, Ned isn't hearing a word. Major Harper's so hot against this thing that he brought it up, with me, yesterday on the battlefield."

"Major Harper doesn't really know her," I softly remarked.

Harry swore with military energy. "I told him he didn't, and he fairly snorted. *We* don't know her, he says; you nor I nor his sister nor his niece nor his daughters, oh, we don't know her at all; and neither do we know Ned; Ned has graceful manners, and she's a born actress, and we're simply infatuated by their romantic situation. Good Lordy! he got up on his Charleston pride-of-family like a circus-girl on stilts, and 'Edgard Ferry-Durand has got a great public career before him,' s's he, 'and no true friend will let him think of taking a wife who is all history and no antecedents, a blockade-runner, a spy, and the brand-new widow of a blackguard and a jayhawker she had run away from practically on her wedding-night.' Hy Jo'! the way he went on, you'd 'a' thought he was already Ned's uncle-in-l'—" The speaker's face took a sudden distress—"Great Cæsar!" He pointed up to the second-story front room and slipped down from the shelf just as Estelle came out to us with her aunt's message for me to come in.

"How's the fair patient?" I hurried to ask as the three of us went.

"Why, Mr. Smith, she's actually been sitting up—in the twilight—at the open window—while Aunt Martha and I smoothed up her bed." Harry groaned.

"She's still very weak," said Aunt Martha when we came to her; "the moment her bed was made up she asked to lie down again."

"Yes," softly exclaimed Camille, "but, oh, aunt Martha, with such courage in those eyes!"

"Smith," privately asked the agonized Harry, "what would you do if you were in my place; go and cut your throat from ear to ear?"

"No," I said, as black as an executioner, "but I wish you'd done it yesterday."

LIII.

"CAPTAIN, THEY'VE GOT US"

MORE days slipped by. Neighbors pressed sweet favors upon us; calls, joyful rumors, delicacies, flowers. One day Major Harper paid us a flying visit, got kisses galore, and had his coat sponged and his buttons re-animated. In the small town some three miles north-west of us he was accumulating a great lot of captured stuff. On another day came General Austin and stayed a whole hour. Ferry took healing delight in these visits, asking no end of questions about the movements afield, and about the personal fortunes of everyone he knew. When the General told him Ferry's scouts were doing better without him than with him—" I thought he would smile himself into three pieces," said the General at the supper-table.

On a second call from Major Harper, when handed a document to open and read, he went through it carefully twice, and then dropping it on the coverlet asked —" and Quinn? "

" Oh, Quinn's turn will come."

" Ah! Major, that is not fair to Quinn! " said Ferry. Yet when he took up the paper again he gazed on it with a happy gravity; it made him a captain. " By the by," he said, " that Yankee horse that Dick Smith captured at Sessions's; I'd like to buy that horse from you, Major." They made the sale. " And there's that captured ambulance still here, Major, with its team eating their heads off."

" Yes, I'm going to take that away with me to-day."

This meant that Charlotte's negro man and his daughter, her maid, had come with her spring-wagon, and Harry and I would have liked the Major better if he had smiled at this point, as he did not. Yet he was most lovable; sent so kind a message up to Charlotte that Harry and I wondered; and received back from her a reply so gracious that—since we could not wonder—we worshipped. In the evening of that day Ferry and Charlotte were transferred, she into the room behind her, and he upstairs into the one out of which she was taken. That night a slave and his wife, belonging

"Captain, They've Got Us"

to the place, ran away to the enemy. If they should tell the Yankees Ned Ferry was here—! "By Jo'!" said Harry Helm, "I'm glad I didn't cut my throat; I told that darkey, yesterday, Ned's name was O'Brien!"

Toward the close of that day came tidings of the brigade's splendid work at a steamboat-landing on the Mississippi River, how they had stolen in by night between two great bodies of the enemy, burned a vast store of military supplies, and then brilliantly cut their way out; yet we were told to be ready to withdraw into Mississippi again as soon as our newly made captain could safely be moved. Pooh! what of that? Lee was on his way into Pennsylvania; the war was nearly over, sang the Harper girls, and we were the winners! They cheerily saw Helm and me, next morning, ride southward in search of further good news. At a cross-roads I proposed that we separate, and meet there again near the end of the day. He turned west; I went an hour's ride farther south and then turned west myself.

When we met again I knew that he—while he did not know that I—had been to Gilmer's plantation. We wanted to see if the Federals had left a grave there. They had left three, and a young girl who had been one of the dancers told me she had seen Oliver's body carried off by two blue troopers who growled and cursed because they had been sent back to bury it. Neither Harry nor I mentioned the subject when we met at the cross-roads again, for we came on our horses' necks at a stretched out run; the Federals were rolling up from the south battalion after battalion, hoping to find

The Cavalier

Major Harper's store of supplies feebly guarded and even up with us for that steamboat-landing raid. Presently as we hurried northward we began to hear, off ahead of us on our left, the faint hot give-and-take of two skirmish lines. We came into the homestead grove at a constrained trot and found the ladies out on the veranda in liveliest suspense between scepticism and alarm.

"Yes, they're fighting, now, on the edge of town," we said, "but our boys will keep them there." Our host and hostess moaned their unbelief. "However," added Harry, "I'll go tell the old man to hitch up the little mules and—"

"You dawn't need," said Cécile, "'tis done!" and Camille confirmed her word, while the planter and his wife returned to the kitchen yard, where the servants were loading the smokehouse meat into a wagon to hide it in the woods; Miss Harper and Estelle went into the house, summoned by Charlotte's maid. On Ferry's chamber floor sounded three measured thumps of his scabbarded sword.

"Dick, you answer that," exclaimed Harry, reining in half wheeled; "but keep him on his back, if you have to hold him down!" He spurred away to learn whether we had better stay or fly. I threw my rein to Camille and flew up the hall stairs.

Ferry lay in bed with three pillows behind him and his sheathed sword across his lap. "Good-evening, Richard," he said, "you are returned just in time; will you please hand me my two pistol' from yonder?— thank you." He laid one beside each thigh. "Now

"Captain, They've Got Us"

please turn the head of my bed a little bit, to face the door—thank you; and now, good-bye. You hear those footstep' there in the room behind? she is dressing to go; the other ladies they are helping her. Richard, I place them in your charge; have them all ready to get into her wagon at a moment's notice, with you on your horse—and you better take that Jewett horse, too; he came to-day."

I hesitated, but a single flash of authority from his eye was enough and I had passed half-way to the door, when, through the window over the front veranda, I saw a small body of horsemen trotting up through the grove. The dusk of the room hid me, but there was no mistaking them. "Too late, Captain," I said, "they've got us."

"How many do you see?"

"About sixteen. Our two horses will be Yankees again to-morrow."

"Ah! not certainly. Where is your carbine?"

"Just outside this door. They know you're here, Captain, they're surrounding the house." As I reached toward the door I heard his sword crawl out, the door-knob clicked without my touching it, the door swung and closed again, and Charlotte Oliver was with us. The light of the western window shone full upon her; she was in the same dress, hat and all, in which I had seen her the night we rode together alone. Though wasted and pale, she betrayed a flush on either cheek and a smile that mated with the sweet earnest of her eyes. She tendered me my carbine, patted my hand caressingly, and glided onward to Ferry's bedside.

The Cavalier

With my back to them and my ear to the door I hearkened outward. In the front doorway below sounded the jingling tread of cavalry-boots and a clank of sabres.

LIV

THE FIGHT IN THE DOORWAY

CHARLOTTE's whisper came to me: "Richard!" Standing by Ferry's pillow she spoke for him. "If they start upstairs come and stand like me, on the other side."

I nodded and slyly opened the door enough to pass half-way out. Some man was parleying with Miss Harper. "Now, madam, you know you haven't locked up your parlor to maintain an abstract right; you've locked it up because you've got the man in there that I've come for."

"Whom have you come for, sir?"

"Lieutenant O'Brien, of the rebel army. Shall I order this man to kick that door in? Answer quickly."

"Sir, there is no Lieutenant O'Brien in there, nor elsewhere in this house; there never has been."

"Stand aside, madam."

"Stop, sir! I command you! There is no Lieutenant of any name on this place!"

"Oh, yes there is; he goes by various names, but one of them is Ned Ferry. Sergeant, we'll kick together; now!"—Bang!

I leaned back into the room to say "It's all right! Oh, but that sweet woman's a 'coon! Let them batter!"

The Fight in the Doorway

As I thrust my head out again Miss Harper was exclaiming "Oh, sirs, don't do that!"—Bang!—"For the honor of your calling and your flag—" Bang!

"There's no Lieutenant in there." Bang!

"Corporal, go find an axe or something."

"Oh, you need not, sirs, I'll unlock the door."

"Well, be quick about it, and then stand clear; we don't want any woman hurt." The key rattled at the keyhole and then dropped to the floor. "You did that by intention! Give me that key!" He tried the lock. "We've jammed it, corporal, but another good kick will fetch it; now!"—Bang!—crash!—open flew the door.

"Well, I will be damned!" said the officer.

"Sir," said Miss Harper, "you give me no occasion to doubt it." She followed the men upstairs. "Estelle, go back to your sister and cousin; and if you, my dear,"—to our hostess—"will kindly go also and stay with them—"

I closed the door. It had no key, but there was a small catch to the knob and I turned it on while the men were looking into the adjacent rooms. When they reached ours Miss Harper was again at their front. Inside, the three of us silently noted our strategic advantages: we were in the darkest part of the room, the bed's covering was a dull red, Ferry had on his shirt of black silk, the white pillows were hidden at his back, Charlotte and I were darkly clad, the light from our west window would be in our assailants' faces as they entered, and they would be silhouetted against a similar light from the hall's front. We noiselessly cocked our weapons and Charlotte and I each sank to one knee. "The door is very thin," murmured Ferry, "we can fire before they enter; they will get, anyhow, our smoke, and if they fire as they rush in we can aim under their flash."

It was only then that I observed that Charlotte was armed. But the fact made her seem only the more a true woman, since I knew that only for her honor or his life would she ever take deadly aim. Her weapon was the slender revolver she had carried ever since the day which had made her Charlotte Oliver, the thing without which she never could have reached this hour of blissful extremity.

"In here there is a lady, ill," we heard Miss Harper say.

"Is she alone?"

Ferry prompted in a whisper, the three of us cried "Yes!" and he added "Pass one side from the door, Miss Harper, we are going to shoot through it."

"Hello, in there! Lieutenant Ferry, of Ferry's scouts,"—

"*Captain* Ferry," retorted Miss Harper, and I echoed the amendment.

"Damn the difference; I give you one half-minute, Captain Ferry, to say you surrender! If you weren't wounded I wouldn't give you that. Corporal, go get a log out of that fireplace downstairs."

"Oh, shame!" wailed Miss Harper, half-way down the hall.

"Captain," called Ferry, "I give you one quarter-minute to get away from that door." He whispered to

The Fight in the Doorway

Charlotte, pointing to a panel of it higher than any one's head.

"Oh, sirs," we again heard Miss Harper cry, "withhold! Captain Ferry, they have called in four more men!" We heard the four downstairs coming at a run. "Oh, sir—"

"Go away, madam!" bellowed the officer as his men thundered into the upper hall. "Now, Captain Ferry, there are six of us here and three under each of your windows. Do you—?"

"Oh, sir, the lady! the sick lady!"

"That's his look-out, madam. If the sick lady isn't Charlotte Oli'—"

"And if she is?" called Ferry, depressing Charlotte's weapon to an aim barely breast high.

"Then throwing away your life won't save hers! Do you surren'—?"

Ferry made a quick gesture for her to shoot low, but she solemnly shook her head and fired through the top of the uppermost panel, and the assault came.

The log burst the door in at a blow, Ferry and I fired, and our foes sprang in. Certainly they were brave; the doorway let them in only by twos, and the fire-log, falling under foot, became a stumbling-block; yet in an instant the room was ringing and roaring with the fray and benighted with its smoke. Their first ball bit the top of my shoulder and buried itself in the wall—no, not their first, but the first save one; for the bureau mirror stood in dim shade, and the Federal leader made the easy mistake of firing right into it. The error sealed his fate; Ferry fired under

his flash and sent him reeling into the arms of his followers. They replied hotly but blindly, and in a moment the room was void of assailants. Ferry started
to spring from the bed, but Charlotte threw her arms
about him, and as she pressed her head hard down on
his breast I could not help but hear "No, my treasure,
my heart's whole treasure, no!"

LV

RESCUE AND RETREAT

I SPRANG for the door, but the fire-log sent me
sprawling with my shoulder on the threshold. As I
went down I heard in the same breath the wounded
officer wailing "Go back! go in! there are only four
of them! don't leave one alive!" and Miss Harper all
but screaming "Our men! our men! God be praised,
our men are coming, they are here! Fly spoilers, for
your lives, fly!"

And it was true. Their hoofs rumbled, their carbines banged, and their charge struck three sides of
the house at once. Rising only to my elbows,—and
how I did that much, stiffened with my wound, the
doctors will have to explain,—I laid my cheek to my
rifle, and the light of two windows fell upon my gun-
sights. Every blue-coat in the hall was between me
and its rear window, but one besides the officer was
wounded, and with these two three others were busy;
only the one remaining man saw me. Twice he levelled

Rescue and Retreat

his revolver, and twice I had almost lined my sights on him, but twice Miss Harper unaware came between us. A third time he aimed, fired and missed. I am glad he fired first, for our two shots almost made one report, and he plunged forward exactly as I had done over the fire-log, except that he reached the floor dead.

Thereupon came more things at once than can be told: Miss Harper's outcry of horror and pity; Charlotte's cry from the bedside—"Richard! Richard!" a rush of feet and shouts of rage in the hall below; and my leap to the head of the stairs, shouting to half a dozen gray-jackets "Two men, no more! two men to guard prisoners, no more! go back, all but you two! go back!"

A sabreless officer with a bandaged hand flew up the stair and into my face. It was Helm. "The ladies! Smith, good God! Smith, where are the girls?"

"In the smokehouse," cried Miss Harper from her knees beside the prostrate Federal officer; "go bring them!—Richard, Charlotte is calling you!"

I ran to Ferry's door; Charlotte was leaning busily over his bared chest, while he, still holding a revolver in his right hand, caressed her arm with his left. "Dick, his wound has opened again, but we must get him away at once anyhow. Isn't my wagon still here? —oh, thank God! there it comes now, I hear it in the back yard!"

A Confederate waiting on Miss Harper with basin and towels barely dodged me as I sprang to the far end of the hall and shouted down into the yard for Harry. The little mules, true enough, were just rattling round a half turn at the lower hall's back door, having been in hiding behind the stables. A score or so of cavalry were boisterously hurrying off across the yard with a few captured horses and prisoners, and I had to call the Lieutenant angrily a second time, to make him hear me amid their din and a happy confusion which he was helping to keep up in a fairer group. For here were all the missing feminine members of the household, white and colored, and Harry was clamorous with joy, compassion and applause, while Camille and Cécile, pink with weeping, stepped out across the high doorsill of the smokehouse, leading Ned Ferry's horse and mine.

However, there was not the urgency for instant flight that Charlotte had thought there was; night fell; a whole regiment of our mounted infantry came silently up from the rear of the plantation and bivouacked without lights behind a quarter of a mile of wormfence; our two wounded and three unharmed prisoners, or Miss Harper's, I should say, for it was in response to her entreaties that the latter had thrown down their arms, were taken away; the dead man was borne out; lights glowed in every room, the servants returned to their tasks, a maddening fragrance came from the kitchen, and the three nieces flitted everywhere in their benign activities, never discovering the hurt on my shoulder until everything else on earth had been discovered, and then—"Oh, Richard, Richard!" from Estelle, with "Reach-hard, Reach-hard!" from Cécile, and "Mr. Smith!" from Camille, as they bathed and bound it.

Rescue and Retreat

At length a surgeon arrived, gave a cheering opinion of Ferry and of Charlotte, and scolded Harry savagely for the really bad condition of his hand. Then sounds grew few and faint, our lights went out, we lay down fully dressed, and nearly all of us, for a while, slept.

But about two in the morning Harry awakened me, murmuring "Reach-hard! Reach-hard! come! our sick-train's moving. Ssh! General Austin's asleep in the next room!" I asked where Ferry was. "Already started," he whispered, " —in the General's own ambulance, with Charlotte Oliver in hers, on a mattress, like Ned, and the four Harpers in theirs." While we stole downstairs he murmured on "Our brigade's come up and General Austin will attack at daylight with this house as his headquarters."

As we mounted I asked whither we were bound. "Tangipahoa," he said; "then by railroad to Brookhaven, and then out to Squire Wall's."

At the first streak of dawn our slow caravan caught the distant notes of the battle opening behind us. "That's Fisher's battery!" joyously cried the aide-de-camp as we paused and hearkened back. "Well, thank the Lord, this time nobody's got to go back for her doll; she's got it with her; I saw her, just now, combing its hair." We descended into a woody hollow, the sounds of human strife died away, and field and forest offered us only beauty, fragrance, peace, and the love-songs of birds.

The Cavalier

LVI

HÔTEL DES INVALIDES

A SHATTERED crew we were when in the forenoon of the third day we reached our goal. Harry's hand was giving him less trouble, but both my small wounds were misbehaving as stoutly as their limitations would allow; my aches were cruel and incessant, my side was swollen and my shoulder hot. Miss Harper was "really ill," said the surgeon, but for whose coming with us we should hardly have brought our whole number through alive. Both Ferry and Charlotte were in a critical condition. "Take you in!" said our tearfully smiling Mrs. Wall; "why, we'd take yo' whole crowd in ef we had to go out and bunk undeh the trees owse'v's! . . . Oh, Mr. Smith, you po' *chi—ild!* . . . Oh, my Lawd! is this Lieutenant Do-wrong! Good Lawd, good Lawd! I think this waugh's gone on now jess long enough!"

In the house she gave the younger Harpers a second kiss all round. "You po' dears, yo're hero-ines, now, and hencefo'th fo'evehmo'!" Harry and I agreed they were; it was one of the few points on which we thought alike. We even agreed that Estelle's grasp of earthly realities was not so feeble as we had thought it.

"Fact is," I said to him, on our first day at the Walls', as he was leaving the soldiers' room, where I sat under the surgeon's inspection, "you were totally mistaken about her."

"Yes, I was," he replied; "she's got more sense in a minute than Camille's got in a week," and shut the door between us.

My blood leaped with rage, yet I sat perfectly calm, while the surgeon laughed like a hyena. "As soon as you can let me go, Doctor," I frigidly said, "I shall look up the Lieutenant. I consider that remark ungentlemanly, and his method of making it as worthy only of a coward."

The surgeon cackled again. "If that man," I dispassionately resumed, "was not perfectly sure that I am too honorable a gentleman to give Miss Camille the faintest hint of what he has said, sooner than say it he would go out and cut his throat from ear to ear."

"Well! you oughtn't to get mad at him for thinking you a gentleman."

"He sha'n't take a low advantage of my being one. You think he's open and blunt—he's as sly as a mink. He praises the older. sister at the younger's expense, when it's the younger one that he's so everlastingly stuck on that he can't behave *like* a gentleman to any man to whom she shows the slightest preference." We heard a coming step, but I talked on: "Sense! poor simpleton! he knows he hasn't got "—the door opened and Harry stepped partly in, but I only raised my voice,—"hasn't got as much brains in his whole head as there is in one of her tracks."

With something between a sob, a sputter and a shriek he shut himself out again. Harry was never deep but in a shallow way, and never shallow without

The Cavalier

a certain treacherous depth. When Ned Ferry the next day summoned me to his bedside I went with a choking throat, not doubting I was to give account of this matter,—until I saw the kindness of his pallid face. Then my silly heart rose as much too high as it had just been too low and I thought " Charlotte has surrendered! " All he wanted was to make me his scribe. But when we were done he softly asked, " That business of yours we talked about on the Plank-road —it looks any better? "

I bit my lip, turned away and shook my head. " Well, any-*how,*" he said, " I am told there is no-body in your way."

I faced him sharply—" Who told you that? " and felt sure he would name the tricky aide-de-camp. But he pointed to the room overhead, which again, as in the other house, was Charlotte's. I blushed consciously with gratitude. " Well," I said, " it makes me happy to see you beginning again to get well."

Within the same hour I met unexpectedly two other persons. First, Harry Helm; who, before I could speak, was deluging me with words, telling me for the twentieth time how, on that evening of the indoor fight, coming with a platoon of Mississippians which he had procured merely as a guard, he was within a hundred yards of the house before our shots in the bedroom told him he was riding to a rescue. Then suddenly he began to assure me that in what he had said about the two sisters he had sought only to mis-lead the surgeon, who, he declared, was more utterly dead-gone on Camille than both of us put together.

Hôtel des Invalides

We parted, and within the next five minutes I confronted the maiden herself.

She came from upstairs with a mixed armful of papers, books and sewing, said she had been with Charlotte, and said no more, only made a mysterious mouth. I inquired how Charlotte was. She shrugged, sank into a seat on the gallery, let her arm-load into her lap, and replied, " Ah! she lies up there and smiles and smiles, and calls us pet names, and says she's perfectly contented, and then cannot drop half asleep without looking as though she were pressing a knife into her own heart. Oh, Dick, what is the matter with her? "

" What do you think,—Camille? "

" Oh—I—I'm afraid to say it—even to Estelle, or aunt Martha, or—"

" Say it to me," I murmured.

" Oh, if I could only trust you! " she said, shaking her head sadly and trying to lift her arm's burden again without taking her eyes from mine. It went to her feet in a landslide, and out of one of the books fluttered three stems of sweet-pea each bearing two mated blossoms. I knew them in an instant, and in the next I had them. She would not let me pile the fallen freight anywhere but into her arm again, nor recover her eye before she was fully re-laden. Then she set her lips freezingly and said " Now give me back my flowers."

I meekly gave them and she turned to go into the house; her head gradually sank forward as she went, and her unparagoned ear and neck flushed to a burning red. On the threshold, by some miscalculation, her burdened arm struck the jamb, and the whole load fell again. I sprang and began to gather the stuff into a chair, but she walked straight on as though nothing had occurred, and shut the nearest door behind her.

In those days used to come out to see us Gregory, in his long-skirted black coat and full civilian dress; of whom I have told a separate history elsewhere. Very pointed was Camille's neglect of both Harry and me, to make herself lovely to the dark and diffident new-comer, while Estelle positively pursued me with compensatory sweetness; and Gregory, whenever he and I were alone together, labored to reassure me of his harmlessness by expatiating exclusively upon the charms of Cécile. She seemed to him like a guardian angel of Ferry and Charlotte, while yet everything she said or did was wholly free from that quality of other-worldliness which was beautiful in Estelle, but which would not have endured repetition in the sister or the cousin. There Harry and I, also, once more agreed. Cécile never allowed herself to reflect a spirit of saint-liness, or even of sacrifice, but only of maidenly wisdom and sweet philosophy.

"If it weren't for Charlotte," whispered the Lieutenant, "I could swear she was created for Ned Ferry!" and when I shook my head he, too, declared "No, no! if ever a match was made on high Charlotte was made for him and he for Charlotte; but, oh, Lord, Lord! Reach-hard Thorndyke Smith, how is this thing going to end?"

That was the problem in the mind of every looker

on, and the lookers-on were legion; the whole wide neighborhood came to see us. Gregory and others outstayed their furloughs; the surgeon lingered shamelessly. Of course, there were three girls besides Charlotte, and it was pure lying—as I told Helm—for some of those fellows to pretend that Captain Ferry's problem was all they stayed for; and yet it was the one heart-problem which was everybody's, and we were all in one fever to see forthwith a conclusion which "a decent respect to the opinions of mankind" required should not come for months.

"Pooh!" said Harry, "'a decent respect to the opinions of mankind' requires just the reverse!" and the surgeon avowed that it was required by a decent respect to her powers of endurance; he was every day afraid her slow improvement would stop and she would begin to sink. He admitted the *event* could wait, but he wished to gracious we could have her decision.

I said suppose it should be negative. "Oh, it won't!" exclaimed both he and Harry. "When it comes to the very point—"

Gregory's approach interrupted us, but I remembered a trait in Charlotte of which I have spoken, and gave myself the hope that their prediction might prove well founded.

The Cavalier

LVII

A YES AND A NO

BUT now Charlotte's recovery took on new speed. Maybe her new brightness meant only that her heart was learning to bear its load; but we hoped that was just what it was unlearning, as she and Ferry sat at chess on the gallery in the afternoons.

One night the fellows gave a dance in Brookhaven. We went in two wagons and by the light of mounted torch-bearers, and Charlotte and Ferry stood at the dooryard gate and sent after us their mirthful warnings and good-byes. It set some of us a-hoping—to see them there—a dooryard gate means so much. We fairly prayed he might compel her decision before she should turn to re-enter the house. But the following morning it was evident we had prayed in vain.

On the next afternoon but one we heard that a great column of our soldiers was approaching on the nearest highway, bound up the railroad to Joe Johnston's army from the region about Port Hudson, and Charlotte instantly proposed that our ladies deal out food and drink from some shady spot on the roadside. It was one of those southern summer days when it verily seems hotter in the shade than in the sun—unless you are in the sun. The force was wholly artillery and infantry, the last Confederate infantry that region ever saw in column under arms; poor, limping, brown-faced, bloody-footed boys! their weapons were the only clean things, the only whole things, about them

A Yes and a No

except their unbroken spirit; and when the very foremost command chanced to be one which the Harpers had seen in New Orleans the day it left there marching in faultless platoons and spotless equipments through the crowds that roared acclaim and farewell, our dear ladies, for one weak moment, wept.

"Here come the real heroes, Harry," said my crippled leader; "we are dandies and toy-soldiers, by the side of those infantry boys, Doctor, we cavalry fellows;" and we cavalry fellows would have hid if we honorably could. Yet hardly had he spoken when he and a passing field-officer cried out in mutual recognition, and from that time until the rear-guard was clear gone by we received what the newspapers call "a continuous ovation." A group of brigade officers went back with us to Squire Wall's, to supper, and you could see by the worship they paid Charlotte that they knew her story. Her strength was far overtaxed, and the moment the last fond straggler had gone we came in out of the splendid moonlight.

"Now, Charlotte, my dear," began Miss Harper, "you are too terribly tired to—why, where is Charlotte; did she not come in with us from the—gate?"

Ferry, too, was missing. Mrs. Wall made eyes at the inquirer, Estelle and Cécile began to speak but deferred to each other, and Camille, putting on a deadly exhaustion, whined as she tottered to her smiling guardian, "Kiss your sweet baby good-night, auntie dear, and "—with a hand reached out to Estelle—" make Naughty come, too." She turned to say good-night to Cécile but spoiled her kiss with an unintended laugh.

The Cavalier

The surgeon, Harry and I bowed from the room and stepped out to the water-bucket and gourd. From there we could see the missing two, lingering at the dooryard gate, in the bright moonlight. As we finished drinking, "Gentlemen," murmured Harry, "I fear our position is too exposed to be tenable."

The surgeon started upstairs. "I'll join you directly, Doctor," Harry said, and in a lower voice added "Smith and I will just lounge in and out of the hall here to sort o' show nobody needn't be in any hurry, don't you see?"

But the other jerked his thumb toward the half-closed parlor, where Miss Harper and Cécile sat close to each other absorbed in some matter of the tenderest privacy. "They'll attend to that," he muttered; "come on to bed and mind your own business."

Harry huffed absurdly. "You go mind yours," he retorted, and then more generously added, "we'll be with you in a minute." The surgeon went, and the aide-de-camp, as we began to pace the hall, fairly took my breath by remarking without a hint of self-censure, "Damn a frivolous man!" Then irrelatively he added, "Those two out at that gate—this is a matter of life and death with them;" and when I would have qualified the declaration, he broke in upon me—"Right, Dick, you're right, it *is* worse; it's a choice between true life and death-in-life; whether they'll make life's long march in sunshine together or in darkness apart."

Well, of course, it was no such simple question, and never could be while life held so many values more splendid than any wilfulness could win. There lay the

A Yes and a No

whole of Charlotte's real difficulty—for she had made it all hers. But when I tried in some awkward way to say this Harry cut me short. "Oh, Dick, I—eh—you bother me! I want to tell you something and if I don't hurry I can't. Something's happened to me, old fellow, something that's sobered me more than I ever would 'a' thought anything could. I want to tell you because I can trust you with a secr'—wh'—what's the matter, did I hurt your wound? Honestly, I want to tell you because—well—because I've been deceiving you all along: I've deceived you shamefully, letting on to like this girl more than that, and so on and so on."

"Yes, you thought you were deceiving me."

"Oh, well, maybe I wasn't, but I want to tell you to-night because I'm going to camp in the morning. Oh, yes,"—he named the deepest place known—"the sight of those webfoot boys to-day was too much for me; I'm going; and Dick, when I told her I was going—"

"*Told whom?*"

"Aw, come, now, Dick, you know every bit as well as I know. Well, when I told her I was going I didn't dream I was going to tell her anything else; I give you my word! Where in the "—same place again—"I ever got the courage I'll never tell you, but all of a sudden thinks I, ' I'm never going to get anything but no, anyhow, and so, Dick, I've been and gone and done it!"

I leaned on the stair-newel, sorry for the poor fool, but glad of this chance. "Why, Lieutenant, not many men would have done as well. You felt honor-bound not to slip away uncommitted, so you took your dose like a hero and licked the spoon." I felt that I was salting his wound, but we were soldiers and—I had the salt.

He drew a sigh. "Yes, I took my dose—of astonishment. Dick, she said yes! Oh, good Lord, Dick, do you reckon they'll ever be such full-blown idiots as to let me have her?"

I sank upon the steps; every pore in my body was a fountain of cold sweat: "Have whom?"

"Cécile." He was going on to declare himself no more fit for her than for the presidency of the Confederate States, which was perfectly true; but I sprang up, caught him (on my well side) by one good hand, and had begun my enthusiastic congratulations, when Charlotte appeared and we swerved against the rail to let her pass upstairs. In some way as she went by it was made plain to us that she had said no. "Goodnight," ventured both of us, timorously.

"Good-night," she responded, very musically, but as if from a great distance.

LVIII

THE UPPER FORK OF THE ROAD

Ferry, as he passed us, called my name, and I started after him. At Charlotte's door we heard the greeting of her black maid. The maid's father, who of late had been nightly dressing Ferry's wound and mine, came to us in Ferry's room; and there my Captain turned to greet me, his face white with calamity.

The Upper Fork of the Road

He took me caressingly by a button of my jacket. "Can you have your wound washed to-night before mine?"

"Why, certainly, if it's the least—"

"Yes, thank you. And down here in this room instead of upstairs?"

"Captain Ferry! if you knew how horribly it smells, you—"

"Ah! don't I know?" he said, and as I sat naked from throat to waist with the old negro laving the sores, Ferry scanned them narrowly. "They are not so bad, Dick; you think a few hours in the saddle will not make them worse?"

"Not if they're spent for you, Captain."

"Yes, for me; also for much better. We shall ride for—"

"You ride? Oh, Captain, you are in no condition—"

"Tst!" he laid a finger on my lips; "'twill not be hard; we are not going on a scout—to jump fences." He began to make actual preparations, and presently helped me draw my shirt into place again over the clean bandages, while the old man went out after fresh water. "I am a hundred times more fit to go than to stay," he suddenly resumed. "I must go. Ah, idleness, there is nothing like idleness to drive a man mad; I must have something to do—to-night—at once." I wish I knew how to give the words with his quiet intensity.

I began to unclothe his wound. "May I ask one thing?"

"Ah! I know you; you want to ask am I taking

that upper fork of the road. I am; 'tis for that I want you; so go you now to the stable, saddle our horses and bring them."

When I reached the front steps with them Ferry was at the gallery's edge, Miss Harper, Cécile and Harry were on three sides of him, and he was explaining away our astonishing departure. We were going to Hazlehurst, to issue clothing and shoes to those ragged and barefoot fellows we had seen that afternoon, and the light of whose tentless camp was yonder in the sky, now, toward Brookhaven. We were to go that way, confer with their officers, telegraph from town for authorizations to be sent to us at Hazlehurst, and then to push on to that place and be ready to issue the stuff when the trains should come up from Brookhaven bringing the brigade. While he spoke Camille and Estelle joined us. "No," he said, "to start any later, 'twould be too late."

To Harry's imploring protest that he, Ferry, was not fit to go to Hazlehurst horseback, he replied "Well! what we going to do? Those boys can't go to Big Black swamp bare-*foot*."

Our dear friends were too well aware of the untold trouble to say a word about his coming back, but Miss Harper's parting injunction to me was to write them.

The whole night and the following day were a toilsome time for us, but by fall of the next night the brigade had come in rags and passed newly clothed and shod, and in a room of the town tavern we dressed each other's hurts and sank to sleep on one bed. The night was hot, the pain of my wounds was like a great stone lying on them, and at the tragic moment of a frightful dream I awoke. "Captain," I murmured.

"Yes?"

"Did she give no reason?"

"No." A silence followed; then he said, "You know the reason, I think."

"Yes, I think I do; I think—"

"Well? don't be afraid to say it."

I got the words out in some form, that I believed Charlotte loved him deeply, as deeply, passionately, exaltedly, as ever a true woman loved a man—

"Ah, me!" he lifted his arms wide and knitted his fingers on his brow.

"And there is the whole trouble," I added. "She will not let you marry the woman whose—"

"Whose husband I have killed. . . . Ah, God! . . . Ah, my God! why was I chosen to do that? . . . And you think, Dick, it was not a question of time; that I did not ask, maybe a little too soon?"

"No, not as between sooner and later; and yet, in another way, possibly, yes." Without either of us stirring from the pillow I tried to explain. I pointed out that trait in Charlotte which I called an impulse suddenly to surrender the key of her situation, the vital point in her fortunes and fate.

"Yes. . . . Yes," Ferry kept putting in.

I went on to say that she seemed now to have learned, herself, that it was on this shoal she grounded at every low water of her physical and mental powers; as when over-fatigued, for instance; and that I should not wonder if she had bound herself never again at such a time to let her judgment follow her impulses. He laid his hand on me: "Stop; stop; you stab too deep. I thought to take her by surprise at that very point, and right there she has countermined. My God! can it be that I am served only right?"

"No," I replied, although it was a thing I would have said Ned Ferry would not do, "no, no, it is she who has served both you and herself cruelly wrong. Captain, I believe that when Miss Harper has talked it over with her she will see her mistake as we all see it, and will call you back."

"Ah, me! Ah, me! Do you believe that, Dick?"

"I do, Captain; but at the same time—"

"What, what? Speak out, Dick. You blame me some other way?"

"Oh, no, indeed! I am the one to blame, the only one. If you had not, both of you, been so blameless —so splendidly blameless—I should hardly have let myself sink so deep into blame; but I knew you would never take the last glad step until you had seen the last sad proof that you might take it. Oh, Captain, to-night is the third time that in my dreams I have seen *that man* alive."

I do not know how long after that we lay silent, but it seemed an endless time before he exclaimed at last "My God! Dick, you should have told me."

"I know it; I know I should! But it was only a dream, and—"

"Ah! 'twas your doubt first and the dream after! But let us think no more of blame, we must settle the doubt. We shall begin that to-morrow." On my venturing to say more he interrupted. "Well, we can do nothing now; at the present, sleep is our first business." However, after a little, he spoke again, and, I believe, purely in order to soothe me to slumber, speculated and counselled with me for the better part of an hour concerning my own poor little love affair.

At breakfast he told me the first step in his further plans would be for us to take the train for Tangipahoa, with our horses, on our way to our own camp; but just before the train came the telegraph brought General Austin's request—which, of course, carried all the weight of an order—for Ferry to remain here and make ready for further issues of quartermaster's stores. He turned on his heel and twisted his small mustache: "That means we are kept here to be kept here, Richard."

It was a mistaken kindness, from our point of view, but it had the merit that it kept us busy. In two days the post-quartermaster's affairs and supplies were reduced to perfect order for the first time in their history. For two days more we ran a construction train and with a swarm of conscripts repaired two or three miles of road-bed and some trestle-work in a swamp; and at every respite in our strenuous activities we discoursed of the girls we'd left behind us; their minds, their manners, their features, figures, tastes and talents, and their walk and talk. So came the end of the week, and while the sun was still above the trees we went on down, inspecting the road beyond our repairs, on our own hand-car to Brookhaven. With heads bare, jackets in our laps, and muddy boots dangling over

The Cavalier

the car's front edge, and with six big negroes at the levers behind us, we watched the miles glide under our wheels and grow fewer and fewer between us and the shrine of our hearts. "Sing, Dick," said Ferry, and we chanted together, as we had done at every sunset these three days, "O my love is like a red, red rose." We could not have done it had we known that yonder glorious sun was setting forever upon the fortunes of our Southern Confederacy. It was the fourth of July; Lee was in full retreat from Gettysburg, Vicksburg was gone, Port Hudson was doomed, and all that was left for us now was to die hard.

LIX

UNDER CHARLOTTE'S WINDOW

At the tavern, where we went to smarten up and to eat, we chanced upon Gregory. He was very shy of Ferry, because Ferry was a captain, but told me the latest news from the Wall place, where he had spent the previous evening. Harry and the surgeon were gone to camp, the Harpers were well, Charlotte was—better, after a bad turn of several days. We felt in duty bound to stay within hail of the telegraph office until it should close for the night; and when the operator was detained in it much beyond the usual time, Ferry, as we hovered near, said at length, "Well, I'm sorry for you, Dick; 'tis now too late for you to go yonder—this evening."

"Didn't you intend to call, too?"

Under Charlotte's Window

"No," he said; yet the moment the operator turned the key in his door we sauntered away from the station, tavern, town, and out into the rain-famished country. We chose a road on high ground, under pines; the fact that a few miles of it would bring us to Squire Wall's was not sufficient reason for us to shun it, and we loitered on and on, discoursing philosophically on man and woman and the duties of each to other. Through habit we went softly, and so, in time, came up past a small garden under the house's southern side. Here silence was only decorum, for every window in the dark upper rooms was thrown open to the sultry air. The house's front was away from the direction of the town, and at a corner of this garden, where the road entered the open grove, the garden fence turned north at a right angle, while the road went on through the grove into wide cornfields beyond.

We kept to the garden fence till it brought us along the dooryard front, facing the house. Thus far the whole place seemed fast asleep. Along the farthest, the northern, side a line of planted trees ran close to a narrow wing of but one room on each of its two stories, and the upper of these two rooms was Charlotte's. Where we paused, at the dooryard gate, we could not see this wing, but we knew its exterior perfectly; it had a narrow window in front, looking into the grove, and a broader one at the rear, that overlooked an open stretch of the Wall plantation. The place seemed fast asleep, I say, but we had not a doubt we were being watched—by the two terrible dogs that guarded the house but never barked. By this time they should have recognized us and ought to be coming forward and wagging faintly, as who should say "Yes, that's all right, but we have our orders."

"Ah!"—Ferry guardedly pointed to the ground at the corner of the house nearest Charlotte's room; there were both the dogs, dim as phantoms and as silent, standing and peering not toward us but around to the wing side in a way to make one's blood stop. We drew deeper into the grove and made a short circuit that brought us in line with Charlotte's two windows, and there, at the farther one, with her back to us, sat Charlotte, looking toward Hazlehurst. The bloodthirsty beasts at the corner of the house were so intently waiting to spring upon something, somebody, between them and the nearer window, that we were secure from their notice. We had hardly more than become aware of these things when, in the line of planted trees, out of the depths of the one nearest the nearer window, sounded a note that brought Charlotte instantly to her feet; the same feeble, smothered cry she had heard the night she was wounded. She crossed to the front window and listened, first standing erect, and then stooping and leaning out. When we saw her do that we knew how little she cared for her life; Ferry beckoned me up from behind him; neither of us needed to say he feared the signal was from Oliver. "Watch here," he whispered, and keeping the deepest shade, started eagerly, with drawn revolver, toward the particular tree. I saw the dogs discover and recognize him and welcome his aid, yet I kept my closest watch on that tree's boughs and

Under Charlotte's Window

on Charlotte. She was wondering, I guessed, whether the call was from some messenger of Ferry, or was only a bird's cry. As if she decided it was the latter, she moved away, and had nearly re-crossed the room, when the same sad tremolo came searching the air again. Nevertheless she went on to the farther window and stood gazing out for the better part of a minute, while in my heart I besought her not to look behind. For Ferry and the dogs had vanished in shadow, and outside her nearer window, wavering now above and now below the sill, I could just descry a small pale object that reminded me of that missive Coralie Rothvelt had passed up to me outside the window-sill at old Lucius Oliver's house exactly a month before. From the upper depths of the nearest tree this small thing was being proffered on the end of a fishing-rod. Presently the rod must have tapped the sill, with such a start did she face about. Silently she ran, snatched the dumb messenger, and drew down the window-shade. A moment later the room glowed with a candle, while her shadow, falling upon the shade, revealed her scanning a letter, lifting her arms with emotion, and so passing out of the line of view.

I waited on. So absorbed was I that I did not hear the coming of a horseman in the fields beyond the grove, nor the click of a field gate; but when the strange quietude of Ferry and the dogs had begun to reassure me I became aware of this new-comer approaching the dooryard. There he reined in and hallooed. I knew the voice. An answer came from an upper window.

The Cavalier

" Is this Squire Wall's? " asked the traveller. " Well, Squire, I'm from General Austin's headquarters, with orders to Captain Ferry."

" Captain Ferry ain't stopping with us now, sir, he's 'way up at Hazlehurst."

" Yes, sir. I didn't know but he might 'a' come down to spend to-morrow with you, it being the Sabbath. My name's Gholson, sir; I've got letters for the Miss Harpers; yes, sir; and one for Private Smith, from his mother, in New Orleans."

" My sakes! yo' pow'ful welcome, Mr. Wholesome; just wait till I call off my dogs, sir, and I'll let you in."

When the dogs came at the Squire's call I breathed relief. Ferry appeared behind me and beckoned me deeper into the grove. He sank upon a stump, whispering " That was worse than ten fights."

" Who was it? " I asked. " Where is he? "

He pointed to the field gate through which Gholson had come. In the field a small man was re-closing it cautiously, and now he mounted and rode away; it was Isidore Goldschmidt, of the Plank-road swamp. I was wondering why he had behaved in this skulking way, when Ferry, as if reading my thought, said, " Isidore can't afford to be found seventy-five miles inside our lines with no papers except a letter from a Yankee officer—and not knowing, himself, what's in it."

" Oh! why should he risk his life to bring such a thing to her? "

" Because three months ago she risked her life to save the life of his father, and now, since only last week, that Yankee has saved the life of his mother."

Tidings

I asked who this Yankee might be. "Well, that is yet more strange; he is the brother of Captain Jewett."

We were moving to the house; at the steps we halted; the place was all alight and the ladies were arriving in the parlor. A beam of light touching Ferry's face made his smile haggard. I asked if this Jewett was another leader of scouts.

"No, he is a high-rank surgeon. Yet I think he must have heard all about her; he wouldn't send that letter, that way, just for grati-*tude*."

"Yes," I responded, pondering, "he may easily have learned about her," and I called to mind that chief-of-staff of whom Charlotte had told us. Then, remembering her emotional shadow-play on the window-shade, I added, "He knew at least what would be important news to her—Captain, I have it!"

He made a motion of pain—"Don't say it!" and we read in each other's eyes the one conviction that from a surgeon's personal knowledge this man had written to warn Charlotte that Oliver was alive.

LX

TIDINGS

ALL the glad difference between hope stark drowned and hope sighing back into life lightened Ferry's heart; he gripped my shoulder—the sound one, by good luck, —and drew me into the dining-room, where the whole company were gathered to see Gholson eat. Our entry was a fresh surprise. As we drank the flatteries of seven lovely welcomes, from behind Gholson I reconnoitred Charlotte, and the fullest confirmation of our guess was in the peaceful resolve of her eyes. I noted the Harpers, all, and dear Mrs. Wall's sweet freckled face, take new gladness of the happy change, while unable to define its cause.

But now came raptures and rhapsodies over the opened letters. Ferry's orders had not been expected to reach him to-night, Gholson said, and so we insisted they and my letter should remain in the saddle-pockets while Gholson ate, and while the good news, public and personal, of the Harpers' letters went round.

"But I thought the' was fi-ive letters," said the Squire as we were about to leave the board; at which Mrs. Wall mumbled to him to " hush up; " for the fifth was to Cécile.

"Yes," guilefully said Charlotte, "Richard's letter!" and we all followed Gholson to where his saddle lay on the gallery. There he handed out Ferry's document and went on rummaging for mine.

"The two were right here together," he said, "and Mr. Smith's was marked 'valuable' and had something hard in one corner of it. Camille brought a candle, Estelle another; Gholson rose from his knee: "Smith, it's gone! I've lost it! And yet "—he slapped his breast-pockets—" no, it's somewhere in the grove; it's between here and that cornfield gate! I counted all the papers just this side of that gate, and I must 'a' dropped yours then!" Cécile brought a third light and we sallied forth into the motionless air,

Tidings

Estelle with a candle and Gholson, Camille with a candle and me, Cécile with a candle and Mrs. Wall, Miss Harper and the Squire, and Charlotte and Ferry. In the heart of the grove Estelle gave a soft cry, sprang, stooped, straightened, and handed me the letter.

"Yes," exclaimed Camille as the three candle-bearers gathered close, "that's your mother's writing," and as we fell into marching order again, with the lights still in the front files, I opened it. It was thick and soft with sheet after sheet of thinnest paper. With these was a sealed letter, unaddressed, containing in one corner what seemed to be a ring. Around all was a sheet of writing of later date than any other. Wonderful, my mother's lines declared, was the Providence that had brought her wounded boy among such priceless friends; and wonderful that same Providence that now gave her the chance to send three weeks' daily letters in one, and to send them by a hand so sure that she ventured to add this other note, a matter so secret that it must be delivered only by my own hands, or hands which I could trust as my own, to Charlotte Oliver. We glanced back in search of Charlotte. She and Ferry were well in the rear of the procession, moving with laggard steps, she lighting his page with a borrowed candle, and he evidently reading not his orders, but the Federal surgeon's letter. "Oh, don't speak yet," murmured Camille, "let them alone!"

At the garden gate the most of the company passed on into the house, Gholson among them. His face, as for an instant he turned aside to me, betrayed a frozen rage; for Ferry and Charlotte tarried just at our backs, she seated on the "horse-block" and he leaning against it. A stir of air brought by the rising moon had blown out their light. Gholson left me, and Camille waited at my side while I tried to read by the flare of her guttering candle. "Come, my dear," said Miss Harper from half-way up the walk, but Charlotte called Miss Harper.

"You'd better go in, Camille," insisted the aunt as she passed us, but Charlotte had just asked for our candle to relight her own, and she said to Miss Harper, "Let them stay, won't you?" and then to Ferry, "They might as well, mightn't they? Oh, now,"—as Camille handed her my mother's letter—"they must!" She toyed with the envelope's thinner edge without noticing the ring in the corner. "My dears," she said, looking frail and distressed, yet resolute, "I have positive intelligence—not through Captain, nor Richard, nor Mr. Gholson,—I'll tell you how some day—positive intelligence that—the dead—is not dead; the blow, Richard, glanced. I was foolish never to think of that possibility, it occurs so often. He was profoundly stunned, so that he didn't come-to until he was brought to a surgeon. It's from that surgeon I have the news; here's his letter."

"Charlotte, my dear," interrupted Miss Harper, "tell us the remainder to-morrow, but now—"

"No, sweetest friend, there will never be another chance like this; Captain Ferry's orders carry him to Jackson at daylight to-morrow, and—and we may not meet again for years; let me go on. When the gash was sewed up, the hand was really the worse hurt of the two, and after a few days he was sent down on a steamer to New Orleans with a great lot of other sick and wounded, and with the commanding general's warning not to come back on peril of his life. 'Tisn't easy to tell this, but you four have a particular right to know it from me and at once. So let me say "—she handed Ferry my mother's letter as if it were a burdensome distraction—" I'm not sorry for the mistake, Richard, which we all so innocently made; and you mustn't be sorry for me and be saying to yourselves that my captivity is on me again; for I'm happier tonight than I've been since the night the mistake was made."

She dropped a hand to Ferry's to receive again the neglected letter, and chanced to take it by the corner that held the ring. With that she stared at us, fingered it, rended the envelope, gave one glance to her own name engraved inside a plain gold ring of the sort New Orleans girls bestow upon those to whom they are betrothed, and springing to the ground between our two candles, bent over the open page and cried through a flood of tears, " Oh, God, have mercy on him, he is gone! He is gone, Edgard! Oh, Edgard, he is gone at last; gone beyond all doubt, and our hands—our hands and our hearts are clean! "

Ferry tossed away his candle and turned upon her, but she retreated into Miss Harper's arms laughing through her tears. " Oh, no, no! we've never hurried yet, never yet, my master in patience, and we'll not hurry now! Go and come again. Go, wait, hide your

The Cavalier

eyes till I cry 'whoop,' and come again and find me, and, I pledge you before these dear witnesses, I'll be 'it' for the rest of my life!"

With the letter again held open, and bidding Miss Harper and Camille read with her, she swept a fleet glance along the close lines that told how Oliver, half cured of his wounds, had died in a congestive chill, of swamp-fever, the day he landed in New Orleans. "See, see, Richard, here your mother has copied the hospital's certificate."

She read on aloud how two private Federal soldiers, hospital convalescents, had come to my mother telling her of his death, and how he had named my mother over and over in his delirium, desiring that she should be given charge of the small effects on his person and that she would return them to his father in the Confederacy. My mother wrote how she had been obliged secretly to buy back from the hospital steward a carte-de-visite photograph of Charlotte, and this ring; how, Oliver not being a Federal soldier, she had been allowed to assume the expense and task of his burial; how she had found the body already wrapped and bound, in the military way, when she first saw it, but heard the two convalescents praising to each other the strong, hard-used beauty of the hidden face, and was shown the suit of brown plantation jeans we all knew so well; and how, lastly, when her overbearing conscience compelled her to tell them she might find it easier to send the relics to the wife rather than the father, they had furtively advised her to do as she pleased.

Tidings

"Charlotte," said Miss Harper, "the thing is an absolute certainty! Even without your likeness or—"

"Ah, no, no, not without this! the ring, the ring! But with it, yes! This is the crowning proof! my ring to him! Oh, see my name inside it, Camille; this little signet is Heaven's own testimony and acquittal! Look, Richard, look at it now, for no living soul, no light of day, shall ever see it again—"

"Sweet heart," replied Miss Harper, "very good! very good! but now say no more of that sort. God bless you, dear, just let yourself be happy. Good-night —no, no, sit still; stay where you are, love, while Camille and I go in and Richard steps around to the stable and puts our team into the road-wagon; for, Captain Ferry, neither you nor he is fit to walk into Brookhaven; we can bring the rig back when we come from church to-morrow."

"No, Richard," said Charlotte, "get my wagon and the little Mexicans." Then to Miss Harper and Camille, "Good-night, dears; I'll wait here that long, if Captain Ferry will allow me." She turned to him with the moonlight in her eyes, that danced riotously as she said in her softest, deepest note, "You're afraid!" and I thanked Heaven that Coralie Rothvelt was still a pulsing reality in the bosom of Charlotte Oliver.

The Cavalier

LXI

WHILE DESTINY MOVED ON

NED FERRY and I never saw Squire Wall's again. When our hand-car the next morning landed us in Hazlehurst the news of Gettysburg and Vicksburg was on every tongue, in every face, and a telegram awaited Ferry which changed his destination to Meridian, a hundred miles farther to the east. He kept me with him at Hazlehurst for two days, to help him and the post-quartermaster get everything ready to be moved and saved if our cavalry should be driven east of the Jackson Railroad. But it was not, and by and by we were sundered and I went and became at length in practical and continuous reality one of Ferry's scouts —minus Ferry. Oh, the long hot toils and pains of those July and August days! the scorching suns, the stumbling night-marches, the aching knees, the groaning beasts, the scant, foul rations, the dust and sweat, the blood and the burials. To be sure, I speak of these hardships far more from sympathy than from experience, so much above the common lot of the long dust-choked column was that of our small band of scouts. After July our brigade operated mainly in the region of the Big Black, endeavoring, with others, to make the enemy confine his overflow meetings to the Vicksburg side of that unlovely stream. How busy our small troop was kept; and what fame we won! On a certain day we came out of a dried swamp in column and ambled half

While Destiny Moved On

across a field to see if a brigade going by us at right angles in the shade of a wood at the field's edge might be ours. It was not, though they were Confederates; but one of its captains was sent out toward us with a squadron to see who we might be, in our puzzling uniform, and when, midway, he made us out and called back to his commander, " Ferry's scouts! " the whole column cheered us. I feel the thrill of it to this hour.

How busy we were kept, and how much oftener I wrote to Ferry, and to Camille, than to my mother. And how much closer I watched the trend of things that belonged only to this small story than I did that great theatre of a whole world's fortunes, whose arches spread and resounded from the city of Washington to the city of Mexico. In mid-August one of Camille's heartlessly infrequent letters brought me a mint of blithe news. Harry and Cécile were really engaged; Major Harper, aunt Martha, General Austin, Captain Ferry and Charlotte had all written the distant father in his behalf, and the distant father had capitulated. Furthermore, Captain Ferry's latest letter to Charlotte had brought word that in spite of all backsets he was promised by his physician that in ten days more he could safely take the field again. But, best of all, Major Harper, having spent a week with his family— not on leave, but on some mysterious business that somehow included a great train of pontoon bridges— had been so completely won over to Charlotte by her own sweet ways that, on his own suggestion to his sister, and their joint proposition, by correspondence,

The Cavalier

to Ferry, another group of letters, from Miss Harper, the Major and the General, had been sent to the Durands in New Orleans—father, mother, and grandmother—telling them all about Charlotte; her story, her beauty, her charms of manner, mind, and heart. And so, wrote my correspondent, the Wall household were living in confident hope and yet in unbearable suspense; for these things were now full two weeks old, and would have been told me sooner only that she, Camille, had promised never to tell them to any one whomsoever.

A week later came another of these heartlessly infrequent letters. Mr. Gregory, it said,—oh, *hang* Mr. Gregory!—had called the previous evening. Then followed the information that poor Mr. Gholson—oh, dear! the poor we have always with us!—had arrived again from camp so wasted with ague as to be a sight for tears. He had come consigned to "our hospital," an establishment which the Harpers, Charlotte and the Walls had set up in the old "summer-hotel" at Panacea Springs, and had contrived to get the medical authorities to adopt, officer and—in a manner—equip. They were giving dances there, to keep the soldiers cheerful, said the letter, in which its writer took her usual patriotic part, and Mr. Gregory—oh, save us alive! And now I was to prepare myself: the Durands had got the bunch of letters and had written a lovely reply to Captain Ferry, who had sent it to Charlotte, claiming her hand, and Charlotte had answered yes. If I thought I had ever seen her beautiful or blithe, or sweet, or happy, I ought to see her now; while as

While Destiny Moved On

for the writer herself, nothing in all her life had ever
so filled her with bliss, or ever could again.

Ferry did not arrive, but day by day, night by night,
we stalked the enemy, longing for our Captain to return to us. Quinn was fearless, daring, indefatigable;
but Quinn was not Ferry. Often we talked it over
by twos or fours; the swiftness of Ferry's divinations,
the brilliant celerity with which he followed them out,
the kindness of his care; Quinn's care of us was pa-
ternal, Ferry's was brotherly and motherly. We loved
Quinn for the hate and scorn that overflowed from his
very gaze upon everything false or base. But we
loved Ferry for loving each and every one of us beyond his desert, and for a love which went farther
yet, we fancied, when it lived and kept its health in
every insalubrious atmosphere, from the sulphurous
breath of old Dismukes to the carbonic-acid gas of
Gholson's cant. We made great parade of recognizing
his defects; it had all the fine show of a motion to re-
consider. For example, we said, his serene obstinacy
in small matters was equally exasperating and ridiculous; or, for another instance,—so and so; but in
summing up we always lumped such failings as " the
faults of his virtues," and neglected to catalogue them.
Thinking it all over a thousand times since, I have
concluded that the main source of his charm, what
won our approval for whatever he did, however he did
it, was that he seemed never to regard any one as the
mere means to an end—except himself.

If this history were more of war than of love—and
really at times I fear it is—we might fill pages telling

The Cavalier

of the brigade's September and early October operations in that long tongue of devastated country which narrowed from northeast to southwest between Big Black on our front and the Tallahala and Bayou Pierre behind us. At Baker's Creek it had a bloody all-day fight, in which we took part after having been driven in upon the brigade. It was there that at dusk, to the uproarious delight of half the big camp, and with our Captain once more at our head, for he had rejoined us that very morning, we came last off the field, singing "Ned Ferry's a-comin' down de lane."

On a day late in October our company were in bivouac after some hard night-riding. Some twenty-five miles west of us the brigade had been resting for several days on the old camp-ground at Gallatin, but now they were gone to Union Springs. Ferry, with a few men, was scouting eastward. Quinn awaited only his return in order to take half a dozen or so of picked fellows down southward and westward about Fayette. Between ten and eleven that night a corporal of the guard woke me, and as I flirted on my boots and jacket and saddled up, said Ferry was back and Quinn gone. I reported to Ferry, who handed me a despatch: "Give that to General Austin; he has gone back to Gallatin—without the brigade—to wait—with the others"—his smile broadened.

"Captain,"—I swallowed a lump—" what others?"

"Well,—all the others; Major Harper, Colonel Dismukes, Harry Helm, Squire Wall, Mrs. Wall, the four Harper ladies, and—eh,—let me see, is that all?—ah, no, the old black man and his daughter, and—eh,—the

two little mule'! that's all—stop! I was forgetting!
What is that fellow's name we used to know? ah, yes;
Charlie Toliver!" In a moment he sobered: "Yes,
all will be yonder, and I wait only for Quinn to get
back in the morning, to come myself." In the fulness
of his joy he had to give my horse a parting slap.
"Good-night! good-bye—till to-morrow!"

I galloped away filled with an absurd foreboding that
he was too sure, which may have come wholly from
my bad temper at being started too late to see our
ladies before morning. However, at two that night,
my saddle laid under my head, and haversack under
the saddle, I fell asleep with all Gallatin for my bed-
chamber, the courthouse square for my bed, the sky
for my tester, the pole-star for my taper, hogs for
mosquitoes and a club for a fan.

LXII

A TARRYING BRIDEGROOM

Joyous was the dawn. With their places in the hospital filled for the brief time by Brookhaven friends,
here were all our fairs, not to speak of the General,
the Colonel, the Major, idlers of the town and region,
and hospital bummers who had followed up unbidden
and glaringly without wedding-garments. Cécile,
Harry, Camille "and others" prepared the church.
The General kept his tent, the Major rode to Hazlehurst, and the Colonel, bruised and stiffened by a late

The Cavalier

fall from his horse, lounged amiably just beyond talking range of the ladies and grumbled jokes to Chaplain Roly-poly, whose giggling enjoyment of them made us hope they were tempered to that clean-shaven lamb.

However, there came a change. By mid-forenoon our gaiety ran on only by its momentum. The wedding was to be at eleven. At ten the Colonel, aside, told me, with a ferocious scowl, that my Captain ought to have arrived. At half-past he told me again, but Major Harper, returning from Hazlehurst, said, "Oh, any of a hundred trifles might have delayed him a short time; he would be along." The wedding-hour passed, the wedding-feast filled the air with good smells. Horsemen ambled a few miles up the road and came back without tidings. Then a courier, one of Ferry's scouts, galloped up to the General's tent, and presently the Major walked from it to the tavern and up to Charlotte's room, to say that Ferry was only detained by Quinn's non-arrival. "It's all right," said everyone.

Another hour wore on, another followed. The General and old Dismukes played cards and the latter began to smell of his drams, Harry and Cécile walked and talked apart, Camille kept me in leash with three other men, and about two o'clock came another courier with another bit of Ferry's writing; Quinn had returned. He had had a brush with jayhawkers in the night, had captured all but their leader, and had sent his prisoners in to brigade headquarters at Union Church, while he returned to Ferry's camp bringing with him, mortally wounded—"O—oh! Oh—oh!"

A Tarrying Bridegroom

exclaimed Charlotte, gazing at the missive,—" Sergeant Jim Langley!"

"Does Ned say when he will start?" asked the Colonel, and Charlotte, reading again, said the sergeant, at the time of the writing, was not expected to live an hour. Whereupon the word went through town that Ferry was on his way to us.

"Smith," said the Colonel, just not too full to keep up a majestic frown, "want to saddle my horse and yours?" and very soon we were off to meet the tardy bridegroom. The October sunshine was fiery, but the road led us through our old camp-ground for two or three shady miles before it forked to the right to cross the Natchez Trace, and to the left on its way to Union Springs, and at the fork we halted. "Smith, I reckon we'd best go back." I mentioned his bruises and the torrid sun-glare before us, but he cursed both with equal contempt; "No, but I must go back; I—I've left a—oh, I must go back to wet my whistle!"

We had retraced our way but a few steps, when, looking behind me as a scout's habit is, I saw a horseman coming swiftly on the Union Church road. "Colonel," I said, "here comes Scott Gholson."

Without pausing or turning an eye my hearer poured out a slow flood of curses. "If that whelp has come here of his own accord he's come for no good! Has he seen us?"

Gholson had not seen us; we had been in deep shade when he came into sight, and happened at that moment to turn an angle that took us out of his line of view. In a minute or so we were again at the small bridge over the embowered creek which ran through the camping-ground. The water was low and clear, and the Colonel turned from the bridge as if to cross beneath it and let his beast drink, yet motioned back for me to go upon it. As I reached its middle he came under it in the stream and halted. Guessing his wish I turned my horse across the bridge and waited. Gholson was almost within hail before he knew me. He was a heaving lump of dust, sweat and pain.

"Has Ned Ferry come?" was his first call. I shook my head. "Oh, thank God!" he cried with a wild gesture and sank low in the saddle; but instantly he roused again: "Oh, don't stop me, Smith; if I once stop I'm afraid I'll never get to her!"

I stopped him. "Why, Gholson, you're burning up with fever."

"Yes, I started with a shaking chill. I'm afraid, every minute, I'll go out of my head. Oh, Smith, Oliver's alive! He's alive, he's alive, and I've come to save his poor wife from a fate worse than death!"

"Gholson, you *are* out of your head."

"Oh, yes, yes, yes! and yet I know what I'm saying, I know what I'm saying!"

"You do not! Gholson, Oliver's been food for worms these four months. I know he wasn't dead at Gilmer's; but he died—now, let me tell you—he—"

"Smith, I know the whole story and you know only half!"

"No, no! I know all and you know only half; I have seen the absolute—"

"Proofs? no! you saw things taken from the body

of another man in Oliver's clothes! Oliver swapped places with him on the boat going down to the city so's he could come back to these parts without being hung by the Yankees; swapped with a sick soldier, one of a pair that wanted to desert; swapped names, clothes, bandages, letters, everything. It was that soldier that died of the congestive chill and was buried by your mother with his face in a blanket—as, like enough, mine will be before another day is done—Oh, Lord, Lord! my head will burst!"

"Gholson, you're mistaken yet! That soldier came to my mother—"

"No, he never! the other one went to her, in cahoots with Oliver, and worked the thing all through so's to have the news of Oliver's death, so called, come back here to the Yankees and us; and to his wife, so's she *would* marry Ned Ferry to her everlasting shame, and people would say they was served right when he killed 'em at last! O—oh! Smith,—"

"Listen to me!" I had tried twice to interrupt and now I yelled; "was it Oliver, and a new gang, that Quinn fought last night, and have you got him at Union Church?"

"Quinn didn't know it, for Oliver got away, but they got the Yankee deserter, and brought him in when everybody was asleep but me, and I cross-examined him. Oh, my friend, God's arm is not shortened that he cannot save! He maketh the wrath of the wicked to praise him! The man was dying then, but thank God, I choked the whole truth out of him with a halter over a limb, and then for three mortal hours I couldn't

start because the squad that took him out to—Who
—who is that?"

The Colonel moved from under the bridge, spurred
up the bank, and turned to us with a murderous smile.
"Howdy, Gholson." The smile grew. "Had to stay
with the hanging-squad to keep his mouth shut, you
was going to say, wa'n't you? But you knew Captain
Ferry would be delayed waiting for Quinn, too; yes.
Does any one know this now besides us three; no!
Good, we're well met! Smith and me are going to
Union Church, and you'd better go with us; I've got
a job that God A'mighty just built you two saints and
me for; come, never mind Gallatin, Ferry's not there,
and when he gets there Heaven ain't a-going to stop
that wedding, and hell sha'n't." Gholson had barely
caught his breath to demur when old Dismukes, roaring
and snarling like a huge dog, whipped out his revolver,
clutched the sick man's bosom, and hanging over him
and bellowing blasphemies, yelled into his very teeth
"Come!"

We galloped. A courier from the brigade-camp met
us, and the Colonel scribbled a purely false explanation
of our absence, begging that no delay be made because of it. As the man left us, who should come up
from behind us but Harry, asking what was the matter. "Matter enough for you to come along," said
the Arkansan, and we went two and two, he and Gholson, Harry and I. We reached camp at sundown, and
stopped to feed and rest our horses and to catch an
hour's sleep. Gholson's fatigue was pitiful, but he
ate like a wolf, slept, and awoke with but little fever.

Never Told Till Now

The Colonel kept him under his eye, forcing on him the honors of his own board, bed and bottle, and at nine we galloped again.

Between eleven and twelve the Colonel, Harry and I were in a dense wood, moving noiselessly toward a clearing brilliantly lighted by the moon. I was guide. A few rods back in the woods Gholson was holding our horses and with cocked revolver detaining a young mulatto woman from whom the Colonel had extorted the knowledge which had brought us to this spot. The clearing was fenced, but was full of autumn weeds. Near the two sides next us, tilted awry on its high basement pillars, loomed an old cotton-gin house, its dark shadows falling toward us. A few yards beyond towered and gleamed a white-boled sycamore, and between the two the titanic arms of the horse-power press widened broadly downward out of the still night sky. The tree was the one which old Lucius Oliver had once pointed out to me at dawn.

LXIII

SOMETHING I HAVE NEVER TOLD TILL NOW

At the fence I ceased to lead, and we crept near the gin-house from three sides, warily, though all the chances were that wherever Oliver lay he was heavy with drink. The Colonel stole in alone. He was lost to us for, I should say, five minutes; they seemed thirty; then there pealed upon the stillness an uproarious laugh mingled with oaths and curses, sounds of a

plunge, a struggle, a groan, and old Dismukes calling
"Come, boys, I've got him! Take it easy, take it easy,
I've got him on the floor by the hair of his head; call
Gholson!"

Gholson brought the mulatress. In the feeble rays
of an old tin lantern, on some gunny-sacking that lay
about the gin-room floor, sat old Dismukes cross-
legged and smiling, with arms folded and revolver
dangling from his right hand, at full cock. On one
side crouched Harry and I, on the other side Gholson
and the slave woman. Facing him, half sat, half knelt
Oliver, bound hand and foot, and gagged with his own
knotted handkerchief. The lantern hung from a low
beam just above his face; his eyes blazed across the
short interval with the splendor of a hawk's. The
dread issue of the hour seemed all at once to have taken
from his outward aspect the baser signs of his habits
and crimes, and I saw large extenuation for Charlotte's
great mistake. From the big Colonel's face, too, the
heaviness of drink was gone, and its smile grew almost
fine as he spoke.

"Ten minutes for prayer is a good while to allow
you, my amiable friend; we ain't heard for our much
speaking, are we, Brother Gholson? Still, we've given
you that, and it's half gone. If you don't want the
other half we won't force it on you; we've got that
wedding to go to, and I'm afraid we'll be late."

The bound man sat like a statue. The slave girl
went upon her knees and began to pray for her master,—with whom she had remained after every other
servant on the place had run off to the Federals,—

supplicating with a piteous fervor that drew tears down Harry's cheeks. "Humph!" said the Arkansan, still smiling straight into Oliver's eyes, "she'd better be thanking God for her freedom, for that's what we're going to give her to-night; we're going to take her and your poor old crippled father to the outposts and turn 'em loose, and if either of 'em ever shows up inside our lines after to-night, we'll hang 'em. You fixed the date of your death last June, and we're not going to let it be changed; that's when you died. Ain't it, Gholson? Whoever says it ain't fixes the date of his own funeral, eh, boys? I take pleasure in telling you we're not going to hang your father, because I believe in my bones you'd rather we'd hang him than not. Mr. Gholson, you're our most pious believer in obedience to orders; well, I'm going to give you one, and if you don't make a botch of it I sha'n't have to make a botch of you; understand?"

Gholson's lips moved inaudibly, his jaws set hard, and he blanched; but the Colonel smiled once more: "I've heard that at one time you said, or implied, that Captain Ferry had betrayed his office, because when he had a fair chance to shoot this varmint he omitted, for private reasons, to do it. And I've heard you say, myself, that this isn't your own little private war. So, —just change seats with me."

They exchanged. The slave girl sank forward upon her face moaning and sobbing. Harry silently wept. "Now, Gholson, you know me; draw—pistol."

Gholson drew; I grew sick. "Ready,"—Gholson came to a ready and so did the Colonel; "aim,"—

The Cavalier

Gholson slowly aimed, the Colonel kept a ready, and Oliver, for the first time took his eyes from him and gazed at Gholson. " Fire ! " Gholson fired ; Oliver silently fell forward ; with a stifled cry the girl sprang to him and drew his head into her lap, and he softly straightened out and was still. " Oh, sweet Jesus ! " she cried, " Oh, sweet Jesus ! "

The amused Colonel held the lantern close down. " He's all right, Brother Gholson," was his verdict ; the ball had gone to the heart. " Still, just to clinch the thing, we'll calcine him, gin-house and all."

Gin-house and all, we burned him up. On our horses out in the open road to the house, we sat, the girl perched behind the Colonel, and watched the fire mount and whirl and crackle behind the awful black arms of the cotton-press. The Arkansan shook his head : " It's too fine ; 'tain't a dog's death, after all. Lord ! why didn't I think of it in time ? we'd ought to 'a' just dropped him alive into that lint-box and turned the press down onto him with our horses ! "

When the pile was in one great flame we rode to the dwelling, and the girl was sent in to bid old Lucius begone. The doors stood open, a soft firelight shone from his room. We saw her form darken his chamber threshold and halt, and then she wailed : " Oh, Lawd God A'mighty ! Oh, Lawd God A'mighty ! "

" Stop that noise ! Gholson, hold the horses. Come, Lieutenant, come Smith, maybe he's killed himself, but it seems too good to be true. Here, girl, go cram what you can get into a pillow-case, and mount behind my saddle again ; be quick, we're going to burn

Never Told Till Now

this hornet's nest too." Harry and I had already run to the old man's room, and, sure enough, there lay the aged assassin hideous in his fallen bulk, with his own bullet in his brain.

Once more the Arkansan shook his head at the leaping flames. " Too good, too good for either of 'em, entirely; we've let 'em settle at five cents on the dollar. Here girl,"—he reached back and handed her a wad of greenbacks,—" here's your dividend; you're a preferred creditor." He had rifled the pockets of both the dead men, and this was their contents. " Now, boys, we'll dust, or we'll be getting shot at by some fool or other. We're leaving a fine horse hid away somewhere hereabouts, but we can't help that; come on."

In due time the Colonel, with the slave girl, and Harry with her pillow-case of duds, turned toward Fayette, and Gholson and I toward the brigade, at Union Church. Then, at last, my old friend and coreligionist let his wrath loose. He began with a flood of curses, lifting high a loaded carbine which we had found with Oliver and which he was ordered to turn in. As he gave his ecstasy utterance it grew; he brandished the weapon like a Bedouin, dug the rowels into his overspent beast and curbed him back to his haunches, fisted him about the ears, gnashed with the pain of his own blows, and howled, and stood up in the stirrups and cursed again. I had heard churchmembers curse, but they were new church-members, camp converts, and their curses were an infant's cooing, to this. Unwittingly he caused his horse to stum-

The Cavalier

ble, and the torrent of his passion gathered force like rain after a peal of thunder; he clubbed the gun to bring it down upon the beautiful creature's head, and when I caught it on the rise he wrenched it from me as if I were a girl, threw it fifty feet away, sprang to the ground and caught it up, fired it in the air, and with one blow against a tree sent the stock flying, threw the barrel underfoot, leapt upon it, tore his hair and his hat, and cursed and champed and howled. I sat holding his horse and feeling my satisfaction rise like the mercury in a warmed thermometer. Contrasting this mood with the cold malignancy and resolve of his temper in the soldiers' room at Sessions's, I saw, to my delight, that our secret was forever imprisoned in his breast, gagged and chained down by the iron of his own inextricable infamy. At dawn he awakened me that he might persuade me to reject the evidences brought against his character by his doings and endurings of the night, and that he might rebuild the old house of words in which habitually he found shelter, too abysmally self-conceited ever to see his own hypocrisy. We breakfasted with the "attatchays"; after which he had barely secured my final assurance that our friendship remained unmarred, when old Dismukes and Harry mounted at the Colonel's tent, and the old brute, as they trotted out into the Gallatin road, beckoned me to join them.

By Twos. March

LXIV

BY TWOS. MARCH

THE Arkansan was happy. "Come up, Legs," he bawled to me as soon as we were beyond the pickets, "come up from behind there; this ain't no dress parade."

"Are they married?" I softly asked Harry at the first opportunity, but he could not tell me. He knew only that Ferry had been expected to arrive about an hour before midnight; if he arrived later the wedding would be deferred until to-day. On our whole ride we met no one from Gallatin until near the edge of the town we passed a smiling rider who called after us, "You-all a-hurryin' for nothin'!"

We dropped to a more dignified gait and moved gayly in among our gathering friends, asking if we were in time. "No—o! you're too late!—but still we've waited for you; couldn't help ourselves; she wouldn't stir without you."

The happy hubbub was bewildering. "Where's this one?" "Where's that one?" "See here, I'm looking for you!" "Now, you and I go together—" "Dick Smith! where's Dick Sm'—Miss Harper wants you, Smith, up at the bride's door." But Miss Harper only sent me in to Charlotte.

"Richard, tell me," the fair vision began to say, but there the cloud left her brow. "No," she added, "you couldn't look so happy if there were the least

thing wrong, could you?" Her fathoming eyes filled
while her smile brightened, and meeting them squarely
I replied " There's a-many a thing wrong, but not one
for which this wedding need wait another minute."

"God bless you, Richard!" she said; "and now
you may go tell Edgard I am coming."

Old Gallatin is no more. I would not mention without reverence the perishing of a town however small,
though no charm of antiquity, of art or of nature were
lost in its dissolution. Yet it suits my fancy that old
Gallatin has perished. Neither war nor famine, flood
nor fever were the death of it; the railroad and Hazlehurst sapped its life. Some years ago, on a business
trip for our company—not cavalry, insurance,—I went
several miles out of my way to see the spot. Not a
timber, not a brick, of the old county-seat remained.
Where the court-house had stood on its square, the early
summer sun drew tonic odor from a field of corn. In
place of the tavern a cotton-field was ablush with blossoms. Shops and houses had utterly vanished; a solitary " store," as transient as a toadstool, stood at the
cross-roads peddling calico and molasses, shoes and
snuff. But that was the only discord, and by turning
my back on it I easily called up the long past scene:
the wedding, the feast, the fiery punch, the General's
toast to the bridal pair, and the heavy-eyed Colonel's
bumper to their posterity! It was hardly drunk when
a courier brought word that the enemy were across Big
Black, and the brigade pressing north to meet them.
Charlotte glided away to her room to be "back in a

moment"; into their saddles went the General, the Colonel, the Major and the aide-de-camp, and thundered off across the bridge in the woods; Charlotte came back in riding-habit, and here was my horse with her saddle on him, and the Harpers and Mrs. Wall clasping and kissing her; and now her foot was in Ferry's hand and up she sprang to her seat, he vaulted to his, and away they galloped side by side, he for the uttermost front of reconnoissance and assault, she for the slow but successful uplifting of Sergeant Jim back to health and into his place in the train of our hero and hers. In the little leather-curtained wagon, with the old black man and his daughter, and all her mistress's small belongings, and with my saddle and bridle, I followed on to the house where lay the sergeant, and where my horse would be waiting to bear me on to Ferry's scouts.

I saw the Harpers only twice again before the war was over. Nearly all winter our soldiering was down in the Felicianas, but by February we were once more at Big Black when Sherman with ten thousand of his destroyers swarmed out of Vicksburg on his great raid to Meridian. Three or four mounted brigades were all that we could gather, and when we had fought our fiercest we had only fought the tide with a broom; it went back when it was ready, a month later, leaving what a wake! The Harpers set up a pretty home in Jackson, where both Harry and Gholson were occasional visitors, on errands more or less real to department headquarters in that State capital; yet Harry and Cécile did not wed until after the

The Cavalier

surrender. Gholson's passion for Charlotte really did half destroy him, while it lasted; nevertheless, one day about a year after her marriage, when I had the joy of visiting the Harpers, I saw that Gholson's heart was healed of that wound and had opened in a new place. That is why Estelle, with that danger-glow of emotion ever impending on her beautiful cheek, never married. She was of that kind whose love, once placed, can never remove itself, and she loved Gholson. Both Cécile and Camille had some gift to discern character, and some notion of their own value, and therefore are less to be excused for not choosing better husbands than they did; but Estelle could never see beyond the outer label of man, woman or child, and Gholson's label was his piety. She believed in it as implicitly, as consumingly, as he believed in it himself; and when her whole kindred spoke as one and said no, and she sent him away, *she* knew she was a lifelong widow from that hour. Gholson found a wife, a rich widow ten years his senior, and so first of all, since we have reached the page for partings, good-bye Gholson. "Whom the gods love die young"—you must be sixty years old now, for they say you're still alive. And good-bye, old Dismukes; the Colonel made a fortune after the war, as a penitentiary lessee, but they say he has—how shall we phrase it?—gone to his reward? Let us hope not.

But what is this; are we calling the roll after we have broken ranks? Our rocket has scaled the sky, poised, curved, burst, spread out all its stars, and dropped its stick. All is done unless we desire to watch the fading sparks slowly sink and melt into darkness. The General, the Major, his brother, their sister, my mother, Quinn, Kendall, Sergeant Jim, the Sessionses, the Walls—do not inquire too closely; some have vanished already, and soon all will be gone; then —another rocket; it is the only way, and why is it not a good one? Harry and Cécile—yes, they still shine, in "dear old New Orleans." Camille kept me on the tenter-hooks while she "turned away her eyes" for years; but one evening when we were reading an ancient book together out dropped those same old sweet-pea blossoms; whereupon I took her hand and— I have it yet. There, we have counted the last spark— stop, no! two lights beam out again; Edgard and Charlotte, our neighbors and dearest friends through all our life; they glow with nobility and loveliness yet, as they did in those young days when his sword led our dying fortunes, and she, in her gypsy wagon, followed them, binding the torn wound, and bathing the aching bruise and fevered head. Oh, Ned Ferry, my long-loved partner, as dear a leader still as ever you were in the days of bloody death, life's choicest gifts be yours, and be hers whose sons and daughters are yours, and the eldest and tallest of whom is the one you and she have named Richard.